MIK

Mike Grist is the British/American author of the Chris Wren & Girl 0 thrillers. He has lived and worked in the UK, USA, Japan and Korea as a teacher, photographer and writer.

HAVE YOU READ EVERY CHRIS WREN THRILLER?

Saint Justice

They stole his truck. Big mistake.

No Mercy

Hackers came for his kids. There can be no mercy.

Make Them Pay

The latest reality TV show: execute the rich.

False Flag

They framed him for murder. He'll kill to clear his name.

Firestorm

Is the new President a traitor?

Enemy of the People

There's a target on Wren's back. Everyone's a hunter.

Backlash

He just wanted to go home. They stood in his path.

Never Forgive

5 dead in Tokyo. His name's all over it.

War of Choice

A red tide is rising in the east...

Hammer of God

Terror comes from above.

HAVE YOU READ EVERY GIRL 0 THRILLER?

Girl Zero

They stole her little sister. Now they'll pay.

Zero Day

One little girl dead in Haiti. More will follow.

Kill Zero

The past isn't dead, but it can kill...

HAMMER OF GOD

A CHRISTOPHER WREN THRILLER
BOOK 10

MIKE GRIST

SHOTGUN
BOOKS

SHOTGUN BOOKS

www.shotgunbooks.com

ISBN - 978-1-7398496-9-6

For Su and Sej.

1

MIEST

The Soyuz rocket decelerated through the outer atmosphere into space. By the time it achieved orbit, there wasn't enough LOX liquid oxygen/methane propellant mix left to attempt a guided re-entry, but re-entry wasn't the goal.

The goal was to dock.

The rocket had time. On the ground, at Vostochny Cosmodrome in Russia's Siberian Far East, the flight crew waited and watched as their calculations played out. It took seven hours until the Soyuz came within sight of the waiting Miest orbital platform.

An hour of intense coordination followed, as the rocket puffed its docking jets and came into range. Cheers erupted in the control room as the platform's docking arm finally clamped hold of it. Slowly, steadily its cargo bay opened.

Within lay a gleaming cluster of five ten-yard-long, two-foot-wide solid tungsten poles. Each weighed several tons, poured at three thousand degrees and cold-rolled like a Japanese katana, laminating layer upon layer to forge the strongest metal on Earth into something near indestructible.

The Miest platform's secondary arm set to work, reaching

into the rocket's bay and lifting each pole out and attaching it to slots down the platform's sides.

The procedure took several hours. Every movement had to be correct or risk a billion dollars of investment lost. When it was done, there was a collective sigh of relief in the flight deck. The Miest released the rocket housing, no longer needed, expected to lapse out of orbit within hours and burn up on re-entry.

One of the final shots from its onboard docking camera was of the Miest: a ring-based housing with five long tungsten poles attached, like the rotary barrel of an old-style revolver, pointing at the Earth. Even the name itself, Miest, was loaded with threat.

It meant 'Vengeance'.

The Vostochny Director hit the button to kill the feed, then tapped out a message on a separate screen and sent it through. One single word.

ARMED

2

SIBERIA

The train's passage through the Stanovoy mountains carried like rolling thunder up the long valley. Special operator Chris Wren lay in snow atop the pitted concrete roof of a long-abandoned research center, deep in a Soviet-era closed city with no known name, watching the train approach.

Snow fell in thick drifts. The temperature was fifty below and every breath stung Wren's lungs. He'd lost all feeling in his legs an hour ago, but he couldn't move just yet.

Three weeks, it had taken to get into this position on the BAM railway, Baikal-Amur Mainline, three thousand five hundred miles east of Moscow and three hundred west from the Vostochny Cosmodrome; Russia's newest spaceport in the far East.

Three days, it had taken Wren and his two-member team to dig out a trench in the train tracks and haul metal wreckage from the surrounding larch forest, where an imitation Russian drone had been purposefully crashed two months earlier.

Three hours, it had taken to lay the wreckage across the rails in a convincing pattern, even pouring gasoline on ready to light, so it looked like a recent crash. Enough to stop the train. Enough to let Wren and his team perform a clean insert operation, unseen and unknown.

"Readout, Chris?" came a deep voice from below.

Wren took his eyes from the Pulsar binoculars and looked down at the sizable frame of Anais Kiefer, standing in thick snow two stories below. At 6' 7", Kiefer had three inches on Wren and maybe thirty pounds of solid muscle, along with attitude enough to make those numbers problematic.

Two years back he'd waged a domestic terror assault on the US, even burning one of Wren's friends alive. But Kiefer was a linguist and an expert in Russia and her Soviet satellite nations. He spoke Russian, Kyrgyz and Pashto, had lived in Afghanistan for three years under deep cover with the Taliban, and without him on board, they would never have made it this far.

Exigent circumstance were the mother of forgiveness, it seemed. Wren had run the request for Kiefer all the way to the top of the food chain, and just about got him lifted from the Mexican black site he'd put him in.

"About time," Kiefer had said, when Wren met him at the Afghan border. "Don't tell me. Russia."

Wren had laughed.

"Seven minutes," Wren said now. "Package is in position?"

The black speck of the train momentarily disappeared from sight, hidden behind an escarpment of the steep granite mountains.

"Package is wrapped up in bed," Kiefer answered. "I'll head to the truck."

Wren focused on the section of the BAM where the transport train would emerge back into sight. The BAM was a 2,700-mile-long broad-gauge rail line that cut across the eastern Russian steppe like a steel ribbon, in most places 'floated' on permafrost over peat bogs. Completed in 1984 as part of the twelfth five-year-plan, it had been called the 'Construction Project of the Century' by General Secretary Brezhnev, designed as a strategic alternative to the Trans-Siberian railway.

The train Wren was targeting was a five-carriage long-haul freight 4TE10S 24-axle two-section diesel-electric locomotive with an output of 8,824 kW. The track east of the Stanovoy range was not electrified, so the train had to run on diesel for the final thousand miles. Already it had traveled some 97 hours from Moscow, with 13 hours left to go before it reached Vostochny Cosmodrome.

Wren could smell the harsh chemical smell of the train's diesel exhaust carried on the wind.

On cue, the train emerged from behind the escarpment like a thick black snake, engine roaring. It was a mighty beast, hulking out an extra foot either side of the rails. Thick steel plating insulated it fully against small-arms fire and somewhat against IEDs or missile strikes. Of the five carriages, two were troop carriers, each stocked with fifteen of Moscow's finest Spetsnaz Special Operations forces, making for thirty men in total.

It was a Presidential-level escort, served by a carriage-worth of munitions and supplies, all to protect the payload in the central carriage. Persona 3 was Moscow's latest optical reconnaissance satellite, due to be launched from Vostochny Cosmodrome in a week. Russia only had two optical reconnaissance satellites in orbit, capable of resolving detail at one pixel per fifty centimeters. By contrast, US spy satellites had ten times the resolution, at one pixel per five centimeters.

It meant the Russians were nearly blind from space. On the surface, Persona 3 was designed to start correcting that problem, but after the economic, military and political collapse of Russia during the Ukraine war, the true purpose behind Persona 3 was a mystery.

Wren's mission was to shed light on that mystery by intercepting and co-opting the satellite directly; attaching a device internally that was capable of piggybacking and even overriding any command passing through it.

"In position at the truck," Kiefer said, his Southern-tinged voice ringing clearly in Wren's earpiece. "Ready to run amok."

"Make it a good show," Wren said.

After that, all he could do was wait and watch as the train snaked its way up the valley toward them, pumping out thick wads of coal-black smoke. Soon the sound of it became a storm and he felt the vibration carrying up through the research station's walls and into his bones; sheer Russian power unwittingly coming up against American black-ops intelligence.

"Chris?" Kiefer prompted.

"It's coming into the last quarter mile," Wren said. "Hold."

Ten seconds passed. Twenty.

Wren triggered the detonator.

Down below and two hundred yards north, nestled amongst the 'wreckage' of the drone across the tracks, a pair of remote detonator caps fired a small electric charge. It was enough to spark the gasoline and set the 'wrecked' drone alight.

The stage was set.

Wren dropped his binoculars and ran. He'd timed the distance; he'd be hunkered down in a blind overlooking the tracks by the time the train was coming up to the drone, ready to step in if necessary. Kiefer should be on a flanking support road, in the Kamaz truck left by an undercover operative who'd brought it up from a neighboring Oblast then 'lost' it, along with a full colonel's outfit. Kiefer should already be wearing the outfit, complete with side-holstered antique Makarov PM.

"Ready," Kiefer said, just as Wren dropped behind the blind. The train rounded the corner, and almost immediately there was a banshee-like screeching of metal-on-metal as the train's brakes engaged.

"Report, Faraday," Wren shouted over the screech.

"Ready," answered Genevieve Faraday, the third member of their team and the 'payload' of their insertion. She was currently embedded in a narrow trench they'd dug a hundred yards down the center of the rail tracks, now roofed with snow.

Faraday was the CIA's foremost expert in the Persona satellites, with a Yale doctorate in aerospace engineering and a specialism in geostationary mechanics. She had with her a custom-built miniaturized device that could slot into the satellite's housing, replacing an existing part but doubling the function, affording the US both oversight and potential override on the Persona's systems.

Wren had vetted and hand-selected her for the op. She was as all-American as they came: prom queen and valedictorian at her Georgia high school; Fulbright scholar at MIT with a specialization in astrophysics at the renowned Kavli Institute for Astrophysics and Space Research. There was also the bonus ball that she'd already done double-agent duty for the CIA during the war in Afghanistan, collecting intel from Russian astrophysicists while seconded at their giant radio telescope in the Kush mountains.

Her deep expertise was needed as she'd have limited time in the carriage with the Persona, and their schematics were fuzzy and outdated at best. Faraday would have to improvise rapidly to attach and conceal the device. If everything went well, the Russians should have no idea their part had been switched.

"It's slowing," Wren said. "Three hundred yards off still. Looks like the middle carriage will halt twenty yards south of you, Faraday."

"It's getting loud down here," Faraday responded. "Shifting position to beneath the hatch."

The sound reached a deafening pitch then ended abruptly as the engines cut out.

"Rear two carriages are emptying out," Wren called. "Soldiers. There's a lot of them. Kiefer, we need you now."

"En route," Kiefer replied, and the sound of his sirens carried through the speaker.

"Am I clear to access the hatch?" Faraday asked.

"You don't have cover. Kiefer?"

"Almost there," Kiefer answered, then his Kamaz truck burst through a stretch of larch forest ahead, ate up the embankment and skidded to a halt across the snow, almost kissing the side of the train's middle carriage, providing perfect cover for Faraday's insertion.

"You're clear, Faraday, go now!" Wren ordered.

"Getting to work," Faraday answered.

Wren watched as twenty AK-47s trained in on Kiefer from either side, completely unaware of Faraday emerging from her trench beneath the train and working on opening the maintenance hatch into the Persona's storage bay in the secure central carriage.

Kiefer made a show of pulling the truck's keys but left the sirens running, then raised his arms up and stepped out of the truck onto the frosted gravel.

"Put your rifles down," he barked in fluent Russian. Wren was no expert in Russian, but he'd picked up enough to follow along with the script they'd written together. "I am colonel Nimov of Kastrovsky Oblast, and I must see to my crashed plane!"

Not a single rifle wavered. Nobody fired either, and Kiefer turned and strode toward the wreckage of the drone.

"I have the hatch," Faraday said. "The truck's screening me from view. Accessing."

Before Kiefer made ten paces the train's commanding officer dropped out of the lead car, a stolid man in his forties with a hard face and a drawn pistol, a captain by his insignia.

"You are impeding a maximum security transport," he shouted in Russian, red-faced with anger. "Identify yourself immediately."

"Play hardball," Wren said in Kiefer's ear. "I recognize this guy. He'll only bow to strength."

"I am Colonel Nimov," Kiefer belted back. "You are currently witnessing the end stage of a top secret test flight. I guarantee you are not cleared to even know this exists. I have an expert team coming from Vladivostok, they will assess the scene and preserve everything in place, before transporting it back to base."

The captain stared. "Vladivostok? Impossible! That could take days. This train ships under the direct order of the President. There can be no-"

"I am a Colonel, Captain, engaged under Presidential seal! If this prototype drone should be further damaged in any way, I'll have you and every man here court-martialed to Kamchatka!"

The captain's face burned. "This is a military escort, 'Colonel'. We are on a strict timetable. I would ask that you clear your wreckage from the tracks immediately, or we all will suffer."

"I'm in," came Faraday's voice in Wren's ear. If all went well, she should be able to secure the Persona 3 device, escape through the hatch and lock it again within ten minutes.

Wren just needed to buy her that time.

"Delay him, Kiefer," he said.

"Unacceptable," Kiefer blurted. "Every scrap of that plane is top secret. You are not cleared to see it. Your men are not cleared to touch it. The train will wait."

The captain shook his head, spat into the snow and turned to bark orders. At once a contingent of ten ran toward the wreckage. When the captain turned back, he found Kiefer's Makarov aimed squarely at his face.

At once Kiefer became the fulcrum point of a dozen AK-47s.

"I'm in the housing," Faraday said.

"Fast as you can, Doctor," Wren said. "Situation is developing out here."

"Holster your weapon, Colonel," the captain said.

"Don't do it," Wren ordered.

"I will not," Kiefer said.

The moment stretched out.

"Where did you launch from?" the captain asked.

"That's classified."

"Very convenient."

"Far enough that this wreckage is groundbreaking. You are looking at the culmination of a ten-year race to control the skies."

"It does not look like much to me."

Kiefer snorted. "I should claw out your eyes for even seeing it. When the Vladivostok team arrives, your names will be taken and-

"This is easily resolved," said the captain, and unhooked the radio from his belt.

"Follow the script," Wren cautioned.

Kiefer pulled back the hammer on his Makarov. "I would not do that, Captain."

The captain's hand froze on his radio. "Fire now and my men will execute you where you stand."

Faraday cursed down the line.

"What is it?" Wren asked.

"I have the part." Faraday answered. "But the shape is different. I'll have to extract our internals and rewire them."

"How long?"

"I don't know. Five minutes?"

"You heard her, Kiefer. Buy us five minutes."

On the tracks, Kiefer lowered his weapon slightly. "Perhaps I have a solution."

The captain didn't budge. "Name it."

"I will permit five of your men to clear my craft, blindfolded. They must be delicate. Every piece of this plane is worth more than their lives. If any man takes so much as a splinter, I will execute him myself, then hunt down his family and gut them alive."

The captain's jaw tightened. His eyes darted once more to Kiefer's colonel's insignia, then he turned to his men and shouted fresh orders. Five men raced forward and began tossing snow onto the detritus to put out the flames. It took several minutes, then they stripped their jackets to bind their eyes and stepped up to start moving the detritus.

"I'm close now," Faraday said. "Final wiring of the contact plates."

"Slowly!" Kiefer shouted. "Carefully. Place the components, do not throw them."

The soldiers moved more slowly. Still, it happened faster than Wren had expected. Within several minutes every bit of wreckage had been removed, and the men were removing their blindfolds.

"Faraday?" he asked.

"I'm out," she replied. "Sealing the hatch."

"Good luck to you, Colonel," the captain said defiantly and tossed off a sharp salute.

"Best never to speak of this," Kiefer replied.

"Sealed up and burrowing back in," Faraday said, just as the train began to creep forward again.

Wren watched the train chug away until it rounded a jagged rock face, then breathed a sigh of relief. The job was done. He climbed down from the blind and strode over to Faraday's trench, meeting Kiefer at the approximate point she'd dug back in.

"You can come out now, Faraday," he said.

There was no answer.

He scanned the tracks. Maybe she'd burrowed in somewhere further along the trench.

"Faraday?" he tried again, putting his toe into the snow. His foot sank into the hollow where her body should have been. There was no sign of her, and for a long moment he didn't understand. He looked at the snow, then the tracks, then the trail of black smoke left by the train, then the awful realization hit.

"Where is she?" Kiefer demanded.

Wren looked up at him. This was catastrophic. Three months' worth of planning, millions in logistics and they hadn't just failed.

They'd chalked up a win for the enemy.

"Faraday just defected."

3

DEFECTED

Kiefer stared at Wren. Wren gazed after the train. Black smoke still hung in the cold air. The roar of its diesel engine dopplered deeper as the sound waves stretched out. Maybe a quarter mile already. It would slow down up the three-mile-long pass. Then there was a half-mile tunnel under the Stanovoys, and-

"We have to go after it," Kiefer said.

Wren didn't move or answer, locked in thought.

He'd planned this strike as a silent, unseen insertion. Against thirty armed men in a hundred-yard-long tank, it had been the only option. But now Faraday had exposed herself as a double agent.

Wren's mind flashed back over every step to this point. He'd approached Faraday. Recruited her. She hadn't even been interested at first; not because she was afraid, but because she hadn't trusted Wren.

He'd wooed her. Brought in advocates. The DNI himself, Director of National Intelligence Gerald Humphreys, the cabinet-level officer in charge of every Intelligence Community agency in the USA, had spoken to her. When that failed to make any impact, Wren had brought in Sally Rogers, his old lieutenant in the CIA.

Still nothing. Only when he'd offered to step down and let her lead the entire operation had she relented.

"I don't want to lead," she'd said, fixing him with a fiery glare. "I just don't want to be another star engraved on your vanity wall. You've gotten a lot of agents killed, Mr. Wren. I have a family. You keep me safe. Do you understand?"

He'd nodded and promised to do just that. He knew what she meant by engraved stars; one hundred and thirty-nine of them graced the wall of the lobby at Langley, representing undercover agents fallen in the line of duty, whose ultimate sacrifice in the name of national security could never be known. DNI Gerald Humphreys had several on the wall behind his desk.

But all of that meant her defection made no sense.

Had she suckered Wren from the start, playing hard to get while working with the Russians? Had someone gotten to her in between recruitment and activation? Had she had a bizarre change of heart in the moment, or had she-

"Chris, we have to go after that train!" Kiefer yelled.

Wren ignored him. Each option presented different branching paths forward. If she was in communication with the Russians, they would be expecting her. That meant they were expecting Wren's team, which meant a squad could be inbound right now to take him out, or a missile. It could mean the train would be hardened beyond his expectations, impossible to breach, or …

It could mean anything.

He thought ahead to the tunnel. The train's engine settled to a fading storm. In the tunnel, perhaps, they'd have a chance. The only chance. If he could somehow bring it to a halt while it was still in the dark, it might be possible to access Faraday's carriage and retrieve her.

Or kill her.

Kiefer was right. With the knowledge and tech Faraday possessed, she was a prize too rich to cede to the collapsing Russian empire, whether she was a willing traitor or not. The cost to prevent that didn't matter. Maybe they'd both become stars engraved on the Langley wall. This was the job.

Wren snapped back into the moment. "On the truck!" he shouted, and ran.

In seconds they were on board. Wren keyed the truck to life and slammed the gas, lurching them forward.

"What's the plan?" Kiefer shouted over the roar of the engine.

"Stop the train in the tunnel," Wren answered, charging the truck along the snow bank toward the rock face, mind racing just as fast. He'd planned for a secret incursion, but prepared for resistance if the play went wrong. The truck was filled with gear. "You're on explosives duty. Grab us some weaponry and blocks of C4; we'll clear the train one carriage at a time then blow the wheels off until it halts."

"There'll be thirty Spetsnaz operators in our way," Kiefer countered.

"Then they'll die."

Kiefer laughed. "Now you're playing my song."

The truck ran out of road ahead and Wren swung hard onto the train tracks. The icy wooden sleepers hammered the old truck's non-existent suspension, drilling Wren's spine. He gritted his teeth and arced the truck around the cliff just in time to glimpse the train plunging into the tunnel about a mile ahead.

He pushed the gas pedal all the way down, struggling to steer straight on the tracks. Thirty seconds passed, while Kiefer scrabbled through crates of materiel, digging out bandoliers of grenades and blocks of C4.

The truck peeled through the train's trail of smoke then

shot into the pitch black tunnel. The rails jolted them left, streaking sparks off the wall and ripping the wing mirror away, then Wren flicked the lights to high beams, illuminating a bare-bones tunnel stretching into the distance.

"Get rid of the windshield," he said, squinting toward the limit of the lights' range.

"Is this glass bulletproof?" Kiefer countered.

"Let's hope not."

Kiefer leveled his Makarov and pointed it at an angle toward the upper rim of the windshield. "Ricochet's coming at you if you're wrong."

"Do it."

Kiefer fired. The antique pistol discharged a single deafening round, which blew the windshield out in sharp splinters.

"I take it I'm shock and awe," Kiefer shouted.

"Grenades, fast insertion then we take her back." Wren boomed back.

"Aye aye," Kiefer said, and hoisted a rucksack full of C4. "See you on the other side."

He surged up and through the shattered glass onto the rocking hood. Just beyond him Wren finally saw it, looming like a ghost at the edge of his high beams.

The tail section of the train.

4

THREE MONTHS EARLIER

"Tell me again why this operation is necessary, Wren?"

The question hung in the air, stinking out the Office of the Director of National Intelligence, on the fifth floor of the DNI's sprawling campus in McLean, Virginia.

Six unmarked gold stars hung on the wall behind a large pedestal desk, representing black-op agents fallen in the line of duty. Floor-to-ceiling shelves lined the remaining walls, filled with leatherbound books of past presidential briefings. Producing these 'briefing books' was one of the primary duties of the DNI, a cabinet-level position that oversaw all the alphabet soup Intelligence Community agencies.

Wren looked squarely back at the man responsible for the stench in the air, Gerald Humphreys. It had been almost a year since their paths had last crossed, but he looked exactly the same. His alabaster face, pale and hollowed-out with rocky overhangs for cheekbones, gave the impression of unyielding competence. His question contradicted that.

"You're suggesting the threat of a collapsing Russia is not worth countering?" Wren said, choosing his words carefully.

"Not at all," Humphreys said coldly. "No one questions

that Russia's collapse after the death of President Burin is a serious concern. I'm questioning your plan. Inserting a high-value operative onto a moving high-security train in the depths of Siberia does not seem like a balanced use of force. And using you to do it, a man who keeps trying to retire from Intelligence every chance he gets, a 'family' man engaged in a court case against his ex-wife, does not seem wise. What's in this for you, Wren?"

"Nothing's in it for me."

Humphreys snorted. "I don't believe you. If that's all you've got to offer, this meeting is ov-"

"You've seen the intel on the Persona satellites," Wren interrupted. "Something's off here, Gerald, something we're not seeing, and blowing up a train isn't going to help. We need to know what Mother Russia's doing launching satellites right now, in the midst of dissolution. Somebody is paying the bill for this, and we need to know who and why."

A wrinkle of distaste crossed Humphreys' face. "Who and why? Christopher, those answers haven't changed. It's Russia. Snippets of Russia. Rehydrated crumbs of Russian communist spirit. I don't care which. They're coming for us, like they always were, in any way they can, only now it'll be with better satellite comms."

Wren shook his head. "Bullshit. Russia isn't a country anymore, Gerald, it's a bankruptcy fire sale. Every high-ranking Party member is stripping their oblast for parts and selling them to anyone who'll buy. Bratva, the Triads, Iran, even the South America cartels? They're all buying in, and it's been going on since NATO forces stabilized Moscow seven months ago. We may have secured the nukes, but everything else? The cosmodromes? Satellites in orbit? Rockets. Launch pads. Flight telemetry. Advanced physics simulations. Exotic weapons. It's all for sale." He took a steadying breath. "Russia as we've known it is gone. Whoever's driving that train and launching satellites, it isn't Russia, they're just a corpse getting picked over by hyenas. This is something else, and we need to figure out who and what they are, before the smoking gun is a mushroom cloud on American soil."

Humphreys' glacier-blue eyes didn't shift from Wren's. "That's not what the Intelligence Community says. It's not what I'm advising the President. But let's say that you're right. Let's even say this mad train heist insertion is a good way to forestall the next 9/11. The question remains about your motivation. You keep quitting. You're suing your wife for joint custody of your children. An operation like this, you'll be dark for at least the next several months. No court dates. No legal arguments. You'll lose your case."

Wren's jaw tightened. He'd anticipated this. "I'll get a continuance."

"They'll never grant it."

"They will. My ex-wife's lawyers are working to unseal my government record, and that will take at least a month. I can do both."

Humphreys shook his head. "You can't unseal a CIA record for family court. That's impossible."

"It's happening. When they get it, there's enough unredacted violence in there to ensure I never see my kids again."

"Again, impossible. Your work's Top Secret classification. It can't be unsealed, it barely even exists."

"I'm not going to argue with you on this, Director. The point is, I have the time to handle this op."

Humphreys' expression soured. Wren felt the mission, teetering on a knife's edge then Humphreys cursed again. "I'll take it to the President. If she OKs it, you're committed. There's no backing out for any reason. You live and breathe this mission until it's done, is that understood?"

Wren nodded firmly. "I wouldn't have it any other way."

"Good. Now get ou-"

"There's one more thing."

Humphreys snorted. "Of course there is. What?"

"I need Anais Kiefer released."

"Kiefer? The giant psychopath you put away?"

"Yes."

"Didn't he burn one of your Foundation cultists alive?"

"It's not a cult. And yes, he did, but he wasn't in his right mind then."

Humphreys snorted. "And he is now, after two years in a black site?"

"Yes. I've been monitoring him. He's mission ready. And he was always a patriot. He just got confused about what that meant. When it comes to external actors, I have no doubt about his loyalty."

"I don't like it."

"I understand that, but with his language skills, experience and our working relationship, he's my best bet to get the job done."

Humphreys' eyes narrowed. "This is not just a ploy to get him released so you can kill him?"

"If I wanted him dead, he'd be dead, Director," Wren said, offering Humphreys his official title as a fig leaf. "Now, can I write him into the plan?"

Humphreys threw up his hands. "Why not? But on your own head be it if this mission actually happens, and he starts burning more people alive."

"Thank you."

"Now I've got work to do. Get out of my office."

5

THE TRAIN

The Kamaz truck closed on the train until it hit with a metallic crunch; the headlights butted against metal, dampening their spread to a spilled white glow. Anais Kiefer wasted no time in leaping from the hood onto a step on the rear carriage, where he set to work attaching C4 bricks to the train's bodywork closest to the wheels.

Wren hit the cruise control, tentatively released the wheel then lifted his foot off the gas. The ride grew even wilder as the truck batted side-to-side off the walls, but he didn't need long, climbing up through the windshield onto the hood.

A gap opened up to the train and Wren leaped, just clearing it. The truck rattled and banged into the distance.

"Both flanks mined," Kiefer said, swinging back around to come face to face with Wren on the narrow rear step. With three inches on Wren, he loomed menacingly in the darkness and smoke.

"One more on the lock plate, then I'll see you up top," Wren said.

"Aye aye," Kiefer said, dipping once more into his rucksack, while Wren climbed up the ladder on the rear. The top of the tunnel ripped by some two feet above the ceiling of the train, with barely enough room for his thick barrel chest to fit. He pulled himself further along, and in moments was joined by Kiefer, laying flat as the train roared deeper into the mountain.

"I never said sorry," Kiefer shouted. "For burning your friend alive."

"You still haven't," Wren shouted back, then triggered the detonators.

The rear of the train kicked as all three C4 patties blew at once, erupting in noise, fire, stinging flecks of rock shrapnel and thick black smoke. Wren's ears thundered, his cheek was numb from the punch of the train's roof, and the wheels were squealing below, beginning a terrifying slalom from side to side as the carriage crashed against one wall then the next.

"Go!" Wren shouted, pushing himself back off the roof and dropping into the blasted-open doorway.

The carriage ahead was a troop carrier, lined either side with seats and floored with the scrabbling bodies of Spetsnaz soldiers trying to find their feet. Wren stripped a grenade off his chest bandolier, pulled the pin and threw it into their midst. Five seconds counted down, and Wren swung out behind the mangled rear wall.

The eruption convulsed the train, along with the wet tearing of bodies and shattering of glass. The flash of light, a fresh blast of smoke and a rain of body parts shot out of the open door.

Wren plunged in and Kiefer followed close behind.

The bucking floor was awash with blood and ruptured bodies. Several stunned Spetsnaz fighters staggered through the smoke, trying to bring their weapons to bear. Wren's shoulder slammed into the gut of a big man and followed up with three bullets fired point-blank through his chest.

He went down and Wren ran on, firing into the froth of

bodies. Screams filled the tight metal confines and bullets cracked out and ricocheted. Wren shot one man as he reached upward, then elbowed another through the broken window and under the screeching wheels.

He'd almost reaching the midpoint of the carriage when something in the trailing undercarriage caught on the tracks and yanked hard left.

The whole car slammed into the tunnel wall gouged in, screaming along at a crazy diagonal. All the lights went out along that side, any remaining glass in the reinforced porthole windows shattered and a reverse waterfall of sparks shot up from below as the train's axle scraped along the rails.

"Chris!" came Kiefer's shout from behind.

Wren looked ahead to see the muzzle of an AK-47 pointing point-blank at his face. The man holding it had long enough to smile, then his finger tightened on the trigger and his head blew backward.

"Call that an apology!" Kiefer shouted over the storm, the barrel of his Desert Eagle smoking, then followed up with a grenade pitched like a fast ball into the midst of a surging squad of Spetsnaz fighters, pouring in from the next carriage over. "Now get down!"

Wren flattened. The grenade blew and there was the same crumping sound of the air compressing, the shattering of glass and the wet rending of bodies. Blood slashed across the back of his neck, then he was up again, charging into the smoke and chaos.

A Spetsnaz with one hand gone lunged, landing a punch on Wren's shoulder, but he rolled it and slammed the man down, stamping on his throat. Another sprang up, firing his AK-47 in a rainbow spray, but Wren leaned back and sent a single shot through the man's head.

He fell back and Wren surged on, wading through the dead and dying until something else in the train's undercarriage shifted, forcing the front corner of the car down. Stone and metal shrieked in an unbearable cacophony, sparks backwashed through the red-hot window frames, then the front corner hit the wooden sleepers and began to smash through with a mad drumbeat that jolted the car on every stroke.

Wren weaved, smoke and impact-drunk, struggling to keep his feet on the twisted floor. He chanced a look back, where Kiefer was battling through the fog. Beyond him the rear of the carriage was on fire; a blasted-out ring with only darkness beyond, showered with sparks. The truck was long gone. No way back.

He looked ahead just in time to see the roof rip away on the rock tunnel. The metal furled sparked and bounced back along the dark rails, and it took Wren long seconds to figure out what had happened, then something hammered him squarely in the temple.

The blow slapped him flat onto his back like a little kid, instantly circling the drain of unconsciousness. It was a harder hit than anything he'd felt in years, but his training kicked in swiftly and he rolled sideways before a foot could stamp down on his neck.

It landed right by his eyes.

He looked up. The man looming over him was huge, a bear even compared to Kiefer, at least seven feet tall and built like a rocket, with a thick black beard, jet-black eyes and a single strange black sigil tattooed on his forehead. Wren backpedaled on all fours to get away, but the man was too fast, faster than any giant Wren had ever seen.

He lunged to grab Wren's ankle. Wren twisted but the giant yanked harder, dragging him up the carriage. His head cracked off a row of seating before he kicked free.

The big foot stamped down a second time and this time Wren reacted too slow, rolling but still taking the full weight of the giant on his right hip. The shock forced a fresh gulp of air into his lungs, which gave him the push to surge upwards, throwing everything he had into a big uppercut punch.

It hit the giant's chin square with enough force to dent a tractor, but his head barely lifted an inch. Wren followed with a jab at his throat, but the big man's incredible speed struck again, landing a punch in Wren's sternum first and hurtling him back to slap the carriage floor.

The big foot came down once more and Wren took it on his ribs. He felt them flex, and the thought came that this might be where his ticket got punched, on a burning train deep in some Siberian mountain under the foot of a Russian giant. His kids would never know.

The big foot came down toward his face.

Then Anais Kiefer hit the giant from the side. The giant's foot caught Wren's head a glancing blow, bouncing it off the floor, and he stared up through graying vision as the two of them went toe to toe.

Kiefer was a big man and fast, but the giant moved like he'd been built in a lab; pumped with human growth hormone and stitched with fast-twitch muscle, then programmed with attacks that took advantage of both. Kiefer threw an elbow and the giant swayed just out of reach, countering with a jab to the gut that bent him double. He came back with a kick at the big man's knee, which the giant avoided by driving that knee hard up into Kiefer's groin.

Wren lurched to his feet as the carriage rocked and split around him. Sparks and smoke were everywhere and he could scarcely breathe, then with an almighty bark the carriage tore; metal shearing down the middle, the back half of the car ripping away and leaving his feet near the burning edge.

Ahead, Kiefer went for his signature move on the giant, a feint to the chin, a skipping duck into a gut strike then a roll into a side-on neck-choke. He managed to land it, both thick arms wrapping around his tree-trunk neck and trying to bend his head inward, but it was a tactical error.

The giant was too strong. His neck was corded like iron bridge supports. All he had to do was turn and swing one of those massive piston arms and the point of his elbow would shatter Kiefer's sternum, driving bone spurs into his heart.

The second before it happened, Wren realized Kiefer was looking directly at him, and he knew this wasn't a tactical error, it was a choice.

"Now we're even," Kiefer shouted, and kicked out with his right leg. The blow took Wren in the chest and drove him backward, just as the giant swung his sledgehammer elbow down into Kiefer's ribs. Then Wren was falling through flames at the edge of the carriage and into darkness, until the gravel spun him and everything went black.

6

TUNNEL

Wren woke coughing.

It was pitch black and his body felt wrecked, like a mountain had caved in on him. He couldn't see anything, but he could feel the noxious fumes wheezing in and out of his lungs.

The train carriage was burning still; in an oxygen-low atmosphere, that had to mean a massive dose of carbon monoxide. He was lucky he'd woken up at all.

He pushed himself to his feet. His right ankle throbbed and his left knee twinged, but nothing felt broken. He fished at his belt for his radio and a flashlight. The light was there but the radio wasn't. He flicked it on and saw billows of black smoke pumping around him.

There could be no way back now. Even if the burning train carriage hadn't blocked the tunnel, the smoke would kill him.

He set off at a jog in the opposite direction. Twisted metal scraps laid across the dull iron tracks, fallen from the ruptured carriage. After perhaps ten minutes there was a body, too large and heavy to belong to anyone else.

Wren kneeled by Anais Kiefer's side and checked his pulse. It was there, but weak and thready.

"Kiefer," Wren said. His voice sounded muted in his own ears, and he recognized the ring of tinnitus from too many blasts. "Kiefer, wake up."

The big man didn't budge.

Wren ran the flashlight over his body. His injuries weren't apparent, so Wren ran one hand over his chest where the giant's elbow had landed. His sternum felt intact, which was a wonder. Perhaps some cracked ribs. His limbs looked intact, his throat unobstructed.

He slapped Kiefer's face, but still no dice. It had to be the intensity of the trauma keeping him unconscious. That or a brain injury. Wren looked up.

The air was getting thicker every second. There was no time to wait. Left in the tunnel for much longer, Kiefer would die.

Wren got on one knee, hoisted Kiefer's upper body in a fireman's lift over his right shoulder, took a deep breath then pressed upward. The man's weight was immense, almost buckling Wren beneath it and sending silvery sparks shooting across his vision. His legs trembled but held.

Smoke billowed. Wren advanced. Every step felt like the last he could manage, with his hips, thighs and calves burning at what felt their limit, but this was what he'd trained for all his life.

He kept going, and the smoke gradually thinned. After about a mile he switched off the flashlight and proceeded by the faint light cast from the tunnel mouth ahead. Cold penetrated through his strike suit. The mix of dark and light played tricks on his eyes. At one point he thought he saw a figure up ahead, guarding the tunnel, but perhaps it was only a deer.

After another ten steps he realized it was neither a deer nor a figure at all. It was two.

Laying Kiefer down on the gravel was hard. The relief from the drop of weight was immense; instantly he felt light-headed and springy. Wren lay on his belly beside the big man, still wreathed in curls of smoke, peering at the figures at the tunnel mouth.

Two Spetsnaz soldiers, left to finish the job. They'd made an unforgivable tactical mistake, though, one that had already saved Wren's life. By staying at the entrance to the tunnel, they'd prevented their eyes from adjusting to the dark. If they'd taken up position a hundred yards in, they'd have seen him by now.

He sent up a prayer for the good luck, then slapped Kiefer's face again.

"Wake up, Anais."

Still nothing. The big man breathed but didn't budge. The giant on the train must've hit him incredibly hard. That left Wren checking their assets again.

No rifles and no pistols. One flashlight. No radio. Two grenades remained on the bandolier around his chest.

He looked ahead at the distance to the tunnel mouth, where the two soldiers patrolled back and forth. It was easily a hundred yards. At full pace on even ground it'd take him fifteen seconds. On the gravel of the tracks, debilitated already, call that more like twenty. On open ground, he figured he could throw a grenade a hundred yards, but given the tunnel's low roof, there was no way. Maybe thirty yards max, flung out as a fast ball.

That left him seventy yards short.

He laughed low.

"What do you think, Anais?" he asked. "Die now or wait for the smoke and cold to do the job?"

Kiefer said nothing. Wren tallied the numbers one more time, then started forward at a low crawl.

Ten yards. Twenty. At thirty the men started noticing. Almost enough. Five more and they raised their weapons. Wren snaked the first grenade down by his side, pulled the pin, then lobbed it forward as hard as he could.

Five seconds.

Answering shots rang out, pinging off the rails and smacking the gravel nearby. Then the grenade blew.

Wren surged to his feet and ran. The smoke of the blast covered him. He managed thirty yards in less than ten seconds, then the gunfire started back up. He pulled the second pin, fast-balled the grenade as hard as he could, then accelerated to a sprint.

The grenade blew. Wren watched one man get blown to the side, breaking his neck off the wall. The other was knocked backward. Wren blew out of the tunnel mouth as he was rocking back up and raising his rifle, still ten yards distant.

He fired just as Wren flung a fistful of gravel.

The shot missed but the gravel didn't, cracking off the man's face and veering the next shot further off target. Then Wren landed, driving his right elbow into the man's face and securing the rifle with his right. the man struggled and Wren sent another blow, then another, until the man's head cracked on the frost-hard ground.

He jerked and entered convulsions.

Wren pulled the AK-47 from around his neck and spun. There was a tent erected by the verge of the tracks, with a midnight-blue 4x4 Lada Niva SUV beside it. Wren stamped over and ripped away the canvas, revealing winter sleeping bags and backpacks filled with gear.

These men must've been sent back by the train, having

sourced the SUV from the nearest village only ten miles away.

He ran back the way he'd come. The man he'd elbowed was dead. The other man was shivering uncontrollably, his neck twisted at a vicious angle but his eyes tracking Wren. He ran on.

Anais Kiefer's breathing was shallower still. The cold and the smoke were getting to him.

"Come on, buddy," Wren said. "Let's get you warmed up."

On the first hoist he failed to lift Kiefer, dropping him back to the gravel. Exhaustion was setting in. He tried again, gritting his teeth and willing his way through. Somehow, he lifted him.

The hundred yards out of the tunnel to the tent were punishing. He fed Kiefer inside, then stripped the two dead men for their thermal coats. One had a satellite radio, and he took that too. He pulled one coat on over his own strike suit, wrapped Kiefer in the other, then tucked him into the sleeping bag and looked down at his face.

A deep purple bruise was swelling up around his left eye, along with crusted blood. Wren saw no wounds, so leaned in, held his breath and carefully peeled back Kiefer's eyelid.

His eye was heavily bloodshot, but there. Wren breathed a sigh of relief. For a moment he'd feared Kiefer had taken a bullet to the eye, which could've torn up his brain on the inside. More likely this was just the remnant of a bad beating. Maybe concussion.

Wren pulled away and stepped back onto the tracks. His head spun from the raw cold, and for the first time he really took in his surroundings: a high vantage point overlooking an incredible vista washed with bright, wintry light. Towering peaks soared to either side, scarred with gray granite ravines like jagged wounds on a corpse. Pristine snow blanketed the valley floor far below, where a frozen river glinted like a ribbon of mercury. Aching blue skies hung over the picturesque white landscape of frosted green fir trees, rock and ice.

The rail line continued unbroken ahead, snaking around the steep side of the mountain. No roads, no access culverts cutting up or down the mountain, no smoke trails or signs of civilization anywhere across the panorama.

Wren's lungs burned in the cold air.

If that view wasn't enough to make you believe in God, he didn't know what was.

He checked his watch.

15:17. Already two hours had elapsed since Faraday's defection. Exfiltration was set for twelve hours; an escort out of the forest ten miles north by a turncoat FSB agent, Russian Federal Security Service, the equivalent of the CIA. If the tunnel back through the mountain was passable, which he doubted, it was still a plausible rendezvous.

Wren had no interest in trying to make it, though.

Whatever was happening here, he had to follow it up. It was three hundred miles to Vostochny Cosmodrome. The train could cover that by midnight, if all went well. He'd go in the SUV, which would take longer.

But he had to go.

The sun was close to setting. With no water or food and a deadly Siberian night ahead, he didn't relish it, but there was no choice. Faraday was his responsibility. The destructive capacity of the cosmodrome, when paired with everything Faraday knew about America's network of satellites, was explosive.

The damage she could wield was hard to imagine.

He spun the radio dial, tapped in an encryption key only Gerald Humphreys knew, then squeezed the transmitter.

7

HUMPHREYS

It took an hour to connect, during which Wren gathered deadfall pine and lit a roaring fire. Around it he staked up a wide sliver of metal scavenged from the train to act as a heat reflector, bouncing the warmth into the open tent, where Kiefer lay, still unconscious.

When the line finally did go through to Director Humphreys, Wren strode away to the tunnel mouth.

"What am I doing talking to you now, Wren? You should be en route to exfil."

"Director," he began, giving Humphreys respect to begin with. "We're in trouble. Faraday's gone, maybe defected, and-"

"What?" came the cry across the continents.

Wren winced but explained what had happened, ending with his plan to pursue Faraday and the train to Vostochny.

Silence crackled through the radio for a time.

"Under no circumstance," Humphreys said eventually. "Exfiltrate now. You've already screwed this up beyond belief."

"Faraday screwed us all," Wren countered. "She passed every test we have. She had the highest clearance possible for an agent, with active field experience in a major warzone. She was our golden girl, and we need to figure out what happened. Did they take her unwillingly, in which case how did they know we were even here? It means you've got a mole, Gerald, and you need to clean house. Or did she really plan all this, gaming me, you, the President, just to defect?"

Humphreys cursed.

"Exactly. If so, we need to know why."

Humphreys' laugh sounded hollow across the five thousand miles back to Washington. "We already know the reason why! Russia bought her off, and now they're trying to take us down with them."

"I told you it's not Russia," Wren insisted. "Stop fighting the last war, Gerald. This is a terror group buying up Russia's assets, I know it. If Faraday really was compromised, she's our best lead on figuring out who they are and what they want."

"As far as I'm concerned, you're compromised too, Wren! I want you out of there right now, that's a direct order."

"Didn't hear that, Director. Besides, I'm not asking permission here. This is a heads up from an on-the-ground asset, exercising local tactical initiative. I'm going after her as soon as Kiefer's stable."

"Unacceptable! This is mutiny, Agent Wren."

"So court martial me again, Gerald," he countered, dropping the 'Director' title. "Oh, and there's one other thing." He cast his mind back to the face of the giant on the train, complete with the strange marking on his forehead. "There was a symbol on the man who nearly killed Kiefer, a tattoo on his forehead, like a figure '8' with a small cross on top."

That seemed to stymy Humphreys. "Figure '8' with a cross. What does that mean?"

"I have no idea. I didn't recognize it. Maybe it means

nothing, maybe it's just prison ink, but it could be a lead. We need to look into it too."

"I'll get right on that, shall I, while I'm filing shoot-on-sight papers for a pair of treasonous mutineers?"

Wren grunted. "Kiefer's still unconscious, so don't write him up just yet. And I want Rogers looking into this."

"Rogers?" Humphreys answered. "Agent Sally Rogers?"

"You know another?"

"You've got history, Wren. She arrested you."

Wren couldn't avoid a smile. Sally Rogers was his ex-lieutenant in the CIA, a hugely ambitious young woman with a sweet Midwest face, the frame of a powerlifter and the conscience of a nun. Two years back she'd arrested Wren for extra-judicial killings and dumped him in the same black site they'd put Kiefer in.

"Ancient history," he said, smiling. "I shot you around that time too, breaking out of the black site, and look at us now."

"Don't remind me. I could just leave you and that other traitor high and dry. Let's see you break out of a Siberian gulag."

"Do that and you'll never sleep peacefully again." Wren racked his mind. "Send her out to Faraday's family. We need to know if she defected willingly or not. If she did, that's huge. It could change everything."

"I'll send her. She'll have to be read in on your mission."

"Good. Also, you should station a satellite over Vostochny Cosmodrome. We need to know who's coming and going."

Humphreys cursed. "You think it's that easy? You think I can just requisition a satellite? It can take up to twenty-four hours to maneuver-"

"I'll be in touch," Wren said and ended the call.

Silence reigned in the mountains again. A high wind

brushed snow off the nearby mountaintops like spray off a wave, dashing silver in the moonlight. Somewhere nearby a wolf howled, and Wren shuddered. Other howls followed; the pack catching his scent.

He turned back to the tent and stalked over; only ten yards out did he realize that something was not right.

The fire had banked down already, and the tent had shifted position slightly. Was that Kiefer's sleeping bag spread out on the snow? He lifted his AK-47 and sidestepped to get a better view.

Kiefer was not in the tent.

He swept the icy forest slopes but saw no sign of him and no trail. Had he imagined it all?

"Anais?" he called. "It's Wren. Where are you?"

Long moments passed, then the giant figure of Anais Kiefer unfolded from amongst the bushes to his left, shivering off snow and brambles, the remaining AK-47 hanging by its strap from his shoulder. He looked as pale as a ghost in the moonlight, and there was something off about his eyes, particularly the left one.

"Chris," Kiefer called, his voice devoid of emotion. "Is it you?"

Wren lowered his weapon, feeling relief blur into a new worry. "It's me, Anais. Are you OK?"

Kiefer stared back at him glassily. "Chris. Good. What happened?"

"There was a fight in the train. We fell out but it continued on. You took a bad hit, leaving you unconscious. If you're OK to travel, we need to go after Faraday." He paused. "Do you remember any of that?"

Kiefer just stared.

"Anais?"

"Sorry. I'm thinking." He paused for a long moment. "I don't want to alarm you, Chris, but I can't see very well."

"What do you mean?"

"I don't know. It's like everything's jumbled. If I try to piece it together, I get a sick feeling."

Wren's mouth went dry. "But you can see?"

"I can see static. It's not snowing, is it?" Kiefer held out both hands, like he was trying to catch snowflakes.

"It's not snowing right now. Come on."

"I think it's a brain injury," Kiefer went on. "That's what I've been thinking. But I can't be sure."

Wren thought back to his earlier fear, the bullet in the brain, but with Kiefer's eye intact that seemed impossible. "Maybe a concussion. Listen, we're getting out of here. We can be at the cosmodrome in around five hours. I can drive the first half, and you can handle the second half when you feel better. How does that sound?"

Kiefer just stared again.

"Anais."

"Yeah," he blurted. "OK, Chris. Whatever you say."

Wren felt a chill spreading in his chest. Maybe this was a concussion, or maybe it was something worse.

"I'm coming over there. I'm going to take you by the hand and lead you into the SUV, OK?"

"Sounds good."

Kiefer didn't budge. Wren advanced and took his giant hand. His grip was weak and his fingers were icy. "How long were you lying in the snow, Anais?"

Kiefer tried to orient his gaze toward Wren, but ended up looking past him by a clear foot. "I don't know. An hour? I tried to count. I couldn't read my watch."

"It's OK. It's fine. Come on."

Wren guided Kiefer into the passenger side and belted him in. Kiefer stared ahead with his hands in his lap, as obediently as a child at church. Wren ran back to the tent, gathered the second rucksack and anything he thought they could use along with water bottles and MREs, then tossed it all into the rear seat.

"Are we going now?" Kiefer asked.

"We're going now," Wren said, and started the engine. "Sleep some more if you can. I'm going to recline your seat, OK?"

"OK, Chris."

Wren wound the seat back. Kiefer let it happen. He'd never seen him this weak and helpless.

"I'll sleep now," Kiefer said, and closed his eyes. "I'll feel better, right?"

"That's right. Just rest."

"And I told you I was sorry, didn't I?"

"For burning my friends? You mentioned it."

Kiefer blinked, and a bloody tear ran down from his left eye. "I am sorry. I wish I hadn't done that."

Wren sucked in a breath. This was too much. "Don't think about it. OK?"

"Do you forgive me?"

"Just rest, Anais."

He wound Kiefer's seat all the way back. His breathing leveled out before he'd even hit full recline. That could be a good sign. Wren cranked the AC up to full heat, executed a jolty three-point-turn over the rails then started out over the icy sleepers, chasing the train.

8

FARADAY

Special Agent Sally Rogers stood on the blacktop driveway of mission specialist Genevieve Faraday's home, in Sandy Point, Texas, 20 miles southwest of Houston. It was a four-bed ranch-style home on the outskirts of the city, situated on five acres, with a stable holding two horses, a garage holding three vehicles and a pool.

It was midafternoon on a late summer day, and the hot air smelled of horse manure and cut grass.

"How many inside?" she asked the FBI officer on the door.

"Husband, two kids," the agent replied. "We rounded up her mother too, just one town over. Her father died a few years back. Kids are playing videogames. Husband's drinking. Mom's folding laundry and rearranging the mantelpiece."

Rogers grunted. She knew much of that from the last couple of hours' research, en route from New Orleans; Faraday's father was dead of a heart attack at 67, husband Fred was an alcoholic, maybe related to her excessive professional success, with genius teenaged kids acing their way through Lancôme Academy, the top prep school in the Southwest.

Faraday had met her husband in a bar near the NASA campus in Clear Lake twenty-two years earlier. She'd been a senior flight controller for the Stardust mission back then, steering the Stardust rocket within around hundred miles of Comet Wild 2 to collect particles for study. It was the first such mission of its kind, and required incredibly fine control of the Stardust boosters. The mission had proven a success, and catapulted Faraday into the upper ranks of NASA's experts.

"Thanks," Rogers said, and surveyed the house a final time. It looked all-American, straight out of a cattle drive. Lawn darts stippled the yard and foam chairs floated in the pool. Not the kind of home you'd expect for people knowingly living with a traitor.

Still, here she was.

"I don't know if this is something or nothing," Humphreys had said three hours back. "Wren is on a mission in Siberia, and there may be imminent blowback. You're the only one who's ever successfully controlled him, or even influenced him. I need you on this."

She'd snorted. In her hands at the time she'd held the first piece of evidence on a cold case that dated back to her days at University of New Orleans. There'd been a sorority admissions party at Sigma Kappa, until an active shooter had entered and started shooting with an automatic rifle.

By the end, fifteen young women were dead, with only Sally Rogers left alive, hidden under the bodies of her fellow pledges. The shooter got away clean. No one saw his face. No one laid a hand on him.

The trauma had flattened her in the days that followed, and nothing anybody said could shift it. For days and nights she relived in vivid detail the feel of the body pile cooling and stiffening above her, the sound of the shooter's taunting voice, the smell of the gunpowder and blood. Within two weeks she quit the school, haunted by survivor's guilt. Why should she be alive when all the others were dead?

Within two months she found herself holding a straight razor to her wrist, sitting in a hot bath in a seedy hotel fifty miles from home.

It was there with the blade pressed to her skin that everything shifted to a new perspective; that trying to 'heal' was hurting her. Maybe healing was impossible, or just too hard to bear. But accepting that the shooter had already destroyed her life?

That changed everything. It offered a new way forward, a new path with nothing to fear, because the old her was already dead.

She dropped the razor. Within two hours she cleaned up and signed up for assessment trials at the nearest FBI station.

"Rogers," Humphreys had demanded. "Did you hear me?"

"Yes sir," she'd fired back, folding the visa page and slipping it into her pocket. It lay at the end of a long trail of deductive leaps she'd made over years, tracking the ghost of the shooter across the country, from mass kill site to mass kill site, ending at Nicholls College, Louisiana, where for the first time in eight years she'd heard his voice again on the entrance interview recording, and finally seen his face.

His name was Vincent Blackwell, a seemingly wealthy exchange student from the UK. She hated him more than anything. But he could wait.

Wren needed her.

The leaps in reasoning she'd taken to get this far had all come from him. He'd taught her to bend laws and read people, along with various tricks of manipulation and cold reading. Her own by-the-book, brute force method of door-knocking and questioning would never have taken her this far alone.

"I can't control Agent Wren," she finally said to Humphreys. "But work with? Even channel? Yes. I'm on it."

She pushed through the door into Genevieve Faraday's home. It was beautifully appointed, a foyer with faintly pale gray walls, black and white diamond marble-tile flooring, lined with exquisitely crafted occasional desks and tables topped with potted jungle plants.

An agent nodded at her, waiting by the entrance to the den.

"Rogers," she said, approaching him. "Anything?"

"Mill," he answered. "And not yet, we waited for you."

She gestured toward the den, where the family were congregated on lush pink sofas on a brushed oak herringbone floor. "What have we told them?"

"Only that Faraday's missing. No more."

Rogers considered. She looked around. "She kept a study?"

"Upstairs, next to the master bed."

"Any other place her things were kept?"

"Not that we can see."

Rogers considered. She tried to think like Wren. This was either the home of a genius taken unexpectedly by Russia, in which case there would be nothing but the usual secrets, torrid affairs, embezzled funds and petty vendettas; or it was something far worse.

A genius had lived here as a pretender for who-knew how long, wrapping herself in the traits of an ordinary life, with a family and horses and cars, gathering intel and expertise until the date she turned traitor.

She knew what the rulebook said. Faraday was innocent until proven guilty. She also knew what the FBI search doctrine would require: search her books for hidden compartments, rake through her computers for encrypted data, parse her habits and routines to the second, micro-analyze every punctuation point she made for microdot scripts.

That was standard. People made mistakes and left things behind.

But not Genevieve Faraday. From everything Rogers had read about her, she was simply too smart to leave any trace behind. Her family wouldn't know. Her kids wouldn't know.

The only slip-up Rogers could imagine now was hubris.

"Toss everything that isn't hers, but gently. Keep the family on ice a little longer, but let them see. I need to view her office."

Mill nodded and pointed to the stairs. "This way."

Faraday's office was on the second floor, another stylish and elegant space painted in a darker shade of gray, with several wooden bookshelves filled with books and journals. In between were framed high-resolution photographs taken from the James Webb telescope, showing star nurseries and black holes and the red shift close to the Big Bang.

Rogers sat in Faraday's chair and surveyed her desk. It was a large wooden podium desk padded with green leather, with a large monitor trailing cables, but no computer.

"Laptop?" she asked.

"We don't know," Mill answered. "Her husband said she usually took it with her on research trips."

Rogers grunted. "Where does he think she is?"

"At a symposium in Tahiti. That's what she told him. It's real, I checked, but of course she's not there."

"Of course."

"Where is she, Agent Rogers?"

She looked over at Mill, then looked away. That was far above his clearance level. "I'm OK here for now," she said.

He accepted that as the dismissal it was.

Rogers looked dead ahead, through a large spidery rose window in the wall and out over the property. Directly ahead lay the circular gravel drive, and beyond it a round paddock for the horses to canter in. The stables stood at the head, swing doors firmly shuttered. On the desktop there was one framed photograph, and it was not of a family member, but rather of a chestnut horse with a single line of golden text.

NEBULA - RIP

Rogers smiled. It was touching, in a way. The kind of name a little space-fanatic girl might name her first horse. She checked the frame and behind the photo, but there were no secret messages.

She looked at the blank screen and tried to put herself into Faraday's head. She tried to think like an arrogant genius, and started leafing through the desk drawers. They were neatly organized, with an IN tray on the left, and OUT tray on the right, all business. There were letters of invite to conferences, and dog-eared research papers yet to go to print, but nothing remotely suspicious.

From downstairs came the sound of a grown man sobbing.

Rogers rose and walked over to the bookshelves. She leafed through books but found no hidden compartments or secretive slips of paper. She looked for hotspots in the pattern of dust, but there was no dust anywhere. Faraday was clinically neat. She took the photographs off the walls and reversed them, but found nothing other than full references and citations of where the images came from.

It only reinforced her existing impression of Dr. Genevieve Faraday; she had an impressively neat and organized mind, which revolved around space, her family and her horses. Anything unconnected to those things held no interest for her.

Rogers could sympathize. They were similarly focused, it seemed.

She took a sheet of paper from the desk, picked up a pen and drew a simple symbol: a figure 8 with a cross atop it. She folded it then went back downstairs. An army of FBI officers were dusting surfaces for prints and opening drawer and cupboards.

It was gentle. It was respectful.

In the conservatory overlooking their garden, sitting on a lacey armchair, was Faraday's husband. An FBI officer was with him, but when Rogers appeared in the French doors, she nodded and stood. The husband didn't even notice.

Rogers sat down.

"Fred Faraday," she said coolly, like she was reading his name off a CV. "Car salesman."

He looked up. He was a handsome man, but his eyes and cheeks were a blotchy red from crying. "Who are you?"

"Agent Sally Rogers. I'm lead investigator on your wife's abduction."

"Abduction? Is that what you're calling it now?"

"Yes," Rogers said bluntly. It was hardly by-the-book, but she'd seen Wren use bad news to shock witnesses into cooperating before. "Possibly with her life on the line. Can you tell me anything about her close contacts or potential enemies?"

The tears stopped. "Now her life's on the line?"

"I'm afraid so, Mr. Faraday. This is a very serious situation and time is a pressing factor."

"What is the situation? Nobody's telling me anything."

"I can tell you she's been taken, but that's all for now. I need your help. I need you to tell me anything you can think of, no matter how insignificant it may seem, about unusual contacts she might have made recently, or enemies made, or breaks in her normal routine."

He snorted. "How would I know? She spends most of her days in her office, staring at the sky out of her window. And when she's out of the house, it's to NASA, or conferences, and I have no idea what she does there."

Rogers took a slow breath. He was going to be hard work. "Let's simplify this, then. To your knowledge, did anyone wish her harm?"

He frowned. "Why would anyone wish her harm? She studied stars. She helped launch satellites."

"Space is a competitive field. There's money in it too. This is a lovely home. Quite a conservatory."

He looked around, blinking numbly, taking in his own home. "I suppose so."

"Did she have any contacts that provoked your suspicions? Anything at all?"

"No! Like I said, she was in her room, riding her horses, or out working. That's it."

She studied him. "So there wasn't much home life?"

"That's none of your damn business!"

She nodded and took that in her stride. "OK. What about enemies, Mr. Faraday? Professional jealousy? Hard words, unpleasant conversations, professional rivalries, threats?"

"No! Of course not! Not Genny. She stepped on nobody's toes. She kept herself to herself. Though…" he paused, then looked away again.

"What is it?" Rogers pressed.

He looked back. "She's an introvert. She always was, but she used to fight it more. She'd come out, we'd drink, we'd eat out. But these days, well…" He threw up his arms in an expression of defeat. "She became insular. Her room, her horses, her work; the areas she could exercise total control over. But me, the boys? We were messy. Easy to avoid." He sighed. "Her work was everything. Anything else, she didn't have time for."

Alarm bells began ringing in Rogers' head. Progressively cutting off family contact was a common sign of radicalization. "What do you mean, didn't have time for?"

"Just that," Fred Faraday said, and dropped his head back into his hands. "Sometimes she was curt with us, or other people that I saw. That's all I can think of, though. Not exactly rude, just direct, like we were all just little booster rockets she needed to perfectly calibrate."

Rogers felt herself walking on thinning ice. He was opening up, but she needed to push harder. "Were these changes caused by any particular interaction? A meeting, a major life change?"

He sighed. "No. It comes of being so intelligent, I think. Always ten steps ahead of us common people, stuck on the Earth. Some people didn't like her for it, sure. I struggled. But I can't think anyone would kidnap her for it."

Rogers considered. There was something there, but she couldn't go head-on to dig it out. He'd just clam up. Instead she laid down the piece of paper on the coffee table between them.

"Do you recognize this?" she asked.

Fred Faraday looked at it, blinking slowly. "It's two circles and a cross."

"It is. Do you recognize it?"

"Why would I?"

"No reason. Did you ever see your wife drawing this symbol, or reading messages with it attached, or anything like that?"

"No." He straightened up. "Are we done? I think we've talked enough."

Rogers swept the paper away. "Just one more question, Mr. Faraday. You mentioned your wife could be curt. Potentially rude. Do any particular instances stand out?"

He looked at her blankly. "I don't see how that's relevant."

"I'm trying to understand her, Fred," Rogers said gently. "Build a picture so we can get her back. Anything you can tell me could help."

He sighed. "OK. Particular instances." He rubbed his temples. "Well, there was our wedding. She got angry at the maid of honor, something about flowers. Does that help you find her?"

"Please go on."

He sighed again. "Uh, there was the time the B&B on Hilton Head double-booked us. She was furious. Then soon after that, right after in fact, we came back here and the landscapers had put the paddock in wrong. Then," he exhaled heavily. "sometimes she's angry with the boys. Nothing unusual, only when their grades lapse. She expects a lot."

"She cares about grades," Rogers said softly, though something else was bothering her about what he'd said.

"What parent doesn't?"

"Sure. And what was wrong with the paddock?"

"The paddock?"

"You said the landscapers had got the paddock wrong. How so?"

He spluttered a half laugh. "Right, the paddock. Well, it was years ago. We were getting the grounds refitted, right after we bought this place. We took the holiday so we wouldn't have to be here while it all got torn up."

Rogers felt something shifting in her head. There was something there, something about the paddock and the office and the window looking out. "How many years ago?"

He screwed up his eyes. "Seven, I think. Seven, yeah."

"Well, it looks lovely now."

He heaved the heaviest sigh yet. "All her design. There was a very specific layout she wanted, probably tied into rockets or stars or something, but they interpreted the designs incorrectly. They made the paddock more of a square, not a circle, and they put the doors and windows to the stable on hinges."

The alarm bells grew louder in Rogers' head, suggesting a new idea. "On hinges? Why would that matter?"

"I don't know. Because she had this idea of taking the doors off completely. Maybe the opening looked like a star to her? Same with the paddock, I guess; it looked like a planet?"

"But the paddock is round now. She made them fix it."

"Of course she did. She was furious." Fred Faraday paled. "She got a lawyer and sued them. In the end they had to pay damages and redo it all."

"That's quite serious," Rogers repeated. "Do you have any idea why it mattered so much to her?"

"Like I said, she wanted control, dominion really, over her little slice of the world. She was a little OCD when I first met her, but it was charming. That part of her ballooned as the years passed, until she was trying to micro-manage everything, like the precise layout of a paddock. The whole thing was humiliating for everyone. But it mattered so much to her."

Rogers stood up, the idea almost fully formed in her head now. "I see. Thank you for your time, Mr. Faraday." She stepped out of the conservatory and walked over to Agent Mill in the foyer.

"I want you to open the stable doors," she told him. "They're not on hinges, so you can just take them out. The windows to either side too."

He frowned. "You want me to remove the stable doors."

"And the windows. Now, please."

"Yes, ma'am."

He hurried off. Rogers went back up the stairs into Faraday's office, where she sat at the desk again and looked out of the rose window; the same window Genevieve had gazed out of for hours at a time, according to her husband. Staring at the sky.

But maybe it wasn't the sky.

Mill came into view, heading across the paddock to the stable. Rogers watched as he lifted first one door, then the other, then the windows to either side, and stacked them against the wall. It created a curious, cross-shaped opening into the stable.

Rogers' throat went dry.

There it was. Hubris, in plain sight. The one thing Genevieve Faraday saw every day that nobody else would ever notice. You had to sit here to see it: the circle of the drive, the circle of the paddock, and the open cross of the stable door. She looked down at the symbol she'd drawn, a figure 8 with a cross atop it.

It was a perfect match.

She brought up her phone, took a photo then sent it with a message to Humphreys.

"It's defection. Tell Wren I'm certain of it. She's been planning this for at least seven years."

9

VOSTOCHNY

After a spine-crunching five hours behind the wheel of the Lada, Wren was drained. Beside him Anais Kiefer breathed low and evenly, which seemed reassuring. He hadn't woken once, and Wren hadn't had the heart to rouse him.

Now Vostochny lay ahead.

Russia's newest cosmodrome was nestled into a confluence of several valleys surrounded by jagged mountains. Wren opened his door and stepped out. It was dark and quiet in the small hours, the pass around him windless and still. The BAM offshoot's tracks ahead descended through a perimeter fence and into a small station at the edge of the compound.

The train stood there, motionless and black as a spent bullet casing, its rear carriage starkly bitten off by the explosion. No guards, no driver, no sign of Faraday. Wren scanned the perimeter fence, unlit and seemingly unmanned. A cluster of dark buildings in the center of the valley were broken by a handful of lights shining through second and third-floor office windows. A half mile further on loomed a solitary Soyuz-2.1a rocket, standing twenty stories tall in the moonlight, like a sentinel over Russia's collapse.

"The train's here, Anais," Wren said, his voice sounding strange in the silence. "Almost no lights, though, and hardly any people."

Kiefer said nothing.

Wren leaned back into the Lada. He'd already refilled the tank once, leaving it half full.

"Stay here," he said softly. "Sleep. You'll be fine."

There was more color in Kiefer's cheeks now, and his breathing had grown even. Wren left the AC running, gathered his AK-47 and a Makarov pistol, then gently closed the door and started down through the snow.

He vaulted the security gate across the tracks without any challenge, reaching the train in moments, where he climbed up into the bitten-off carriage, switched on his flashlight and advanced. All the bodies were gone, but the blood and char marks of his grenade explosions remained. The door to the next carriage along was open, another empty troop carrier, and beyond that lay the central car. Inside a long, heavy-duty cradle hung from the ceiling on chains, while the walls were coated with a thick layer of padding.

An empty berth for a Persona satellite.

The hatch Faraday had climbed up through lay beneath the cradle, giving access like the service pit in a motor pool.

But no Persona. Had it already launched?

Wren cleared the rest of the train, finding every carriage empty. He dropped back to the snow and advanced on the main compound. The parking lot was almost empty but for a few Ladas and a Moskvich 3 model sedan with diplomatic plates.

Automatic lights flickered to life as he neared the central entrance, revealing CCTV cameras watching down, but no alarms rang out. Wren felt like he was boarding a ghost ship.

He pushed through the central glass doors, and more lights splashed to life at his arrival, illuminating a cavernous, glass-ceilinged lobby. Carved friezes hung on the walls depicting Soviet rockets shooting to the moon. The size of the space offered a show of strength, but it was cold like a mausoleum and smelled of mold.

Past a security turnstile, several large offices spread to left and right behind glass walls, but all were empty and dark. Wren padded deeper, feeling like an interloper in a graveyard. He scanned the signs as he went, and despite his spotty Russian, he could make out 'кабина экипажа'.

FLIGHT DECK.

Two sets of stairs deposited him on the top floor, at a long corridor lined either side with glass-walled executive offices that ended in a white double door. Above it was a sign with both red and green portions, signaling mission underway or mission pause. Neither was lit.

Wren advanced. To his surprise, the offices to either side had been ransacked. Books, shelves, drawers and papers lay on the floor haphazardly. A sound came from ahead; male voices laughing. He froze in place, straining to hear. Four, maybe five, and drunk. Their laughter grew louder, then there was a woman's scream.

Wren sped up. The shouting grew and the screaming intensified, until barely five yards ahead a man stepped out of an open office. He wore the black tactical uniform of Russian Spetsnaz, the same as the men on the train, but it was rumpled and loose; belt untethered, jacket unbuttoned and shirt hanging free. In his hands he held a crystal decanter half-filled with amber liquid.

Wren understood what it meant. Some of the Spetsnaz had stayed behind to loot the cosmodrome, taking advantage of anything and anyone left behind.

The shrieks of the woman grew louder. The soldier opened his mouth to shout a warning.

Wren fired.

The bullet took the man in the belly and doubled him over. Wren ran toward him, drove a knee into his face then burst into the office.

Four more Spetsnaz stood around a desk in various stages of undress, with a young woman in a torn skirt and blouse lying on the worktop between them. The man standing between her legs looked confused, while the other three were reaching for their weapons.

Wren sprayed a burst across them all.

They dropped, leaving one man remaining. He stared in disbelief then went for his weapon, but Wren was already upon him, hammering the grip of the rifle into his face. His cheek bone crunched and blood spurted out and he went down with a strangled cry.

Wren dropped with him, pulling zip-ties off his belt and swiftly hog-tying his wrists to his ankles. He then moved to the others, securing their weapons, several two-way radios and a set of car keys, checking for signs of life as he went. Two were already dead and two were on their way. Wren secured them to be sure, then stood.

The woman on the desk was struggling to cover herself, but shaking uncontrollably.

"It's OK," Wren said as soothingly as he could. "Everything's OK now. Do you speak English?"

The woman tried to sit up but fell back, barely catching herself. Wren pulled off his thermal jacket and gently held it out. She allowed him to wrap it around her shoulders.

"I speak ... English," she said, with a strong Russian accent.

"Good," Wren said. "My name's Christopher. What's your name?"

She stared at him, then answered. "Ivanya."

"Ivanya. That's a beautiful name. First thing, Ivanya, do you know who these men were?"

She shook her head.

"You don't know. But they came on the train, is that correct?"

"Da. Yes. On the train."

"Are there any others in the building right now?"

A look of terror spread across her face. "I do not know."

"OK. It's OK. I think there aren't, or they'd have come here by now. I'm sure we're safe."

"Who are you?" she countered. "American, yes?"

"I'm American. I'm looking for a woman called Genevieve Faraday. She's an American too, an astrophysicist, and I believe she was brought here on that train by these men. Have you seen her?"

The woman stared.

"Did you see anything?" Wren went on gently. "Do you know what happened here?"

"Launch," she said.

"Launch? The Persona launched already?"

She nodded.

"How is that possible?"

"Possible? Everything was, uh, ready. Prepared. It launched."

Wren took a step back. That was dumbfounding. He could only have been 7 or 8 hours behind the train. For them to load and launch the satellite into space in that time was incredible. But then…

"Why so fast? What was the urgency?"

She made a face. "I do not know. I am, what do you say? Cleaner. I clean offices."

Wren looked at the remnants of her clothing scattered on the floor. There was a ripped blouse, a navy jacket, navy suit pants and tall black high heels. He ran back the conversation in his head.

"You're a cleaner, but you wear a suit and know about the Persona?"

That confused her for a moment, but she doubled down. "Da. Is name of rocket. Everyone knows."

"It's not the name of the rocket," Wren said, and kneeled to pick up her blouse. There was a name badge attached which read, 'ОЛЬГА КУЗНЕЦОВА - ПОЛЕТНЫЙ ДИСПЕТЧЕР', which translated to 'Olga Kusnetsova - Flight Controller'.

He looked her in the eye. "Persona's the name of the payload. Olga, why are you lying to me?"

The woman's expression shifted from one of fear and uncertainty to anger.

"You are American. You have destroyed my country. You-"

Wren ignored her as she fell into a rant. He thought it through. The Persona was undoubtedly gone. There was a Soyuz-2.1a rocket on the 1S launchpad, but Vostochny had another launchpad, 1A. Launch was certainly possible.

"But it did launch," he said firmly.

She stared at him defiantly, then changed her answer. "No. They loaded into truck. Carried away."

Now that Wren had a baseline for her, the lie was obvious. He pointed at the four dead men around them, with one unconscious. "These men were going to rape you. Probably they would've killed you. I saved you. Still you're loyal to them."

"I am Russian," she sneered.

"Russia doesn't exist anymore," Wren said, then took her by the arm. "Come on. Let's go see what you launched."

10

FLIGHT DECK

The flight deck stretched in three tiers of workstations down to a wall-sized screen. The lights were off but the screen was on, showing helicopter footage of some kind of festival in what looked like a desert. There was orange sand underfoot, and thousands of people circled around a giant brass statue of an upright cow, easily fifty foot tall. The people were dressed in bizarre steampunk clothing, all skimpy leather and frills and feathers, like extras from a Mad Max movie. Radiating out around the giant cow were numerous music stages, tents, booths and, further out, a vast field filled with tents.

Wren had no idea what he was seeing. Russian text ran along the bottom of the screen, accompanied by the blue and white '1' logo for Channel One, Russia's premier state-owned news channel.

A man sat in the front row, tall and gaunt, seemingly watching the footage.

"Who's that?" Wren whispered to Olga.

She said nothing.

Wren led her down toward the front of the deck, Makarov

raised. "Hands up," he said, then repeated the order in rough Russian.

The figure didn't budge.

Wren circled around. "I said hands up," he said again, then cleared the front row and got his first good look at the man.

He was in his sixties, coiffed perfectly in a designer suit and sitting ramrod straight with his hands resting placidly in his lap. His gaze was fixed on the screen, but his left eye was circled with purple bruising, crusted with dried blood and so completely bloodshot that it was solidly red.

Wren flashed back to Kiefer. It was the same symptoms on the same eye, the left. A cold sense settled in his stomach as he drew closer. The man's face was pale and his breathing shallow. There was a gilt name badge on his jacket breast, which read Д. АНТОН ВОРОНИН - ДИРЕКТОР.

Doctor Anton Voronin - Director.

Wren cursed, recognizing the name, and strode closer, pulling Olga with him. "Doctor Voronin," he said. "My name is Christopher Wren. I'm looking for Genevieve Faraday. What happened here? Who did this to you?"

The director finally registered him. "You," he said in soft, clipped English. A line of pinkish fluid wept from the side of his left eye as he spoke. "You are CIA?"

Wren ignored that. "Who did this to you, Doctor, and why?"

The man laughed weakly. "Who? I wonder. Perhaps…" he paused, his eyes darting side-to-side until they finally settled on Olga Kusetsnova. "Kusetsnova!"

"Da, Director."

"You are … out of uniform."

"Spetsnaz forces were assaulting her," Wren said. "Director, why were they here? Why were they looting your facility?"

The director's gaze switched to Wren. "Месть," he said, then looked back at the screen.

"I don't know that word. What does it mean?"

The director ignored him, so he turned to Olga.

"Miest," she said. "Vengeance."

"Vengeance?"

She looked at Voronin, but his left eye seemed to disturb her, and she turned back to Wren. "Vengeance, but it is not the act. This is name of Russian orbital platform."

"What orbital platform?"

"I do not know. We launched Persona to Miest aboard Soyuz-2.1a. That is all I know. I want to go home now."

Wren studied her eyes. He didn't think she was lying, but there was something else. Her gaze kept darting to the director. "You know what happened to him?"

She shook her head sharply; a little too quickly for Wren's liking.

"I'm thinking he isn't always like this," Wren pressed. "It's his eye, isn't it?"

"Perhaps he struck his face."

Now she wouldn't look at the director.

"That's bullshit. I've got a friend waiting outside the compound with the same injury to his left eye. Now he can't see, can't think properly, and he's been sleeping for ten hours straight. It was right after he met a giant man with a tattoo on his forehead."

The woman froze in Wren's grip.

"You've met him?" Wren pressed.

"Nyet. No! Let me go."

Wren took her other arm in his hand. She flailed and tried to headbutt him, but he swayed back. "Olga, calm down. The giant with the tattoo, what do you know?"

"Nothing! I saw nothing."

"I don't believe you."

Now her eyes were tearing up. "Let me go."

"Not going to happen until you tell me what you know."

She let out a cry of frustration, tried to send a kick up into Wren's crotch which he easily blocked with his knee, then got control of herself.

"I was at station," she blurted, nodding toward one of the desks in the second row. "This giant man came in with Spetsnaz, also your expert, 'Faraday'." She spat the name like she hated it. "Before launch. All was arranged. We were prepared, excellent pay day, last job for Vostochny. Director Voronin met them, but there was argument. He wanted to know target coordinates."

"What target coordinates?" Wren demanded.

"I do not know! This was not my job. I am engines and upward telemetry. I do not know Miest or purpose of Miest or anything else. Just launch."

Wren shook his head, the notion of target coordinates spiking the tempo of his pulse. "Stop lying. If you're involved with the launch, with the engines and telemetry, you must've known at least what the cargo was. I've done my research on satellites, Olga. I know that it all matters, how mass, orientation and shape affects thrust, inertia, rotation, fuel, drag. What was on board that rocket?"

She stared furiously then snapped. "Tungsten!"

"Tungsten?"

"Five rods of tungsten. Long. Two tons each."

Wren's jaw worked the air. Tungsten was the hardest metal on Earth. "What possible reason could there be to send five rods of tungsten into orbit?"

"I do not know."

"But you must have a guess."

"I did not guess. I do not know!"

Wren frowned. It made no sense, but he believed her.

"OK. I'm thinking the Director knows. Exactly what happened between him and the giant?"

Kusetsnova glanced at Voronin. "Director is man of peace. Man who cares about landing Russian cosmonauts on the moon. This is same for me. So he insisted to know coordinates. Giant refused. Director refused to launch. Then giant man took him." Tears spilled down her cheek. "Held his head and did something to his face. I could not see, nobody could. It was very fast. Director was screaming, making terrible noises, then suddenly stopped. He became like this."

She pointed at Voronin.

Wren's blood ran cold. Few things could explain what they were seeing. He dropped to one knee before the director, pulling Olga down with him, and gently probed around the man's left eye. Voronin didn't budge, but another bloody tear leaked free.

"Did you see drugs, maybe?" he asked Kusetsnova. "A pill or an injection, maybe administered through his eyeball?"

"Through his eyeball?"

"A long syringe, something the giant could keep in his sleeve."

Olga shuddered. "No, I did not see this."

Wren considered, standing again. The Director had known about 'Miest'. He'd known something awful was coming, and Wren had to get it out of him.

"Director, can you see me?" he asked.

"Nyet," the man said, then shifted. "Yes. But you are very far away."

"That's fine. Do you know what you're watching on this screen?"

"Miest," he said, echoing Kusetsnova. "Vengeance."

"Vengeance for what?"

The director opened his mouth then closed it.

"Do you know your name?" Wren tried.

The director looked like he was about to frame a sound, but said nothing.

"Do you know your station? Where you are? Do you know what day of the week it is?"

The director said nothing.

"What about the tungsten rods on board Soyuz-2.1a? Five large tungsten rods, Director. What were they for?"

The Director shuddered. "Tungsten, density 19.25 grams per centimeter squared, high melting point of 6192 degrees Fahrenheit. Tungsten is one of the few substances capable of making Earth re-entry almost intact."

Wren listened and thought. Was that an answer? His mind raced back over the research he'd done in advance of this mission, and everything he'd told Humphreys the Russians were selling off: the cosmodromes, satellites in orbit, rockets, launch pads, flight telemetry, advanced physics simulations and exotic weapons.

His mind stuttered on that last.

Exotic weapons were the stuff of science fiction, the Star Wars program that Reagan had considered in the 80s. One amongst the range of exotics was 'kinetic' weapons: solid rods of a highly toughened metal, like tungsten, that could be dropped from orbit to circle, make re-entry and strike a target with no guidance of any kind.

Hammers of God, they'd been nicknamed by the press at the time. Given the vast height of orbit, and providing for enough weight, such rods could strike directly from the skies with the kinetic force of an atomic bomb.

Wren's mouth went dry.

Reagan had canceled the program. It was always believed the Russians had too. But had they?

"Kinetic weapons," he said, his voice low. "Director, is that what we're looking at here? Heavy rods they can drop on targets?"

The Director's eyes wavered.

Wren spun to the big screen, feeling the urgency fire his pulse faster. "Do you know what that event is?" he asked Kusetsnova.

"Festival," she said.

"I know that. Is it a target?"

"Target? I do not know. This is Channel 1 News, but is on loop."

"It's what?"

"Footage is looped from earlier. I saw this many hours ago."

Wren's mind raced. It couldn't be a coincidence that Director Voronin had demanded to know 'target' coordinates, been denied, then been left watching this looped footage in a semi-lobotomized state. It smacked of petty revenge; the giant rubbing his victim's face in the loss.

"Do you know what festival it is?"

"Da. Of course. Is written."

"Where is it?"

"America."

The sense of dread stamped on Wren's chest. "America where?"

"Desert of Nevada. Is called 'Burning Man' festival. Today is last day. They will burn big cow statue at dusk."

Wren's mouth went dry. The footage showed midday, but if it was a loop? He brought up his watch; adrenaline played games with perception of time, and the long night of the Siberian north didn't help. It was almost 9 a.m. local, but halfway around the world to Nevada, it would be 5 p.m.

Coming up for dusk.

His eyes widened on the screen. Judging by the huge field of tents and the scale of the temporary structures in the desert, there could be almost a hundred thousand people clustered around that golden cow.

The sense of threat cascaded.

Wren dragged Kusetsnova to her station, sat her down then zip-tied her to the chair. The screen was dead but there had to be a way around that. "Find where the Persona went, where Miest is and when it's going to fire. Find me everything, Olga, or a hundred thousand deaths are going to be on your head. Do you understand?"

She nodded. "Da, but-"

Wren tuned her out, pulled the scavenged radio off his belt and put the call through to Humphreys.

11

SPETSNAZ

As the call bounced through redials and automated code checkers, Wren stepped into the office where four dead Spetsnaz agents lay.

The fifth lay amongst them, hog-tied and still. Too still.

Wren kicked him in the stomach and air whuffed from his lungs, then he began coughing. Wren reached down, lifted him bodily then slammed him onto the desk where he'd been about to rape Kusetsnova. The man began to thrash, but that stopped when Wren wrapped one meaty hand around his throat and pressed down hard enough to crush his airway.

"If you don't speak English, this will be a short conversation," he said. "If you do, I want you to blink once."

The man stared at Wren. Already his face was turning red. Wren stared back. Twenty seconds passed. Wren bore down.

Finally the man blinked. Wren ignored it. He blinked again, then many times in rapid succession, until finally Wren let up slightly.

Air rushed into the man's lungs and he gasped.

"The giant," Wren said. "The man with the tattoo on his head. I need to know everything you know."

The Spetsnaz operator shook his head, coughed twice,

then found his voice. "I don't know. I don't know … this man."

Wren squeezed again.

"Wait!" he croaked. "I can tell you … things. Useful things."

Wren relented slightly. "Go."

"I need to … breathe."

"Correct," Wren said, but didn't let up at all.

The guy's eyes widened but he pushed on. "Da … We had … orders. Giant was on … train. We had orders … to follow him."

"Ordered by who?"

"Commanding … officer."

"Give me a name."

The man stared.

Wren squeezed. "Name."

"Arrgh. Yes. Alexey Platnov!"

Wren didn't recognize the name. "Rank?"

"No rank. We are … Spetsnaz. He is FSB … administrator level."

"Why've I not heard of him?"

Anger entered the man's eyes. "Because you … destroyed us. FSB is gone. President Burin is dead. Nothing is left."

"Boo hoo. So you recognize me?"

"You are … assassin. Man who killed … Burin."

"I didn't kill him, actually," Wren offered, as if it made any difference. "That was a colleague of mine. But Platnov, where is he based?"

"He was … Moscow. He came to … train also."

"He was on board with the giant?"

"Not at … same time."

"But he described the giant?"

The man nodded.

"How did he describe him? Does he have a name?"

The man squeezed out a word. "Matthew."

"Matthew? That's it?"

"Yes."

Wren considered. "Why did this 'Matthew' want Faraday?"

"Who?"

"The woman! The woman on the train."

Now the soldier was confused. "What woman?"

"The woman who boarded your train in the Stanovoys. The train halted, right, three hundred miles out? We inserted her, and she didn't get off."

"I do not know … about this. But if you-"

Wren squeezed him silent. He had to think. The man turned red again, elbows thrashing, but Wren was in no mood. He relented slightly.

"Where did he go, this Matthew? Why didn't you join him? Why not return to Moscow with the others?"

"Job was … done," the man rasped. "Spetsnaz are … done. Had our … payment. No point … going back. FSB is … dead."

Wren grunted. Exactly what he'd been telling Director Humphreys. As if on cue, the radio squawked.

"What extension?" came a tinny voice.

Wren brought up the radio. "Director Humphreys, secure line, this is special agent Christopher Wren, codeword clockjaguar 365 with urgent intelligence."

The line clicked and redirected. Wren turned back to the man on the desk.

"You may not have seen a woman board your train, but you saw this 'Matthew' with a woman, correct? An American woman?"

The man nodded reluctantly. "Yes."

"OK. Did Matthew take her with him?"

"Yes."

Wren considered. Now they were getting somewhere. "And was there a launch from this facility in the last eight hours?"

"Yes!"

"Did that launch include the Persona satellite from the central car of your secure train?"

"Yes, yes!"

All that was further confirmation of Kusetsnova's story. "Where did Matthew and Faraday go?"

"Out of … cosmodrome. There is only … one road."

"You didn't hear a destination?"

"I did not … listen. This man, Matthew … he is dangerous."

"Dangerous how?"

"He does things. Bad things. To your friend. To cosmodrome director."

Wren leaned closer. "Do you know what he did?"

"No. People are … different after. Broken."

"I know. Who else went with Matthew and the woman?"

The man's eyes rolled up to the left, accessing a memory. "Six, I think. Quiet men. Not Spetsnaz."

"His own men."

"Yes, exactly."

The radio squawked again.

"Any noticeable characteristics? Did they have tattoos like Matthew?" he tapped his forehead.

"No … only him."

"Do you know what that tattoo means?"

"No! Now … please. Let me … go."

Wren let go of his throat. A familiar voice was on the radio now. He backed into the

corridor and brought up the radio.

"Humphreys?"

"It's me, Wren," Humphreys' familiar bass voice. "I'm

registering you at Vostochny Cosmodrome. What have you done?"

"It's not what I've done, it's what's coming. I've got strong reason to believe there is an imminent kinetic weapon attack coming on the Burning Man festival in Nevada, most likely around or just before dusk, when they light their cow statue."

Crackly seconds passed that couldn't be accounted for by the distance between them.

"Cow statue?" Humphreys came back with. "Kinetic weapon?"

"I know it sounds ridiculous, but by my calculation there could be a hundred thousand people there. Maybe just one of them's the target, maybe they all are. There was a launch of a Persona satellite from Vostochny in the last few hours, likely heading for an orbital platform called 'Miest', which means vengeance. Did you see the rocket go up?"

"We know they launched from Vostochny. Was it really a Persona satellite?"

"No. As far as I can tell, they sent up five two-ton tungsten rods. Drop those from orbit, and given the huge kinetic power they'll generate coming down, they'll blow a target like an atom bomb."

Seconds ticked by. "Wait, Wren. You're saying they're dropping a rod of metal out of space, but with precision? I don't buy it. I've seen satellites fall out of the sky. They break up, burn up, they might kill some wildlife in a forest in Nova Scotia. They're no threat."

Something clicked into place in Wren's head. "Not if they're made of tungsten, Gerald. But you're right. Without incredible precision in the moment they release the rod, the angle it descends, the speed it picks up, the angle it hits the atmosphere, they'll be useless." He mind raced. "That's why Reagan canceled the program. The orbital mechanics required are mindboggling. The whole thing is impossibly complex, with too many factors to calculate. It's science fiction. Except, they have Faraday."

Humphreys said nothing for a long moment, then he cursed.

"Exactly," Wren said. "One of the foremost experts on orbital mechanics in the world. With her running their numbers, I believe they can strike with precision."

Another curse came. "Five rods, you said? Can we shoot them down?"

"Five went up in the last launch, as far as I know. As to shooting them down, I don't know. Maybe? It's a pole coming straight down at terminal velocity." Wren made rough calculations on the size of a two-ton rod. "A radar profile no bigger than a lamp post from side on, as big as home plate from below. No heat signature, no electronics, nothing to target. We'll barely see it, then it'll hit."

Humphreys cursed again.

"I'm going after Faraday. She's the key to this; take her out, and hopefully they'll lose their ability to target. She's currently with a group of seven fanatics led by the tattooed man I told you about, going by the name 'Matthew'. They left the cosmodrome hours ago."

"Going where?"

"Working on it. I've also got the name of the FSB director who arranged the train. His name's Alexey Platnov, out of Moscow. No idea where he is now, but he may know more about the purchase order to set all this up, which might help us locate Faraday."

Moments passed by. "This is a lot, Wren. Do you have evidence for any of this?"

"I'm looking at a brilliant orbital scientist taken, an abandoned cosmodrome, a fake Persona satellite rushed through launch just hours ago, a squad of Spetsnaz on the lam because they've just had a big payday, and two witnesses who saw it all."

"Two Russian witnesses," Humphreys cautioned.

"Three if you include the Director of the whole facility."

"Why wouldn't you include the Director?"

"He's gone mad, or something very like it. Matthew did something to him. The point is, I believe what I'm seeing and so should you."

Seconds ticked by. "And what does Kiefer think of all this?"

"Kiefer's still unconscious. Matthew did something to him too, the same thing he did to the Director, which has left him half blind and confused."

"Did what?"

"I don't know. Drugs, maybe, delivered by a syringe through his eye? Could be oxygen restriction leading to hypoxic brain damage? He did it quickly for both men, then left, like they were no longer a threat. Maybe that's a pattern of behavior you can key into a search matrix."

"Of course," Humphreys said. "I'll just type in 'causes hypoxic brain damage' to the search box and see how far we get."

Wren ignored that. "You need to get the warning out to Burning Man, Gerald. They won't believe it, as far as I know those are hippy types and counterculture warriors, with plenty of anti-government sentiment mixed in. You'll need to send an army of federal agents, local police and national guard to move them off."

Humphreys snorted. "Not only will they not believe it, they'll resist. It'll be like trying to herd coyote, and if there really is an attack coming from space, it'll only put hundreds of our own people into the strike zone."

Wren cursed. That was a good point.

"Put Sally Rogers on it."

"She's standing by to act. I'll send her."

That was reassuring. "Good. Give her resources, Gerald, and watch the clock. Dusk is in a few hours, they'll hit before then."

"I'm aware when dusk is."

Wren refocused. "What about the tattoo, the figure 8 on Matthew's head? My witnesses confirm it, but no one knows what it means. Did you find anything?"

"Nothing yet. We've got symbologists working it up."

"It could be key to tracking him, and understanding Faraday's flip. Could you find anything in her record on why she'd defect?"

"There's news on that. Sally Rogers went out to her ranch already and interviewed her family. On the surface, she's as clean as they come. Some charitable giving, plenty of time with her family, work, riding horses, but that's not all. Apparently she laid out her ranch in the precise same shape as your figure 8 and a cross."

A chill passed down Wren's spine. "She did what?"

"I know. Seven years ago, she freaked out at some contractors when they got it wrong. Two circular paddocks with a cross-shaped entrance to the horses' stable. Apparently, it was only really visible through the rose window in her study. So she could look at it all the time."

"Seven years," Wren breathed. "Gerald. This is bad."

"I know."

"Seven years of radicalization. Seven years at the top of her field, and as a CIA operative. I thought I convinced her to come work with me, but…"

"She played you, Wren."

"She brought me the intel about the Persona launches!" Wren countered. "Look at it that way, and the whole mission was her idea."

Humphreys grunted. "She needed a way into Russia. She needed to be on that train. You delivered her."

Wren cursed. He'd seen no signs of radicalization.

"Seven years," he repeated. "The symbol matters. You need to get those symbologists in a room with a range of experts, spin up a think tank. You'll need Faraday's peers, experts in orbital mechanics, cult experts, a psychologist, whatever you can think of, have them bounce ideas off each other and try to figure out motives and targets."

"I'll do that. How will you follow this 'Matthew'?"

"Only one road leads out of the cosmodrome, so I'll start there." Wren tried to put aside Faraday's betrayal and racked his mind. "Did you get a spy satellite up over Vostochny yet?"

"I told you, it takes time."

"So send a spy plane! We need oversight."

"Not possible, too visible. I'm not ready to rile the Russian bear in its death throes."

"Well get ready, Gerald. Miest is coming whether we like it or not."

Humphreys grunted. "So find Faraday. Get us a fix on this 'Miest' platform. Maybe we can shoot it down."

"I'll be in touch."

12

SOUTH

Wren returned to the Spetsnaz officer. The man had managed to kick himself off the desk to land on his chest on the floor, where he was struggling to inch-worm his way across the room.

"Please," he said, looking up at Wren. "I can give you more. I can-"

"You were going to rape that woman," Wren interrupted, drawing his Makarov. "That'd earn you up to twenty years in prison in the US, but that's not happening here, is it?"

"I helped you!"

"Not enough."

Wren fired a single shot through his skull, killing him instantly.

Back in the flight deck, the main screen had shifted, displaying satellite imagery looking down on a snowy mountainscape. The Director remained in the same place, gazing calmly ahead, while Kusetsnova worked at her station.

"What are we looking at?" Wren asked, striding down to her.

"Did you kill him?" she asked.

"Yes. What is this?"

She nodded. "Thank you. This is our satellite feed above Vostochny. I cannot access anything else. There is lock in our systems, but I can see this."

"Nothing on Miest or the Persona?"

"Only this."

Wren peered at the screen. The contours of Vostochny were vaguely familiar. There was the looming Soyuz-2 rocket, casting a shadow as the wintry sun finally peeked above the mountains, there was the central building they were in currently, and there in the corner…

Wren's heart pounded. "Zoom in there, bottom-right quadrant," he tapped her screen.

She zoomed in. It was exactly what he'd feared. The truck he'd driven in was encircled by another squad of black Spetsnaz soldiers. The doors of the truck were open, with one man kneeling in the snow.

Anais Kiefer.

There were eight soldiers in the squad. One of them drove the grip of his rifle into Kiefer's face, knocking him over.

"Wind that footage back," he ordered, his voice cold. "Find where the giant and Faraday went and track them as far as you can."

"I will try. But-"

"Take this." Wren handed her one of the Spetsnaz radios. "Answer when I call, or I'm coming back for you."

Then he spun and set off at a sprint.

He was out of the building in less than two minutes, into the parked Spetsnaz truck in thirty seconds. The keys he'd taken slotted neatly into the ignition and fired up the engine. He hit the gas, spun the wheel and accelerated away from the central building.

In seconds the train whipped by on his right, then he bounced onto the BAM tracks, cranked his lights to full flood and pushed the pedal all the way down. The truck shot up the slope to the pass, where three of the Spetsnaz were now holding Kiefer up and one was throwing punches like he was a speed boxing bag.

At two hundred yards out Wren crashed through the gate in the perimeter fence. Ahead Kiefer took the blows like a sack of grain. His head lolled. His jaw was bloody. Wren's grip on the wheel tightened. At one hundred yards he wound his window down and waved at the soldiers. They waved back. Only at thirty yards did they realize he wasn't slowing. By then, it was too late.

The truck flew up onto the pass at fifty miles an hour, struck three of the soldiers full on and swept them off the cliff. Their screams rang out until the truck crashed in the valley below.

Wren rolled out his momentum in the snow after diving clear, rose to his feet and fired. The Spetsnaz were stunned at this shift and unready. Wren took out three more before they realized what was happening, by which time only two remained. One raised his rifle and Wren drilled him through the forehead. The other wrapped his thick arm around Kiefer's throat and barked something in Russian.

Wren just advanced, closing the gap.

The man kept shouting. Kiefer watched Wren approach impassively. At five yards out the Spetsnaz went for his side-arm and Wren charged, ramming his shoulder into both him and Kiefer and driving them back. The Spetsnaz fell across the rails and threw an elbow at Wren's face.

It landed, stunning him, but Wren reached around the dizziness and grabbed the man's head, lifting it then slamming it down on the metal rail. There was a thud, and the man went for Wren's throat. Wren did nothing to block him, just slammed his head down again.

The thud was louder, and the hands around Wren's neck

weakened. They wrestled for a moment, but Wren powered through to hammer the man's head one more time.

This time there was a crack. The man shrieked. Wren hammered once more, bringing a final earsplitting crunch, after which he began to convulse.

Wren wasted no more time. He stood up and hoisted Kiefer to his feet.

"Anais, I'm sorry, are you OK?"

Kiefer stared past him, just like before. "Chris," he said in a voice curiously empty of emotion. "I thought you'd gone."

"Of course I'm here. We're in this together. How do you feel?"

Kiefer stood motionless, arms by his side. He made no move to touch his jaw.

"Anais, how do you feel?"

Kiefer tried to fix his wandering gaze on Wren, but it seemed like he was fighting against a strange current, dragging his eyes off target. "I feel different. Am I standing, Chris? Or am I lying down?" He looked down at his legs. "I can't tell."

Wren followed his gaze, as if he'd find Kiefer standing on something other than his legs. "You're standing. You still can't see?"

"Things are jumbled. I can't feel my legs either. I can't feel 'me'. I know that sounds strange. But it doesn't feel like I'm really here."

Wren had never seen anything quite like this before, and it unnerved him. "It's OK, Anais. You're here, just take my word for it. Come on, let's go."

He gently corralled the big man back into the Lada. The tank was half-full, the air inside still warm. Once Kiefer was strapped in, Wren checked his injuries. They looked superficial; a bloody jaw, a broken nose. "I'm sorry I left you, Anais. I'll stick with you from here on."

Kiefer said nothing, simply placed his hands on his lap and stared ahead.

Wren fired up the truck and took off. There was only one road leading out of the cosmodrome. He squeezed the radio to transmit.

"Olga, are you watching me?"

"You killed them all," came her reply. She sounded numb.

"They got in my way. Tell me you tracked Matthew and Faraday?"

"I found them. Are you leaving me here?"

Wren thought of the looped footage showing Burning Man, and the rush with which they'd launched the Persona satellite, and looked at the sun rising over the mountains. Dusk in the US was coming, and he was running out of time.

"Yes, I'm leaving you. You'll find something to cut the zip-tie with, or you'll call for help. Now tell me, where did they go?"

Seconds ticked by.

"Don't test me, Olga."

"West," she spat. "There is one road for five miles. This is limit of our satellite range. There is crossroad onto north-south route. South leads only to small airfield for use of Director and other high rank workers." She paused a moment. "They went south."

Wren cursed. The Lada picked up speed down the slope. "Do you have eyes on the airfield?"

"No. Now I am done. I will not help you kill more Russians."

The radio died. Wren dropped it. The truck skidded around the train platform, bit on the gritted perimeter road and raced toward the one route out, heading west.

13

BURNING MAN

Agent Sally Rogers sat in the Bell Boeing V-22 Osprey helicopter with her six-strong squad of FBI Gold Team members, staring down at the orange desert of Nevada as they sped toward the setting sun.

Dusk, Wren had said.

"How far to Burning Man?" she shouted to the pilot over the roar of the rotors.

"Seven minutes," the pilot answered. "We should see them soon."

Rogers gritted her teeth and stared. The desert was already striped with the long shadows of cacti and boulders. Off to the north lay towering red mesas, to the south were buttes. The hot wind whipped by at two thousand feet, heavy with the sap of high summer.

"Why Burning Man?" she'd asked Director Humphreys.

"It's your job to figure that out," he'd answered. "Wren suggested it could be an individual in attendance. Probably it's packed full of Silicon Valley types, tech bros and entrepreneur investors and millionaire futurists and weirdo influencers of all types."

"Our best and brightest thinkers then," she'd countered.

"Probably. Or it's the whole event, the symbol of it, or maybe it just makes for the largest gathering of people available outside of a city."

"So why not a city?"

"Figure it out, Rogers," he'd countered. "I'm busy squirreling the Cabinet away in bunkers across the country and moving SAM missile batteries above the White House, trying to figure out how we shoot one of these Hammers down if they decide to target Washington. You have investigative lead."

"Understood."

"There it is," called the pilot abruptly.

Rogers looked dead ahead. Bisecting the muddy orange yolk of the sun across the flat desert horizon stood a bizarre statue. A giant cow, she knew, symbolizing money or control or something the Burning Man attendees wanted to see go up in smoke. She'd checked out their ideology, and it was a huge, weird grab-bag of out-there innovations, conspiracies and political policies.

Down there, artists marched hand-in-hand with liberals and conservatives of all political stripes, with neo-communists, with pansexual polyandrists, with face paint-wearing anarchists, transhumanist weed dealers, blockchain touts, tech evangelists, pleather-dressed eco-fashionistas, Earthship kibbutz farmers and more.

It was a mass conference of the bizarre, partying it up in the desert in front of a totemic 'idol' that was so tongue-in-cheek it didn't really mean anything at all. Rogers had seen plenty of such artistic types at college, and considered them generally sweet if clueless.

She gazed down at the Burning Man site. The people were out in the tens of thousands, dancing and swirling around their cow statue like pilgrims in Mecca. She looked up to the deepening blue of the sky, trying to imagine the 'Miest' station far overhead, potentially unleashing one of its Hammers at any moment.

"One minute out," the pilot called.

A spark caught Rogers' eye and she looked back down, but it was just the cow statue being ignited. This was the climax of each Burning Man. Not only the central statue, but everything involved in the festival and the art created during its seven-day duration would be thrown onto this pyre, all a gift to whatever god or gods the festival-goers believed in.

The cow burned. Rogers' hand tightened around the grip of her Glock 19. She didn't anticipate using it. It wouldn't help. They'd already reached out to the festival organizers and they'd blanked her. Nothing was going to stop their bizarre desert ritual.

Nothing, except maybe-

Something drew her eye.

She looked up. A spike of light flared in the skies far above. Rogers' eyes snapped wide. It was miniscule, a tiny red flare in the heavens but dropping fast. For perhaps a second only she stared, awestruck by the thought of what this might truly be: a lamp post-sized rod of tungsten dropped from orbit.

It blazed hotter and moved faster, heading straight for the center of the Burning Man crowds.

"Incoming," she shouted. "Turn us around! Get us out of here."

The pilot swung the cyclic and the helicopter banked. Rogers brought up her walkie. She already had local teams on the ground, and more on their way, both by road and in the air. She hit the button to transmit on all channels.

"The Hammer's coming, get out, get away!"

Then there was a screaming sound, and a series of massive booms as the sound barrier burst, then the Hammer struck.

14

THE HAMMER

The red-hot tip of the Hammer hit the sand and for a single heartbeat there was nothing, just long enough for Sally Rogers to imagine it was a damp squib; perhaps the Hammer had plunged deep under the surface of the Earth like a bullet into water, burying its momentum harmlessly.

Then there was a sudden, blinding flash, and the festival's heart was engulfed in a colossal fireball. It erupted from the Hammer's entry point and ripped outward with terrifying speed, obliterating the cow statue and the music stages and the people in a churning inferno.

The Earth convulsed.

The fireball tore wider, shredding the outer field of tents and sending parked vehicles tumbling on a ring-shaped tsunami wave of flame, dust and debris that swamped the desert in a suffocating haze.

Then the sound slammed into Rogers' ears, a titanic boom that went on and on, only growing louder as the seconds passed by and the fireball lifted off the ground and rose into the sky, so loud she had to clasp her hands over her ears.

"Brace!" cried the pilot, and a moment later the shock wave hit the helicopter like a monstrous hand swatting a fly.

The helicopter bucked and swayed violently, lurching sideways as the pilot wrestled with the cyclic. Kicked-up dust and shrapnel scoured the aircraft like they'd fallen into a sandstorm, adding a constant barrage of cracks and thumps to the throbbing boom of the primary blast.

Below the wave carried across the desert surface like a flood tide, sweeping the desert clear of topsoil and gouging deep trails with the twisted metal of stages, trucks and cars.

Rogers found herself screaming, braced against the frame of the helicopter as the wave rocketed on, and the helicopter shook, rocked, and finally settled.

The booming ended.

The barrage stopped.

Rogers' mouth closed. For long seconds she just breathed, completely overwhelmed by what she'd just experienced. The other members of her gold team looked awestruck and terrified. They panted and stared out of the windows, where the fireball was rising higher across the purple skies, leaving a long mushroom stalk of flame and dust behind.

An eerie silence fell across the desert. Rogers didn't even hear the thumping of the rotor blades, barely registering the pilot's voice as she said they'd taken damage and needed somewhere to land. Nothing felt the same after witnessing the Hammer strike. She felt numb.

Then, perhaps only twenty seconds after the blast struck, reality pummeled back in. The helicopter was reeling, its transmission knuckle grinding overhead and spewing black smoke.

"Where do I put down?" the pilot demanded, spinning to look at Rogers.

Rogers swept open a gear bag at her feet, pulling out an energy-compensated Geiger- Müller counter. For all they'd heard from Wren about kinetic weaponry, after what she'd just witnessed, and with that mushroom cloud still climbing into the sky, she needed to know if this had been a nuclear strike.

The counter fired up and began to click. Rogers watched the digital readout roll to settle between two figures, 49 to 50cpm, or counts per minute.

Normal background radiation.

"It's safe," she shouted to the pilot. "Put us down wherever you can."

The pilot gave a thumb's up and worked the collective lever, sending the helicopter into a teetering descent. Rogers took a breath, ripped her gaze away from the thick trunk of dust written across the sky, and turned to her team.

"The mission just changed," she shouted over the thunder of the dying rotors. "We're now first-on-scene at a disaster. Survivors, if there are any, will be at the very fringe. No one will have lived through this at the heart. We do what we can and we help coordinate the wider response. Leave all weapons behind. Is that clear?"

"Understood," her sergeant shouted back.

Rogers plucked a bag of med equipment from the stack of gear and handed it to one of her team members as they came down, then dragged the helicopter's own emergency med-kit in a tin from under her seat and handed it to another. It was a paltry amount of equipment, but perhaps it was more than they'd even need.

She brought up her radio and tuned through to Gerald Humphreys. His deep voice came through in seconds.

"What the hell happened out there, Rogers? I'm showing a seismic event of-"

"The Hammer hit," she interrupted, taking a page from Wren's book. "It's like a nuclear bomb, but no radiation.

There's nothing left of the festival, but there could be survivors. Send everyone you've got."

"Nothing left?"

"It got completely erased. There's a mushroom cloud. I'll stream video when we're on the ground."

"I'll send everything we've got. Godspeed, Sally."

The helicopter came down through thick clouds of dust, putting down on a ragged field of sand. Sally Rogers was first out, onto dark sand that shifted and clinked strangely underfoot.

"What's this?" one of her teammates asked, reaching down and coming up with a globular chunk of glass, stretched out like an elongated teardrop and tinted yellow.

Rogers scanned the desert through the drifting smoke and settling dust. Similar chunks of glass were everywhere; some in large round clumps like glazed barrel cactuses, others in large runs like diamond rail tracks leading deeper.

"The sand fused," she said, surprised to hear her voice saying the words. "The heat of the blast smelted it."

The team member abruptly dropped the teardrop and it thudded on the ground. "It's hot."

"Everything will be. It fused then blew outward. Come on, spread out."

Rogers led the way, advancing over the field of sand and glass. Ahead loomed a structure of some kind and she sped toward it; the boxy frame of a large truck trailer lying on its side. Its corners and vertices remained, but the panel walls were gone, seemingly melted away, along with whatever the contents had been. Rogers climbed up the hood and peered in through the passenger-side window, but the cab had been scrubbed back to the bare metal; no chair, no wheel, no dashboard, only the blocky skeleton of the chassis beneath.

She brought up her phone and keyed up the video, then tagged that to Humphreys' line in a livestream.

"I don't think anybody survived," she said.

"I'm putting you live with the Joint Chiefs and the President," Humphreys said. "You're on their screen already."

Rogers was too numb to feel intimidated.

"I'm on the verge of the blast here," she reported, advancing deeper into the clouds of smoke and sand. "Maybe a mile or two out, and there's nothing. The sand's been melted to glass." She kept moving, sighting on something in the gloom. "Wait, there's something ahead."

She ran. The screen jogged up and down but no word came from the other end of the line as the top officials in her country stared on silently. The shape ahead was lumpish, looming upward from the sand like a strange crag. As she neared it grew clearer; some kind of huge metal structure, the surface mottled and bubbled from heat, its contours blending together.

"I know what this is," she whispered, as she finally picked out one blunted horn, barely a nubbin on the statue's flattened skull. "It's the cow."

She circled it, looking up. It was half-buried in the sand, leaning at an angle. "That was sixty feet of solid brass," she said softly as a fine rain of sand and dust pattered off the metal, skittering down to the surface. "It took them a year to forge, some twenty tons of metal. The blast just picked it up and threw it."

Voices came through the line, but Rogers didn't hear. She ran on. It only took a few minutes, by which time the desert winds and the heat convection had begun cutting clear avenues through the smoke and hanging dust. She found herself within one, looking out over a vast expanse that had been utterly decimated.

A crater centered on the Hammer's Ground Zero.

It was easily a half mile across and a hundred feet deep,

and filled with fused, glistening glass. The sun's last rays sparkled on the perfect surface like a vast concave ice rink.

Sand continued to rain from the sky. The mushroom cloud above had flamed out, leaving only a massive brown weight of dust that blocked half the sky. She looked back down. There were no people. No stages or structures. Nothing of Burning Man remained.

"Oh my God," Rogers whispered.

Voices spoke through the phone, but they didn't register any more than the dust falling. She stared, feeling this down to her bones. Seventy thousand people in attendance; that was the number she'd gotten off the organizers before they'd shut her out.

All gone.

"Agent Rogers," came Humphreys' stark voice, snapping her back to the moment.

"Yes," she said.

"You can't do anything there. I've sent another helicopter. Get your team out. You're on point for this. Work with Wren. We cannot allow another of these Hammers to fall on American soil. Do whatever it takes."

American soil. She stared at the crater for a moment longer, then nodded. Humphreys was right. This was the worst attack America had ever received, and one it would remember forever.

There could not be another.

15

AIRSTRIP

Wren whipped through the moonlit mountains west of Vostochny, with Anais Kiefer drooling by his side. Ice on the road made the truck skid but Wren adjusted around a sharp twist, shooting out over an iron bridge between two ridges.

Ahead was the crossroad. Wren raced through and turned left, heading south. The route plunged down between the sheer walls of a widening valley, until the dark oblong patch of a runway ahead became clear, illuminated by a handful of burning firepits.

There was an ice-rimed hangar with light showing through a small window toward the rear. Wren braked the truck twenty yards out, tires spitting ice chips and gravel, then turned to Kiefer.

"Five minutes, OK?"

"Five minutes what?" Kiefer responded. His right eye tried to fix on Wren, while the left was immobile now, seemingly clotted into position.

"To rest. I'll be back."

The air seemed even colder outside the truck, perhaps dropped into an icy micro climate. He looked up at the purple dark skies, spattered with a patina of thousands of stars, hoping for a contrail. The atmospheric conditions made the odds around fifty percent: jet contrails formed best when the engine's hot, wet water vapor exhaust fumes met the thin, cold air of 30 to 40 thousand feet and produced ice crystals.

Most jets cruising at those altitudes left contrails, but many faded swiftly, thanks to low ambient humidity in the air forcing the ice crystals to disperse back as water vapor. The colder the air, though, the more chance the crystals would hang for hours, gently spreading into a wide furrow.

Night was best, as the Earth cooled. The air over Siberia had to be some of the coldest there was, but also the driest.

Wren spun, registering familiar constellations even here thousands of miles from home, along with others he rarely saw given the northerly latitude of 63 degrees, compared to Delaware at 38. There were wispy clouds to the south, and Polaris hung high and clear above the greenish tinge of the Northern lights. For a moment he mistook the crisp froth of the Pleiades cluster for the starting line of a contrail, then looked further afield.

Over the Stanovoy mountains. Any jet rising from this valley airstrip would take time to reach cruising altitude. He looked around, then climbed up onto the truck's hood, then its roof, trying for a better angle on the horizon.

The extra few degrees of visibility made the difference. There, at the very edge of the horizon, was the clear zipper-like tip of a contrail, heading north.

Matthew and Faraday.

Wren dropped down and ran to the hangar. The front roll shutters were down but around the rear there was a door. As he closed on it he considered knocking, but thought better of it and instead sent out a front kick with everything he had.

The door flew open, battering against a wooden worktop and revealing a small office-workshop lit with an orange glow. On the table at the center stood an incomplete scale model of Vostochny, complete with Soyuz-2 rocket. On the walls hung framed photographs showing the construction of Vostochny, and on the surrounding workbenches lay the tools and materials needed to craft the scale model. An old Grundig radio produced a low stream of Russian.

Sitting in a chair with a look of vague annoyance on his face sat an old man, easily 70 years old, with long white whiskers emerging from under a thick gray fur-trimmed 'ushanka' cap. A pipe rested crookedly between his lips, a thin waft of bluish-gray smoke rising from the bow, and a brass jeweler's loupe hung equally loosely in the embrace of his right eye. In one hand he held a precision boxcutter, caught in the act of whittling what looked to be a piece of Soyuz booster tank.

He gazed at Wren and spoke in grizzly Russian, which Wren roughly understood to mean, 'Are you going to close the door?'

"Are you alone?" Wren countered in his amateur Russian, scanning the workshop with his Makarov raised.

The old man laughed and switched to English. "American? You are very far from home."

"I like the scenic route. Call me a tourist if you like; I'm looking to hop a flight right now. Are you alone?"

The old man slowly spread his arms. "Who else would be here? I am, what is the word, lighthouse keeper?" He smiled. "All alone, left to keep lights lit, with hobbies." He held up the rocket tank and the boxcutter.

"Put the weapon down."

"This is not weapon," said the old man, and reached under the table worktop and smoothly brought out a polished silver Tokarev pistol. "This is a weapon."

Wren kicked the table before he could point it, jamming the edge across the old man's chest and tipping him backward. The pistol discharged into the ceiling then his back hit the floor and Wren was there, securing first the Tokarev, then the man's wrists.

"You're no lighthouse keeper," Wren growled, hoisting him back into his chair. He checked for further weapons, pocketed the boxcutter then stepped away. "You're an exile. KGB?"

The old man shrugged, like nothing had happened. "I worked for many agencies, for a time. One day they will recall me."

Wren snorted. "Unlikely. Russia is collapsing, in case you hadn't noticed, and the group who just left on a jet out of this air strip will only bring the death blow faster."

The old man laughed and leaned over, groaning as he scooped up his pipe and put it back in his mouth. "Death blow. Americans always think Russian bear is defeated. You think you stuff and mount us on your wall, like great hunter." He sucked and the pipe crackled as the tobacco flamed red, releasing a puff of blue smoke. "But Russia comes back. I will come back."

"OK," Wren said, watching the door into the hangar. There'd been a gunshot but nobody had come; that suggested it was just the two of them. "I can help you with that."

The old man laughed. "Help me? You already broke my door. Now you have broken my rocket." He gestured to the scale model, where the Soyuz-2 had tipped over. "I doubt I will survive any further American help."

Wren picked up the rocket and stood it up again firmly. "What's your name?"

The man's eyes narrowed. "Call me Ivan."

Wren restrained laughter. It was only one of the most common Russian names. "OK, Ivan. I'm Chris. The people who just flew out of here included a giant man and a woman with red hair, is that right?"

"This might be right," 'Ivan' allowed.

"Good. Well, they have bought access to a Soviet-era orbital weapons array called Miest, sold because your country is mid-collapse, and now they're targeting America. But it's a Russian-made array, Ivan. When one of their missiles strikes, who do you think American will come for?"

Ivan studied Wren, then reached over and tapped the rocket gently. One of the fins snapped off and it toppled again. "See. Here is American help."

Wren stared at him. This exiled spy had been hardened by years of solitude and dreams, and he wore that like a thick protective shell. Drilling through that could take time, but Wren didn't have time. Already the contrail would be dispersing into the dry, cold skies far above.

"I need a plane now. Either you help me, or I kill you and help myself. If they drop a missile on-"

"If?" Ivan interrupted, his eyes shifting to the antique radio in the corner. "What is this 'if'?"

Wren stared at him in the silence that followed, then looked at the radio and tuned into what the voice was saying. It was too low and crackly for him to catch much, but he did hear essential details; enough to tell him everything he needed.

Burning Man. A missile. Death count in the tens of thousands.

His heart sank and his blood ran cold. With a death count that large, it would be the worst strike on American soil ever. He was too late; the Miest had begun its vengeance.

But four more Hammers remained.

He stepped closer and set the Makarov against Ivan's head. "Put me on a plane or die."

The old man laughed. "Who is stuffed and mounted now, American?"

Wren pulled back the hammer on the Makarov. "Five

seconds. Help me and I'll help you get back to Moscow. Refuse and your fantasies end here. Two seconds. One."

"Da," said Ivan, as casually as if Wren had asked him his preference of borscht. "I want one thing."

"What?"

"Give me back East Berlin."

Wren stared at him. "Is that a joke?"

"Perhaps. Is black humor. In times of loss, is Russian way. During famine, many jokes about sexual appeal of potato."

Anger blurred in Wren's chest with a strange lightheaded giddiness. "We were just attacked. People died."

"People always die, American. Is one third function of people. Born, make babies, die. Understand?"

Wren gritted his teeth. He'd have time to process the loss later; now he had to deal with a mad Russian. "OK. So, East Berlin?"

"Da. Does not need replacement wall. I know you Americans struggle to build walls."

Wren frowned. Another joke. Maybe he'd misjudged this man. "I'll buy you a ticket to Berlin. Stay on the east side if you like. The whole city's come a long way. You can buy Levi's and Marlboros anywhere."

Ivan studied Wren like he was weighing the decision. "I will only stay at Ritz-Carlton."

Wren snorted, amused beside himself. "Of course you will. And dine every night at the Waldorf Astoria. Deal?"

Ivan gave his hand. Wren shook it.

"I have planes," Ivan said. "Not fast. Not jet. I will not fly them."

"Not a problem. Just get me in a cockpit."

16

ANTONOV

Ivan led Wren through the door into the hangar, where several planes stood in darkness, veiled with dust sheets and vaguely illuminated by the orange light from the workshop. It looked like a graveyard fleet from the Cold War.

"This is your choice," the old man said, then hit a switch by the door. Bright white lamps spat to life, casting harsh shadows under the fuselages of four vintage planes. None were jets. One was barely a glider. "I recommend Antonov."

"After you," Wren gestured. Not one of the planes looked like they could catch a jet, if they could even fly at all. Ivan strode between the aircraft until they reached the furthest, closest to the roll shutter.

"Antonov An-2 biplane," Ivan said proudly, pulling on the sheet to reveal the glass cockpit, two-wing design and single propeller engine of what looked to be an old-style cropduster. "Soviet design, 1948, sturdy, very worthy of air."

Wren studied the Antonov's bodywork. Not only was it old but it was battered, with an olive paint job that was scarred and peeling, and what looked to be bullet pocks in the steel undercarriage.

"1948," Wren said. "It could've flown in World War 2. The best you've got is a biplane?"

"Is reliable Soviet engineering," Ivan said, and gave the flank of the plane a hearty thump. The metal resounded. "Like AK-47. We Russians understand that when it is not broken, you do not fix it."

"And that's why you didn't invent the iPhone," Wren muttered.

"iPhone is for fools with no patience," Ivan said, and opened the plane's rear door. "Antonov is rock of ages."

Wren frowned and leaned in. The interior had been stripped of seating. "In my experience, rocks don't fly. Where are the chairs?"

"Is drug plane," Ivan said. "Commandeered from small airstrip in Mongolia, Chinese Triad members shipping opium into Russia. All seats removed to make space for opium bales. Here, you see bullet holes?" he pointed at the pocks through the plane's skin. "Also, there are bloodstains."

Wren shook his head. He'd taken brief courses on small jets, but nothing as old as the Antonov. Peering into the cockpit, he saw the most basic flight controls that he recognized, but there was nothing more. Most cars had more information in their dashboards. "I can't fly this."

Ivan laughed again. "Of course not. You are half-dead man, like zombie."

"What?"

"Your eyes," Ivan said, pointing. "Drunk, high, or not sleeping for many days. CIA officer on vital mission?" Wren's face gave nothing away, which only seemed to amuse Ivan further. "You will crash my Antonov. I cannot give this excellent plane to man who will only crash into mountain."

Wren stared at him, trying to read between the lines, whether this was another joke or not. "You said you wouldn't fly either."

Ivan shrugged. "Perhaps I am now also keen for scenic route. I do not wish American bombs to land on Russia. Our resurgence would be much delayed. I will never return to Moscow, if this happens."

Wren laughed, then stopped when Ivan cast him a dark glare. "Of course. You want to go back to Moscow."

"As hero."

"As a hero, by way of Berlin. OK. So, you will pilot it?"

"Da. Where is destination?"

"I don't know. North somewhere. Do you know where the last group were going?"

"Nyet. Of course not. For them, I am janitor dusting down plane they left here three months ago. I know nothing."

Wren's gaze narrowed. Maybe he'd misjudged this man. "They left the jet here for three months? Do you have any records of that?"

"Records of secret plane being left in secret facility? No."

"Then who ordered it? You must know who told you to watch their plane."

"Order was not to watch it. Ignore it, but fuel it. And order comes from Vostochny Cosmodrome Director, Comrade Voronin."

Wren sighed. "He's broken, as good as dead."

Ivan smiled. "See. One third of life."

Wren shook that off. "But you'll still help me? You know these people are not acting in Russia's best interests."

Ivan sighed. "They are not. You are not. Maybe I am not. They are looters before corpse is cold. You are great American glory hunter, like Indiana Jones. I am old lost spy full of bitter regret. This is good cast for Hollywood movie, no?"

"So let's go earn our Oscar," Wren said. "All I have to go off is their contrail."

Ivan laughed, looked at Wren then laughed even harder

when he realized he was being serious. "Contrail? Of jet? We will chase with this," he smacked the rump of the Antonov again, "following ice vapor in air?"

"That's the plan. I'd say we better get going, wouldn't you?"

Ivan laughed once more, then smiled. "Da! This is what I like about Americans. No common sense, full of dumb confidence."

Wren frowned but had no real argument to offer back. "What about fuel?"

"I will fuel Antonov. Collect your friend. Board him. We will go."

"How did you know I had a friend?"

Ivan winked. "I am not only old man with crafting hobby. I am spy, so I spy. I watch Vostochny. I watch you. Now, go."

Wren's frown deepened, then he ran. Back at the truck, Kiefer was exactly where he'd left him, hands in his lap, staring ahead like a posed mannequin. When Wren spoke to him, he only said one thing.

"I don't feel right."

"I know," Wren soothed. "We'll get help."

"Help," he repeated, then allowed Wren to guide him out of the truck. He didn't shiver in the cold. He said nothing more. Wren got the impression if he sat him on the snow, he'd just stay there until he froze.

It took several minutes to reach the Antonov.

"Fueled," said Ivan, pulling a hose out of the gas tank and letting it drop to the floor. Beyond him, the roll shutter was open, revealing the airstrip with its fire pit barrels still burning, marking the runway. Ivan looked out toward it. "I will not come back here, will I?"

"Vostochny's been abandoned. If you return, you'll be alone."

"I have been alone long enough. Here."

He pointed to the back of the plane. Wren guided Kiefer in then followed. Ivan climbed into the cockpit and started the engine. The front propeller coughed, rattled then whined to life, spinning faster and faster until it bit on the air and pushed off. They taxied to the tip of the runway, and Wren found belts still attached to the walls. He strapped Kiefer in, then himself.

"Rest," Ivan shouted over the roar of the engine. "I think you will need it for what comes next, American."

Wren already felt himself being lulled by the vibrations and the white noise. The old spy whooped something in wild Russian, then the Antonov rumbled off. It went fast but felt slow to Wren. The twin wings caught the air and the structure strained. Wind whistled through the bullet holes. He spotted a bloodstain in the flooring, then they were in the air and rising.

"Follow the contrail," he shouted, already fighting a wave of exhaustion.

"This is common Russian hobby," Ivan shouted back. "Children follow bread crumbs. Men follow jets. We will see where fairy tale leads."

17

ORBITAL MECHANICS

Wren almost succumbed to the tide of sleep, but thoughts of the radio transmission stating Burning Man had been hit dragged him back up. He lifted his satellite radio and checked the battery. Almost dead. He dialed it to Humphreys.

The line went through swiftly this time.

"Wren," came Humphreys' voice, barely audible over the engine though Wren had the radio pressed close to his ear.

"Tell me it's not true, Gerald. Tell me they didn't destroy Burning Man."

"I wish I could. They hit it, Chris."

Wren cursed. "How bad?"

"Bad. We had visual contact on the Hammer as it came down and it blew like a nuclear bomb, just like you said. Mushroom cloud, total devastation, most likely all 70,000 attendees dead."

Wren cursed again. Too late.

"Sally Rogers was in a helicopter nearby and she got hit by the blast wave. She's OK, but it was close."

Wren said a prayer for small mercies. "Do we have anything on motivation on these attacks?"

"Nothing yet. We're priming assaults on all our primary enemies, Islamists, Russia, North Korea and others, but we don't want to strike randomly. We can't afford another Iraq."

Wren grunted, mind racing. "Rogers needs to get the attendance list for Burning Man, find out if this was an assassination of a single individual. If we can rule that out, then we look into the symbol on Matthew's head, and brainstorm reasons someone might go after Burning Man as a group. Maybe they just really hated hippies." He paused to think. "Did we get anything on Faraday, why and how she flipped?"

"There's nothing on Faraday. No sign of coercion, her family are all in protective custody and not one knew she was planning this. Same goes for her colleagues. She kept it dark. I'll relay the rest to Rogers. Let me put you on the line with-"

"Not yet. My battery's almost dead. I'm on a plane heading north, chasing the contrail of Matthew and Faraday. It's a shot in the dark; I need to talk to someone who knows orbital mechanics, satellites, re-entry physics."

A second passed. "I can get them. Who do you need?"

Wren scanned his memory. He'd spoken to a number of experts in the field in his search for Faraday; there'd been smart people amongst them, even some geniuses, but none with the innate understanding and field experience of Faraday. "I want Kepler or Thorne. You'll also want a symbologist, an expert on counter culture, a cult expert, a Russia expert, as well as anyone who knows Faraday. Put them in a think tank and bang their heads together until something shakes loose, brainstorming motives for this attack, next moves, next targets. We need to clear the fog."

"Agreed, I'll arrange that," Humphreys said. "As for Kepler, he's here already, on the floor below."

"Good. I'm down to a few percentage points, I need to talk to him now."

"The call's going through."

The line clicked. Wren checked his battery. 5%.

"Kepler here."

"Kepler, it's Wren. I'm on a plane heading north out of Vostochny Cosmodrome, chasing Faraday and a terrorist called Matthew. I need to know what they're doing, why they might be leaving Vostochny, and likely destinations."

Seconds ticked by. "I couldn't possibly guess that, Agent Wren," Kepler said. "I already told the Director that I have no special insight into Genevieve's mindset, and-"

"I'm not asking you to delve into her psyche," Wren interrupted. "I want the science. They're shooting tungsten rods from orbit. That's not easy, right?"

"Not easy?"

"Could you do it? Fire from orbit and hit Burning Man, while keeping the launch platform, Miest, undetectable?"

Seconds passed. "I take your point."

"So talk to me. What does it involve? What would it take for you to do it? Can they automate it? Is it something some kid in Alabama could trigger, hitting a button on a smartphone once the app is dialed in, or is it more complex?"

Kepler laughed nervously. He was young and socially awkward, a graduate of Yale at 16, he'd been rushed through first CERN then the NASA mill, before a stint with Blue Origin gave way to a massive grant bursary at Harvard, where he gave boring lectures and originated stunning mathematical proofs of orbital dynamics, taking into account quantum theory in ways few others could match. He was 25 now, quite possibly had never had a girlfriend and wouldn't stand a chance in the field, but he'd still been Wren's second choice for the mission.

"A kid in Alabama? I don't think so. This kind of operation, it's not…" he paused, trying to find the words, "it's not something an AI can do. An algorithm can't do it. You can't just drop data points into a decision tree and pop out an answer."

"Why not?"

Kepler breathed heavily. "It's far too complex. There's an unknowable quantity to orbital dynamics, Agent Wren. Even if a single percentage point is unknowable, and we guess wrong, that would place a strike hundreds of miles off target. Honestly, we're still reeling that she achieved this. There's definitely a level of artistry involved. It's like…"

"What's it like?" Wren prompted, watching his battery drop to 3%.

"It's like shooting basketballs into a hoop, but imagine the hoop is three thousand miles away, with five layers of atmosphere between you and the hoop. The troposphere, the stratosphere, the-"

"I don't need the names of all the layers."

"OK. But each layer has a different density, temperature, elemental composition, and all of those are constantly shifting, depending on time of day, climate and about a thousand other factors we can barely account for. There's also the Van Allen radiation belts, and different orbit heights and velocities, and-"

"Got it. It's hard."

"Almost unknowably hard. You're talking about petabytes, no, exabytes of data just to get started, then a serious supercomputer to crunch that, plus the programming skills to make sense of it. There are no programs I know of that can do that, as there's no commercial application, so she must have written her own code." He took a breath. "Now, could I do what Faraday has done here, you asked? The simple answer is no, not a chance. A machine can't do it, though that would be ideal. The best way to organize a strike decision like this, requiring release of the rod timed to the fraction of a millisecond, would be at the point of departure, meaning the Miest platform itself. Automation would be best, but impossible, not with that one percent missing, that human artistry."

"So what does that mean for where I'm going?"

"It means Faraday is a necessary human component in these strikes, at least for any kind of decent accuracy, and the best place for her to be is at a location closest to the Miest, to minimize distance to transmit the strike decision."

Wren frowned. "So, she should be in space? Aboard the Miest?"

"That would be ideal, but not feasible. The only habitable orbital station is the International Space Station, and she's not aboard that. No, the closest she could be is a point on the Earth most proximal to the orbital platform."

Wren frowned. 1% battery. "So, directly underneath the Miest? You think it might be a geostationary satellite, rotating while locked to a point on the Earth's surface?"

"Highly unlikely. A GEO orbit, or Geosynchronous Earth Orbit, is extremely high, around 36,000 km high. The lag time would be a quarter of a second; that's decades. More likely the Miest will be in an LEO or MEO that overpasses her regularly."

"In English, Doctor."

"Sorry, Low Earth Orbit or Middle Earth Orbit. LEO is anything from 160 to 2,000km, MEO is 2,000 to 36,000km. LEO would be best, the lag is only three thousandths of a second. She could compensate for that."

Wren tried to put that together. "So that means they're going to a high-speed comms center above which the Miest will orbit regularly, most likely in LEO?"

"Correct."

"OK, that gives us a lead on the Miest." Another thought struck him. "How long does one orbit take?"

"One orbit?"

"I'm wondering why there have been no more strikes. She has at least four more Hammers. Is it because the satellite takes time to come overhead again?"

Keys clacked down the radio line. "Excellent question. A satellite at the lowest LEO would take 90 to 120 minutes to orbit the Earth. MEO is anything from 2 hours to 24, but bearing in mind that the further away the satellite is, the longer the transmit time. How long since the last attack?"

Wren checked his watch. "Just over two hours."

"Then we can likely rule out LEO."

A cold shiver ran down Wren's back. "So MEO. That means the next strike is due in hours."

"Most likely within the next eight hours. Any longer and you're into the Van Allen radiation belts, and they're too unpredictable."

"Eight hours," Wren repeated, and set an alarm on his watch. "Make sure Humphreys hears all that. And see if you can find a high-speed comms center on any map on my route north."

"I can try, Agent Wren, but you are talking about Siberia. I don't know of any, and I know all the major space observatories. If I wanted to hide a secret comms base anywhere in the world, I'd put it in northeast Siberia. There's a million valleys in the mountains, almost as unknowable as deep space. Short of us fielding about a million spy satellites on constant overwatch, we'd never see it."

"So tell Humphreys to start moving satellites on my northward route. Nothing matters more than this. And Kepler, you really need to…"

The radio died.

Wren looked down at it. He'd been going to say, 'really need to figure out a way to detect these Hammers as they fall,' but perhaps that was redundant. Without knowing where they were coming from, and a fall time of anything from hours to seconds, there weren't enough SAMs batteries in the world to protect the entire United States.

That fell to him out here and Rogers back east.

Six hours or less.

He looked up at Anais Kiefer. The big man looked like a child, sat with his legs stretched out, hands placidly in his lap. He had no idea of the stakes they were facing. It occurred to Wren that neither had eaten or drank anything in hours.

"Are you thirsty, Anais?"

The big man looked past Wren. "Yes."

"Do you want to drink something?"

"Yes."

Kiefer made no move toward their packs, so Wren reached in and scooped out several water bottles and a few packs of MREs. He opened one of the bottles and held it out to Kiefer. The big man didn't even look at it.

"Don't tell me I have to feed you like a baby."

Kiefer didn't budge.

Wren popped the cap and held the bottle to Kiefer's lips. The big man drank. Water spilled down his chin, but he swallowed most of it. He drank the whole thing, then smacked his lips and let out a big, "Ah!"

Wren laughed. "Was that good?"

Kiefer said nothing more. Wren swigged his own bottle, then popped the first MRE. Tarragon chicken with green beans and rice. He took it in turns to spoon-fed Kiefer and himself. Kiefer ate with minimal mess, occasionally chomping at the spoon in an almost playful manner. Together they got through three MREs.

"No 'Ah'?" Wren asked afterward.

"It wasn't delicious," Kiefer countered.

Wren laughed again, looking into Kiefer's good eye. "You're in there, aren't you? Somewhere."

Kiefer said nothing.

For a few minutes they sat side-by-side, lulled by the vibrations of the plane.

"You don't know what he did to you, do you?" Wren asked softly.

Kiefer said nothing, but he shuddered.

"It's OK," Wren said, and patted his arm. "It's all OK. Rest now."

Soon Kiefer's eyes closed, and his breathing became low and even. Only then did Wren allow himself to drift off too, in a cropduster plane piloted by an ex-Russian spy, chasing a trail of icy dust into the Arctic north.

18

ROSTER

The helicopter's downdraft blasted away the clouds of dust to land on the Nevada desert. Sally Rogers boarded with her team. No one spoke as they took to the skies. Her mind was a whirl and she didn't know how to begin.

"Where are we going?" the pilot asked.

She tried to stamp some discipline on her thought process but struggled to take her eyes off the crater. There was no filling this in. Maybe it would become a national monument. Like the craters on the moon, it would remain for millennia.

"Agent Rogers, where are we going?"

She clicked back into the moment. There'd been an attack and more could come at any moment. She had point. Her mind raced ahead full throttle.

"The nearest airport with a jet," she ordered.

"Routing for Winnemucca Airport," the pilot said, then worked the cyclic and tilted the collective, throwing them into a sharp spin away from the crater and the tumbling brown cloud. The helicopter banked then leaned forward hard, bearing west toward the blood red line of the horizon, where the sun had finally set.

Rogers brought up the radio, still carrying the line to Director of National Intelligence Gerald Humphreys.

"Director, I need to talk to Wren."

"I'm working on arranging that. He's gone dark."

"As soon as you can," she said, trying to think like Wren. They'd gone after terror organizations together before, and he'd taught her that you had to start with the 'why'. The motivation. Once you had that, the rest fell into place. "Has anyone claimed this attack?"

"Nothing yet."

"No chatter?"

"Other than Wren's input? We're completely in the dark."

Rogers cursed.

"We're working to re-establish contact. In the meantime, I need next steps, Agent Rogers."

She took a deep breath and pulled herself together. She could do this without Wren. "OK. We need to get our hands on the Burning Man attendee list; try to figure out if this was an attack on a single individual, a group, or just Burning Man as an icon. I tried to get the organizers to share the roster earlier, but they refused. As far as I know, they were all on site except one."

"All the organizers? Who wasn't there?"

She took another steadying breath. "Tech billionaire Lars Mecklaren, owner of the NameCheck and WeStream social media sites. He's been a silent partner in Burning Man for a decade. He's the only one who might have the list."

"Lars Mecklaren," Humphreys repeated, sounding surprised. "He's a free speech and privacy absolutist, Rogers. He won't cooperate."

"He will for me," she said. "And if he doesn't, on the day his country's under attack, then we hang him for treason."

"Agreed. I'll scramble SEAL team 7, currently shored off San Francisco, to rendition him immediately."

"Plus we need an elite think tank brainstorming motives for this attack. We need to clear the fog of unknown unknowns in the next hour. Get every expert you can think of in a room. Or better yet, multiple think tanks with multiple experts."

"Already working on that," Humphreys said. "We have the people here. I'll portion them out and fire them off."

"You'll want satellite and orbital experts in each group, a symbologist, an expert on counter culture, a cult expert, a Russia expert, as well as anyone who knows Faraday. Bang their heads together until something shakes loose." She thought for a moment. "Do we have anything on tracking the Hammer back to its point of origin?"

"Point of origin for the Miest platform is our highest priority; we should have something back on that and the rest within the hour. Pull no punches with Mecklaren, Rogers. You have the President's absolute backing. She's about to go on national television and announce the attack. As of now, the country's at war. Find us an enemy."

"On it," Rogers said, and put the phone down. The crater was behind them now. Only clear desert lay ahead.

"Go faster," she said to the pilot.

They reached Winnemucca Airport in five minutes, where a Cessna Citation Longitude jet was already fueled and waiting at the head of the single runway strip. Rogers and her team transferred and within another five were back in the air, climbing to thirty thousand feet and accelerating to 600 knots. They'd eat up the 500 miles to San Francisco in less than an hour.

"Anything on Wren?" she asked one of her team, Danny Riggs, a comms expert with a DELTA past.

"Still nothing."

"Have you got the symbologists?"

He checked his tablet. "We've got one in a room at

Langley, symbol and cult expert, yet to be assigned his working group by the Director. Leviticus Farley."

"Leviticus?"

"He's old school."

"Old Testament, more like it. Put him on."

"Here you go."

Riggs tapped a number then handed her one of many phones he kept on his person.

"Hello?" came a tentative voice, high and nasal.

"Mr. Farley," Rogers began, "this is Special Agent Sally Rogers. I understand you've been working on the symbol we provided."

It took a moment, then he spoke again. "Agent Rogers. Is it true that-"

"The symbol, please, Mr. Farley. You'll be in your working group soon where you'll get a full debrief."

"Very well. Thank you." He took a breath, steadying himself. "Now, the symbol you discovered, I have been researching this for the last several hours. An upright figure 8 with a small cross. To my knowledge, this precise configuration exists nowhere. I've never heard of it and neither has any expert in the field. However-"

"Never heard of it? How could that be possible?"

"New symbols arise organically all the time, Agent Rogers. New groups form and create them. Sometimes they create from whole cloth, sometimes they evolve an existing symbol in new ways. If we break the symbols down, an 8 and a cross, the potential number of meanings is massive."

"Give me a sample."

"Very well. The figure 8 on its side symbolizes infinity, or long life, linked to the mythology of ouroboros, the snake eating its tail, and to the Mobius strip. Upright, the numeral 8 has meanings in countless religions and cultures. In Christianity, the Antichrist is the 8th king in the Book of

Revelations. In Islam 8 is the number of angels that carried Allah to heaven. The Buddhist wheel has 8 points, in Hinduism there are 8 elementals, and so on. As for the cross, there is the obvious Christian connection, but in the pre-Christian era it symbolized the numeral 10 for the Romans, and carried the meaning of burial for Bronze Age Europeans. It links to the four cardinal directions, has similarities to the Egyptian Ankh, and more. Conceived as a 'plus' symbol, it means addition or advancement, with additional meanings in computer programming and advanced mathematics."

"That's so many," Rogers said, her mind reeling. "Can you narrow it down to those symbols in combination?"

"Yes. The closest relatives I can find to this multipart symbol are the 'Infinity Cross,' the 'Leviathan Cross', and the symbol for the Transhumanist movement."

Rogers absorbed that. "Send them."

"I'm sending the images now."

The phone beeped and Rogers brought the screen around. The first was a figure 8 on its side with the cross on top, labeled 'Infinity Cross'.

"The Infinity Cross symbolizes Jesus' everlasting love," Farley explained. "The cross is small but rises from the middle, not the top, and the 8, or infinity symbol, is resting sideways, not upright. The group who use this symbol are small and widespread, and preach absolute love, absolute forgiveness, absolute charity. They'd throw themselves in the road to let you walk across their backs rather than see your feet get muddy."

"Hardly mass-scale terrorists, then," Rogers said.

"So the attack is real?" Farley asked his voice squeaking up an octave.

"It's real. I think we can rule out these people." She swiped sideways to the next symbol, labeled the 'Leviathan Cross'. It was very similar to the first, an 8 on its side with a cross rising from the midpoint, but with a double bar crossing it. "What about the next?"

"The Leviathan cross looks similar, but is very different," Farley said, speaking faster now, perhaps aware of the pressure weighing down. "This one invokes Satan, and is used by Satan worshippers the world over. Generally, though, this group are not violent or especially anarchical, they simply follow the law as explained by Satanist Aleister Crowley, 'Do what thou wilt is the whole of the law.'"

"That sounds lawless to me," Rogers said.

"It does, I agree, but in practice it leaves a lot unsaid. These Leviathan-symbol Satanists care more about knocking down the dogma of religion and ensuring other religions don't take too big a role in political and economic governance."

Rogers frowned. "How does that manifest?"

"In small ways. Members typically pay their taxes the same way they accept they have to breathe and eat to live. They do, however, push back against efforts by the church to influence the state. Have you heard of the 'War on Christmas'?"

"Sure, TV gins it up every year."

"Indeed, and it is often led by these Satanists insisting that, alongside traditional displays of the nativity on government property, there are also images of the goat-headed god Baphomet to balance things out. In this, they are following the letter of the First Amendment on freedom of religion and separation of church and state. Members of the Satanic Temple did this again recently at the Iowa state capitol."

Rogers considered. A goat-headed god next to the nativity wasn't nice for god-fearing folks or their kids, but it hardly condemned them. "So they don't bomb people?"

"I have no record of that ever happening. They are wholly non-violent in creed."

"What if violence is 'what they wilt'?"

"It's possible, but I show no record where it ever has. They're shock doctors more than true anarchists, seeking to shake things up. They are responsible for zero terror attacks anywhere in the world."

Rogers thought back to the imagery of Burning Man. From what she understood, it was the kind of place these 'Satanists' would embrace; wild freedom in the desert, a cow-headed 'god' at the center, probably plenty of drug-taking and free love. It was 'what thou wilt' on overdrive.

"So they're unlikely to be bombing Burning Man."

"More likely they'd sponsor it."

"OK. We'll check them out, but they're hardly the prime suspect." Rogers scrolled to the third symbol. If anything, this seemed the closest to the symbol Wren had described, an upright 8 with a small cross in the upper right corner. "What about these transhumanists?"

"They're a small group, extremely wealthy, interested in achieving long, if not eternal, life through technological augmentation. That's what the infinity symbol denotes. The cross here is actually the plus symbol, to mean 'human plus'. Broadly speaking, they believe that the mind or soul will, at some be point, be able to upload onto a computer then download back into a new body, or into some kind of cyborg body with a neural network brain, with far greater capabilities than a human body."

Rogers snorted. "Hence the plus. Sounds like real science fiction."

"It is. We're not even close to extending the human lifespan. These are the people who, right now, are having their brains frozen immediately after death, in the hope that there'll be a death cure before their tissues turn to slush. It's a pipe dream."

Rogers took a breath. "OK. Any reason these people would want to bomb Burning Man?"

"Again, followers of transhumanism seem like they'd sponsor it rather than bomb it. Burning Man, as I understand it, is a hub of creativity and an incubator of new ideas. The diversity of peoples and ways of thinking at this festival have previously sparked and fostered several moments of brilliance. They'd no more bomb it than they'd turn off their own brain freezers."

Rogers laughed at the image of brain freezers, then held it back. "So what you're telling me is that this symbol doesn't exist, and the closest symbols are unlikely to be evolutionary forebears."

"I'm sorry. It seems that way."

"No, that's good. It's something to rule out. Keep looking, though. Go wider, blur the lines, consider broader evolutions. Shortly you'll be in a working group with a range of different experts. Maybe that'll spark something."

"Yes. Thank you, Agent Rogers. I've just seen the President's announcement."

"Ah," Rogers said.

"Kill these people. That's all I want to say."

"We'll kill them together," Rogers said, then ended the line.

The jet engines burred. She looked out the window. The word on what had happened was out, and America's longest night had begun.

19

MECKLAREN

The jet landed within the hour, and there was a convoy of black SUVs waiting to take Rogers and her team to a safehouse five minutes away, where Lars Mecklaren had been renditioned.

The convoy pulled up in a quiet residential neighborhood of modest means. It was dark and quiet out, but Rogers' pulse thumped loud in her ears. Ahead lay their current best lead, but she'd crossed paths with Mecklaren before, and knew what kind of man he was. He was immensely arrogant, considering himself a genius thought leader. Back when the #Reparations group had been sowing violent chaos across America, he'd refused to share any details of how his social media sites had been used as a vector for the terrorists to share their snuff videos.

At least, he'd refused until Wren had visited upon him a terrible threat: to release deepfake footage of him engaged in disgusting activities. He'd buckled then.

Rogers didn't have that deepfake footage now, but she understood the concept. Above everything, Mecklaren was a narcissist. Dying as a martyr for the privacy cause might appeal to him, but doing it unseen, unheard and without applause?

Less so.

She entered the house and passed down a corridor that led up to a room fitted with one-way glass mirrors.

"Agent Rogers," said one of the SEAL Team 7 members, a huge man with swollen biceps and a thick black beard, wearing a tight black t-shirt. "He's feisty."

"Billionaires," Rogers said and strode to the door, turning back briefly before she turned the handle. "Thanks for picking him up. Did he give you any trouble?"

"Only threats of personal legal action. He had a private army on the NameCheck compound, but they stood down as soon as they saw us."

"Of course they did," Rogers said, scanning the other SEAL team members. They looked like beefy ninjas. She turned the handle.

Mecklaren sat at a white table in the white interrogation space, hands steepled before his lips. He was in his early 30s now, not unhandsome, with frizzy hair cropped close and a perpetual sour expression on his lips, like a permanent sneer at how dumb the world was.

"Agent Rogers," he said. "We've spoken before."

"Lars Mecklaren," she said, and sat down. "We have. I understand you've been briefed on what happened at Burning Man."

"I have," he said. "You want access to the attendee roster."

"I do. And you're going to give it."

The sneer momentarily broke for a cocky smile. "I don't think so. Of course I'm distraught to hear of the deaths of so many friends and colleagues. But principles like data privacy don't bow to a high death count."

Rogers narrowed her eyes. "I can see you're distraught.

The smile says it all. Probably ninety percent of your competition just got baked into a big ball of fused glass. I expect you're celebrating."

His smile faltered. "I'm not celebrating. And that's unnecessarily graphic."

"I was there, Mecklaren. I saw it happen. It's necessary."

He took a slow, steady breath. "You may feel that way. Emotions run high, just like they did after 9/11. The fact remains," he re-steepled his hands, as if symbolically taking control of the interview, "I cannot share the Burning Man attendee list with you."

"That makes you a suspect," Rogers said.

"What?"

"Like I just said. Half of Silicon Valley was wiped out; that's a clear motive. I don't need to see the attendee list to confirm that. The way ahead for you now is clear. No more competitors, no more start-ups threatening your dominance. Or perhaps you thought I was only here for the list?" Now she leaned in and steepled her fingers. "I'm here for you, Lars. I want to know how you did it. I want control of the Miest satellite platform. I want the codes to shut down any more of these Hammers from striking."

Mecklaren's smile faded. "Wait, what? You think this was me?"

"Every second I think it more. This nice rendition," she gestured around the room, "comfortable, cozy, genteel? From here it only sinks. First up, we put you in a steel coffin with air holes and load that into a C-17 Globemaster. We fly it south of the border, where we bury you in dirt you'll never again emerge from. No sleep for weeks. Piss and grit for food and drink. Living in your own filth. Cold. The sound of babies crying played loud enough to blow your ear drums, nonstop. When you get filthy and squalid, we'll give you a shower with a high power jet until you're red raw and terrified of the next time you foul yourself. When you feel like talking, we'll listen, but it won't end. Within a year you'll be a shell of what you are now, lose a hundred pounds easily, teeth start falling out, ears blown, eyes blasted by the constant bright lights, skin aged thirty years by the jets. And that's just one year. Past inmates have lived as long as ten. By ten, you'll be jelly. This life, the one you just left, will feel like Alice through the looking glass. Unreal. Your reality will be freezing, hungry, lonely misery, and you'll spend every conscious hour counting the seconds until your heart finally gives out from the strain. And worst of all?" She leaned in. "No one will ever know about the brave stand you took on privacy for a bunch of dead people. To them, you'll just be another name lost in the worst terror attack on US soil in history. Or maybe even the perpetrator, who deserves everything he gets."

Mecklaren's eyes widened. His skin was paling. But he wasn't done yet. "Bullshit. I have habeas corpus. Even if you somehow justify locking me up, I will get out. My lawyers will blow this up. They'll petition the Supreme Court. I've done nothing but stand on principle."

Rogers smiled. "You won't be standing on anything but cold concrete with your bare feet." She raised her voice. "Your lawyers won't breathe a whisper. You're not Alexey Navalny, Lars, and you're certainly no Mandela. Nobody actually likes you; you're just really rich, but all that goes away as of this moment. Bring in the coffin."

There was a hammer on the door, making Mecklaren jump, then the door swung open. Four SEAL team members stamped in carrying a large iron trunk, one to a corner.

"Your bed of roses," Rogers said. "Three hundred thread-count Egyptian cotton. Load him up."

The SEAL team set the trunk down and swung open the lid. Mecklaren's jaw dropped. "You can't be serious?"

"Consider it the comfiest sleep you'll ever have again," Rogers said. The SEAL squad wrapped Mecklaren's arms in their thick fists, lifted him easily and began inserting him into the coffin. He kicked in disbelief, eyes bugging on the space below.

"You can't do this! Stop!"

"Don't be too gentle," Rogers said, and the SEAL dropped him the last few inches. He thumped down on the metal base and scrabbled to get out, but the SEALs batted his hands away and slammed the lid closed.

The screaming began.

Rogers waited. She waited until the screaming stopped and the begging began.

"Last chance, Lars. Talk now or we load you atop a Humvee and railroad you out of America forever."

"OK! OK. I'll give it to you. I'll give you the list. Just let me out!"

20

TARGET

Mecklaren had the attendee list stored on the blockchain, secured in an encrypted digital wallet only he had the passcode to. While Rogers watched, sitting at the interrogation room table with the coffin gaping open by his side, he tapped it in.

The list unencrypted and fired up. Rogers sent it to her team then stood back.

Mecklaren looked wrecked, already aged by ten years.

"What now?"

"Now you go home," she said, and started for the door. "Thank you for your cooperation."

"What? So I'm not a suspect?"

She turned. "You don't have the imagination for this, Lars. You pimp likes and tinker with pixels. Plus we've already run every check imaginable on your whereabouts, your associations and your digital activities. This wasn't you."

He sagged with relief.

Rogers strode out. Her convoy was waiting, and in the backseat was a laptop. She dropped in, scooped the computer onto her lap and directed her driver to the San Francisco FBI Building.

They pulled out and she opened the laptop. The Burning Man attendee roster was already online, an Excel file shared in a secure cloud, within which dozens of Intelligence workers were working, their cursors whipping across the table's cells like bees in a hive, highlighting, cross-referencing and dropping in data.

Rogers surveyed the table. There were 72,394 rows, already organized into various tiers: three classes of attendee, from Carbon at the cheapest level, rising through Graphite to Diamond at the top level. Diamond-level attendees got special backstage access, luxury yurt accommodation, luxury buffets and dinner dates with the 'stars' of Burning Man. There was also a full listing of several thousand service and support staff, as well as a listing of all bands and speakers, along with their road crews.

Several names were highlighted in red.

Rogers dialed in to the analysis room she'd set up in San Francisco. Another trusted team member, Elena Reyes, answered.

"What are these red highlights?" she asked.

"Members who ping in a criminal database, could be one of ours or internationally. We're working to grade them on a color scale, from terror-level violence down to fraud."

"What about motive? That's the best method of grouping. Why would targeting these people help anyone, and how?"

"We're working on that. We're already adding vested interests, ownership, any attendees who have political power or huge followings, and known enemies."

"Good," Rogers said, gaming it through. "Any big fish so far? People with their own protective details, maybe, something that would make a simple sniper hit difficult or impossible? To send a Hammer from orbit had to cost millions. Why go that far unless an easier route was ruled out?"

"Good point. I'll set net worth as an indexable factor alongside influence."

"They'd be Diamond level, or maybe one of the guest speakers. Start with them."

"Makes sense. We should have something in minutes."

"Call me as soon as you have it."

Rogers put the phone down and looked to her comms master, Marcus Chang.

"Nothing from Wren," he said.

Rogers grunted and placed a call to Director Humphreys. He answered within moments.

"Give me good news, Rogers."

"We braced Mecklaren and now we have the attendee list. We're working through it and should have a list of high-percentage targets in minutes. Can you give me an update on the satellite situation? Are we having any success tracking the source of the Hammer?"

"No success yet. The experts are saying there are too many variables to route the Hammer back to Miest. We don't know its angle of entry, how long it orbited before it fell, its starting speed or orientation or weight or even its shape. We know nothing. Effectively, it could've been dropped from anywhere above the Earth and made its way to Nevada, whether easing gently into the atmosphere after several full orbits or diving straight down. When more Hammers fall, we'll get a better picture."

"When," Rogers repeated. It made her feel ill. "Still no one has claimed it?"

"No one but kooks. Keep me informed."

Rogers looked back at the laptop. The data was churning across her screen like lines in the Matrix, as different analysts worked and reordered it in the cloud. She scrolled up and down, watching as order emerged. A new column for net worth had been added, alongside one for 'approximated audience'.

"What's 'approximated audience'?" she asked Chang.

"Followers," he answered. "Many of these potential targets are social media influencers, alongside the speakers, the bands, thought leaders. We're collating their rough audience size. Bigger numbers equals bigger soft power and makes them a bigger target."

"Good."

The top hundred rows of the Excel sheet rapidly populated with Diamond-level guests, juggling rapidly and shifting position as more names were researched and had their net worth and audience sizes filled in.

"Are these all screened for protective details?" she asked. "Protective detail means they were aware of a threat."

A few seconds passed. "I'm not entirely sure how to do that, Boss," Chang said. "There's footage of Burning Man out there, sure, but if they wore plain clothes how would we even know?"

Rogers sucked her teeth, working the problem. "So we go historical. If they ever had a private security detail, visible in any media they appeared in or mentioned in any interview, mark them out. Those are our best targets."

"High value individuals with a habit of hiring their own security. Working."

It took several minutes for that to take effect. Rogers watched with bated breath. She'd been a data analyst for a time. In moments like this, working the whirlwind of figures as they spun toward a deadline, the high could be all-consuming.

Then something shifted and the top of the list began to shrink. High value individuals who'd never hired security began to drop off, until within minutes the list was down to eleven.

Rogers studied them. Some she recognized. Some were completely beneath her radar. All looked like viable targets. Their deaths would have ripple effects. Millions would change hands. Business empires would crumble.

She took a screen shot and sent it to Humphreys, tagged it 'FAO think tanks', then one more name popped up onto the list. Rogers' eyes widened as it climbed swiftly to the middle of the 11. It immediately stood out, a household name who was quite likely the highest profile individual at Burning Man, though far from the richest. Terrorists had tried to kill him many times before, and almost succeeded, taking one ear and the use of his left arm after a stabbing at a recent theater event.

His name was Ravi Sharma. For twenty-three years he'd lived under a fatwa from the Iranian Ayatollah, after publication of his book 'The Shadow Canton' outraged certain Muslims with its allegedly blasphemous depiction of the Prophet Mohammed.

The Ayatollah wanted him dead.

Now he was.

21

SHARMA

For fifteen minutes it was a whirlwind in Rogers' vehicle. First she had to be certain Sharma had actually been in attendance at Burning Man, not just on the attendee list, so she set her team to scour social media postings looking for him.

They soon found him in the background of numerous photographs at the festival, out shaking hands and chatting on the sands without a seeming care in the world.

Then she needed to know that the fatwa was still active.

It was.

Next she checked Al Jazeera and other Middle East independent news agencies, as well as the social media sites of numerous known terrorist agencies and states, to see if anyone had yet claimed his death.

None seemed to even know he was dead.

Last she looked over the top attendees on the list again, searching for any higher value target amongst those listed, but given all the variables in play, and the scale of the assault, she found none that even came close.

She called Humphreys.

"Tell me you've got something, Rogers."

She explained it all in thirty seconds. For a long moment after she finished there was silence, until the Director spoke in his deep rumble.

"How confident are you this Hammer was an Islamist strike targeting Sharma?"

"I can't answer that definitively, Sir," Rogers said, heart pounding now, fully aware that anything she said now could provide a pretext for war, whether righteous or ill-founded. She didn't want to be responsible for another moral quagmire like Iraq. "Of all the individuals at Burning Man, he's the most likely target by a country mile. He's the only one under a fatwa. He's the only one who's experienced assassination attempts previously. But that doesn't guarantee he was the target."

"It's circumstantial, I agree. It's also habitual. Islamic extremists have been trying to kill Sharma for decades. Would they really do it on US soil at this scale, knowing we'll come for them indiscriminately?"

Rogers felt pinned in place. "I don't know the answer to that, Sir."

Humphreys let out a heavy breath. "I do. The answer is yes. Zealots would, even it meant taking massive losses. These people are playing on a generational scale, Rogers, fomenting wars they hope their great-grandchildren will win." He took a breath. "Does it match up with Wren's intelligence, though? A man called Matthew with a cross symbol on his forehead? That's a Biblical name, one of the apostles, and I don't believe the cross features heavily in Islam."

"I understand that, Sir. I'm just looking at the evidence before me."

"It clashes."

Rogers wasn't sure what to say. "One of the symbologists

I spoke to said the figure 8 denotes the number of angels carrying the throne of Allah to heaven. That could make it the perfect symbol for jihadis. As for the cross, I do know that Jesus is an important figure in Islam. They have a different name for him, and to them he's not the son of God, but he still died on the cross."

Humphreys considered. "Some kind of fusion, maybe? A group that blends the religions. It is possible."

Fraught seconds ticked by. Rogers felt the crushing weight of pressure on her shoulders: a bad judgment here could lead to attacks on the wrong enemy, taking their eye off the true source of the Hammer and allowing the real enemy freedom to act freely.

Doubts plagued her.

"We should also consider the choice of Burning Man, Sir. Sharma's an excellent target, but why kill him in the desert with only 70,000 others, when they could have killed him in a city and taken a million? When they could have taken the President herself? It doesn't add up."

"Who knows what calculations they make," Humphreys said. "But your concern is noted. It doesn't add up. Burning Man is hardly the Illuminati."

"Perhaps the think tanks-"

"The think tanks are going round in circles," he interrupted. "They're calculating orbital distances and descent vectors, they're coming up with dozens of potential enemies vaguely linked to symbols, but nothing specific. We're all in the fog of war right now, and we need data to clear it, not more guesses." He paused a moment. "Do you have other targets?"

Rogers took a steadying breath. "I am looking at several groups with symbols similar to the one Wren saw. That's specific. We're preparing intel-gathering raids against them."

"Good, run them," Humphreys said resolutely. "And package everything you've got on Sharma immediately. I'll take it to the Joint Chiefs. We have intel raids of our own ready to go against multiple Islamist groups in a range of countries." He paused a moment. "They'll judge us harshly for this, Rogers, when it's done. Success or failure, our every second will be accounted for. You understand that?"

"Yes, Sir."

"Run down every lead. Do not stop."

The line died.

Rogers squeezed the phone so hard it hurt, looking out of the window at the passing lights of the city but imagining the raids to come; groups of black-clad operators equipped with night vision goggles, sitting in Blackhawk helicopters far from home, rotoring in to their targets and preparing to fast-rope down to the X. Explosive breach of doors would follow as they charged terrorist compounds in Tabriz, Kabul or Sana'a. Operators would clear rapidly through hot, dark rooms filled with women, children and the world's most wanted terrorists.

Shots would ring out. Bullet-riddled bodies would be pulled out of dugouts. The families would scream and be zip-tied and removed. Snipers would clear the decks. The terrorists would be interrogated.

More than anything she wanted to be with one of those strike teams. She wanted the certainty that this was the right course, that the bosses above her knew best and had it right. She'd wanted certainty ever since she'd lost her friends in the New Orleans killing, and only ever found it for a time operating under Wren's command.

But Wren was dark, and there was no certainty. She was on the front line of this, and it fell to her to make sense of it. Failure could damn tens of thousands.

She turned to Chang.

"Package everything together," she said, more confidently than she felt. "Send it to the Director. We're moving on."

"Yes, Boss. Onto what?"

Her mind whirled. She thought back on her conversation with Leviticus Farley.

"Salem," she said. "We're going after the Satanic Temple."

22

SATANIC TEMPLE

Within an hour, Sally Rogers sat at the head of a long desk in a makeshift War Room in the San Francisco FBI office, her team arrayed around her with laptops open and headsets on, all looking at the big screen on the wall.

The strike team stood ready in Salem, Massachusetts.

Voices crackled in her ear; this time it was SEAL team 4, deployed at the same time as 7, from their East Coast base in Little Creek, Virginia. The big screen displayed a selection of their bodycams, with the leader's camera enlarged. It showed a charcoal-gray building standing alone at the corner of an intersection. Rogers recognized it as the target, the Satanic Temple's headquarters, based in a refurbished funeral home, run by a man called Damocles Lysander. Lights were on in the upper floors.

"Go," she said.

The team advanced swiftly and silently. At the door they forewent any warning and hammered it down with a mobile battering ram. The team flooded in, clearing room by room. The interior was decorated with all manner of satanic imagery and statues, with pentagram symbols woven into the rugs, goat-headed Baphomet statues of various sizes in every room, and tapestries showing bloodletting ceremonies alongside smiley drawings from schoolchildren advocating the After School Satan clubs.

Up the stairs, the team found six members of staff on their knees with their hands in the air, in the midst of a modern office with desktop computers and ergonomic chairs, though the walls were decorated with raw stone hung with iron manacles. It looked like some cheap theme park torture chamber.

"Damocles Lysander," barked the SEAL lead. "Where is he?"

One man spoke up. "That's me."

The SEAL lead strode to him and hoisted him easily to his feet, exposing his face to the bodycam. He was early thirties and handsome in a cut-glass kind of way, with short, dark hair, deep eyes under sharp black eyebrows, and a chiseled jawline.

"It's him," said Rogers, checking her perp sheet. "Isolate him for interrogation."

The SEAL team secured the staff and marched Lysander down a hall to a private office, where they put him on his knees, hogtied his wrists to his ankles to keep him there, then set a laptop in front of him and brought up Sally Rogers.

Across three thousand miles, she looked into the eyes of the head of the Satanic Temple.

"My name is Sally Rogers," she said. "Special Agent with the FBI. I've been given sweeping discretionary powers in the wake of the Burning Man attack. We're following a lead on a symbol associated with the attack, one that bears a close resemblance to your 'Leviathan Cross'. If you know anything about the attack on Burning Man, or were in any way involved, now is the time to say so."

Damocles Lysander stared at her through the screen. He

didn't seem scared, which in itself was a concern. Either he was a man of unusual poise, or he'd prepared for a moment just like this.

"Normally, the Satanic Temple would stonewall you, Special Agent," he said. "With every fiber of our DNA, we fight against tyrannical overreach. But tonight is a clear exception. Many of those killed at Burning Man are our brethren. I can name a dozen close friends I have lost this night."

He fell silent.

"So you're denying any involvement?"

"Absolutely." His gaze didn't waver. "But I don't want to waste your time. All our records are open to you. Ask me or my staff any question and we will answer. Whoever dropped a bomb on the Nevada desert, they dropped that bomb on us also."

This wasn't what Rogers had expected. She gave an indication to her team to begin harvesting computers.

"What do you know about orbital weapons?" she asked.

"Orbital weapons? I don't even know what that means."

"What do you know about a symbol very similar to the Leviathan Cross, where the figure 8 is upright, with only one bar on the cross?"

He frowned. "You speak as if the Leviathan Cross is our symbol alone. It doesn't originate with us. We adopt it, but it comes from the earliest eras of Christianity."

Again, that wasn't what she'd expected. "Have you seen this symbol before?" She hit a key to share her screen, showing the symbologist's rendering of the symbol Wren had seen.

Lysander squinted. "I don't know. Perhaps."

"Perhaps?"

"We considered many symbols when forming the Temple

ten years ago. This one is familiar. Perhaps in a similar format?"

"Be more specific."

He smiled. There was a mischievous magnetism to that smile, despite his situation. "I think I could draw it, if my hands were free."

"Cut him free," Rogers said. "Get him a pen and paper."

The SEAL leader cut Lysander' ties and another team member handed him a pen and paper. He looked at the paper for a moment then began to draw. Rogers couldn't see. In seconds he completed the symbol and held up the paper.

"Here," he said.

Rather than a figure 8 at the center, there was now a more angular hourglass shape; two triangles stacked tip to tip atop each other, the upper one upside down. There was the same small cross atop the upper triangle's horizontal bar, but the cross' long vertical bar descended down to the point where the two triangles intersected. Across that long bar, within the upper triangle, ran a short diagonal slash.

It roughly resembled the figure 8 Wren had described. Blur the angles on the triangles and cut the slash, and you were there. Perhaps the natural evolution of symbols could account for that. Or perhaps Wren had simply misread a tattoo on a man's forehead in the heat of battle. She captured the screen and sent it off to Leviticus Farley, the symbologist.

"What does it mean?"

"Let me think," Lysander said. "As I recall, it's a take on the Russian Orthodox cross, which-"

"Russian Christian Orthodox?" Rogers blurted, instantly sharpening.

"Yes," said Lysander, "is that significant?"

Rogers tapped that into another message to Farley and fired it off. "Go on."

"That's all I can remember, I'm afraid. We didn't consider it for long. It was a problematic symbol for various reasons."

"What reasons?"

Lysander' eyes narrowed as he settled to think, then he shook his head. "I really can't remember. Sorry. It was years ago."

Rogers felt the world reorienting around her. Maybe the symbol was real. Maybe it was out there. She just had to hunt it down. "Where did you find this similar symbol?"

"I don't know that, either. I was searching through arcane texts for inspiration."

"Do you have those texts here?"

"Some, I think. We can fetch them." He turned to give an order to his team, but a SEAL stepped in his path.

"Find those books," Rogers ordered. "Escort Lysander every step of the way. Take his team, begin standard interview protocol and open access to his computers to the core team."

The SEALs moved.

Rogers opened a Google image search and dropped the screenshot of Lysander' cross into the search area. It returned results in seconds, but none of them matched. None were close.

She tapped the button to call Leviticus Farley. He answered swiftly.

"Agent Rogers?" he began. "I left the working group as soon as you sent that symbol."

"Do you recognize it?"

"I'm afraid not. That is the Russian Orthodox cross in the middle, representing the majority religion in Russian, followed by more than 90 million people. But the triangles?" Farley paused. "As a whole, it is fascinating. It's hardly even an infinity symbol anymore."

"So what does it signify?"

"Until I can research it further, I'm limited to assessing the components again. Triangles are potent symbols: in some cultures they represent fire, in Christianity their three points and three sides can represent the Holy Trinity. And when one is reversed like this upper one? It can represent femininity, while the upright triangle can represent masculinity. Slide that upper triangle down so they overlap, and you'll have a six-pointed star, or a star of David."

Rogers could hardly believe her ears. "Jews as well?"

"As well?"

"I'm following leads on several other religions already. It seems this one symbol has them all."

"The pieces could," he replied. "In combination, though, they will not. To combine two triangles with the Orthodox cross is highly unusual. I'll reach out to some people. If it's out there, I'll find it."

Rogers let the phone drop into her lap.

They were falling behind; she could feel it. To the best of their knowledge, the Miest platform had contained five hammers. One had been fired, leaving four more, and she still had no solid idea why they'd destroyed Burning Man or what their other targets were, who was doing it or how to stop it.

"Where are you, Wren?" she whispered.

"What's that, Boss?" Chang asked.

"Nothing. No, scratch that. We're on the move." She stood up.

"Where to?"

"The nearest Russian Orthodox church. Maybe they have some idea what this symbol means."

23

RUSSIAN ORTHODOX

There were over a dozen Russian Orthodox churches in central San Francisco, two of them cathedrals, and the nearest of these was barely ten minutes away. Rogers went in a convoy of three blacked-out Escalades, accompanied by both Marcus Chang and Elene Reyes.

The Russian Orthodox Cathedral of St. Vladimir stood out proudly in the urban landscape of clothing boutiques and designer coffee shops, a vaulting work of Byzantine arches capped with three iconic golden onion domes. Each dome was topped with a gilded cross, gleaming in the bright sunlight. Hand-carved details popped in Rogers' vision everywhere, studding the exterior with embellished images of Jesus on the cross and Mother Mary holding him close.

The convoy parked and Rogers led the way through a meticulously landscaped courtyard. The air hang heavy with incense, and the gentle sound of low hymns for Mass carried on the breeze. Granite steps led up to intricately designed wooden doors, each panel telling stories from the Old Testament.

The church's interior was filled with stunning

iconography, displaying numerous unfamiliar saints in elaborate frescoes, murals and stained-glass windows. Candlelit chandeliers spread a warm glow from high arches, lighting a large filigreed wooden screen that blocked all view of the choir, itself carved with more imagery of saints and holy warriors.

Rogers led the way toward the wooden screen, where the priest stood on an elevated wooden walkway, addressing a small congregation. He wore a conical black hat and a long black robe, with a heavy golden cross hung on a large-linked chain around his neck.

At the base of the walkway, Rogers raised her hand.

"Apologies. I need to speak with you.

The priest surveyed her, then his flock, then the retinue of FBI officers trailing Rogers.

"We are at Mass," he said, his voice gentle but authoritative, with a soft Russian cadence.

"It won't take long. It's a matter of national security."

The man looked displeased, but nodded to the side, where a second priest stood. In moments they had swapped position, and the Mass continued as he led them through a wooden door in the side of the main church and into a side chapel.

Here was another wooden screen which filled the wall, with several rows of pews and a display case stocked with golden censers, chalices, icons and reliquary chests. The priest stopped before the wall and crossed his hands behind his back, waiting.

"FBI Agent Sally Rogers," she said, holding out a hand. The priest shook it.

"Father Konstantin Saikov. How may I help you?"

"There's something I'd like to show you," she said, and brought out her sketch of the symbol Damocles Lucius had produced. "I need to know what this symbol means."

Father Saikov took the sketch and studied it. "This is the Orthodox cross," he said.

"Yes," Rogers allowed. "What about the rest of it?"

Saikov squinted. "It is familiar. One moment. Let me confer with a colleague."

He stepped outside. Moments passed, and Rogers felt anxious. She wasn't sure if this was the right thing to be doing. Moments turned into minutes, then Saikov returned, accompanied by three other priests, one in an oval white hat bladed with gold.

"This is our Rector, Father Boris Yermakov. He believes he knows what this symbol means."

The Rector smiled beatifically and nodded. He seemed wizened and friendly.

"He recognizes it?" Rogers asked, her heart leaping.

"He believes so. He does not speak English, so I will translate."

The Rector took the paper and began speaking in soft, hypnotic Russian. After several full sentences, Saikov began to translate.

"He believe this is a take on the 'Calvary Cross', an ancient symbol dating from the early fourteenth century." The Rector pointed and Saikov continued. "This bottom triangle, as he recalls, symbolizes Calvary Hill, where Jesus and the two criminals were crucified. The upper triangle is actually several components combined. Do you have a pen?"

Rogers looked at her entourage. Chang produced one.

"Thank you," Saikov said, then extended it graciously to the Rector, then turned around and bent over slightly, offering his back as a writing surface. The Rector placed the paper against his back as if this was very natural, and began to sketch a new version of the symbol, all while speaking still in his low tones."

The lower triangle remained the same, though the

Orthodox cross was different, and the upper triangle was broken into three parts. The horizontal bar became the bar of cross, while the left and right diagonals were separated and came to resemble the diagonal arms of a broken arrow, with an arrowhead on the left and feather flights on the right.

Saikov turned back around and held out the new symbol.

"Here is a true Orthodox Russian cross with three bars, one of them diagonal," he said, pointing. "These two diagonals," he tapped the arrows that made up the remaining two sides of the upper triangle, "signify the spear that was plunged into Jesus' side."

Rogers' jaw dropped. "What does it mean?"

Saikov waited while the Rector explained, then translated. "He believes it is a kind of Originalism. Taking the faith back to Jesus' death on Calvary hill and enthroning him there. He believes, and I believe this also, it was adopted by a sect of monks in the fourteenth century, men that wanted to reinstate the primacy of Jesus as both Lord in Heaven and King on Earth. They wanted a religious state, with faith leaders in governance rather than kings or politicians."

Rogers stared. She allowed her eyes to defocus. Removing the details of the spear and the extra diagonal bar, it could easily be re-imagined as an 8 with a cross atop it.

"Religious state," she repeated, projecting it forward. "But Christian, not Islamic?"

Saikov frowned. "Why would you mention Islam?"

"This symbol is a lead in an ongoing case. Islam may be connected."

Saikov relayed that to the Rector, who came back and was translated.

"He cannot imagine this symbol being associated with Islam. Not with the Orthodox cross. The only link he can see to Islam is in the extremism. Islamists want a Caliphate. These monks wanted a more religious form of government."

Rogers considered. "That doesn't sound so bad."

"It all depends on the religion. For monks in the Middle Ages, women were animals to be treated as property, with more outspoken women branded as 'witches' and burned alive with no recourse in law. Homosexuals were stoned, people with disabilities were left to die. Alcohol, dancing, music, all relationships outside of marriage, other religions, even other strains of the same religion, were all blasphemous and warranted heavy punishments."

"That's their idea of religion?"

"When this was their symbol?" Saikov tapped the sheet. "Yes. And if those monks were alive today, I am certain they could not think of a better target for total destruction than Burning Man. Their Sodom and Gomorrah, in worship of a false idol. Mass deaths there would only speed the dawn of their new world."

Rogers felt her hackles rise. "I never mentioned Burning Man."

"Of course not," Saikov said. "But it is apparent." The Rector spoke again. "The Russian Orthodox Church stands ready to help in any way, Agent Rogers."

She nodded absently, mind spinning with this new information. "Thank you. I will be in touch."

On the way out she brought up her phone and called DNI Humphreys. Maybe everything had just shifted.

24

STRIKES

"You think what?" Humphreys asked, as the convoy sped south through San Francisco, headed for the airport.

"It's worth considering at least," Rogers pressed. "It links together this man's name, Matthew, the symbol, the Orthodox Russian church, and a motive to attack Burning Man."

"What about Sharma? Are you suggesting we halt the Islamist raids and turn them onto, what, Christians?"

"Not Christians," Rogers countered fiercely. "I'm Christian, and I don't want to lock myself up in my house and never be allowed to read a book again. I don't want to stone people, or replace the Presidency with some kind of Supreme Leader. If Saikov is right about the meaning behind this symbol, though, then we're looking at ultra-extreme Christians, just like ISIS are ultra-extreme Muslims."

"And all of this came from a symbol remembered by Damocles Lysander, the Satanist? That's what you're telling me, correct?"

"Yes."

"Did it never occur to you that he was simply feeding you

the target he wants you to take out? If anything, this would make me more suspicious of him."

"We have him in custody," Rogers countered. "We have all his data."

"But you're not going hard. You're treating him like a friendly."

Rogers was taken aback. "You want me to torture him?"

"You threatened to dump Mecklaren in a black site by way of an iron coffin! Why not the Satanist?"

"Because I think he's got a point. Director, you said to pursue every possible lead. This is one possible lead. Perhaps likely."

"To where? Do you even have any idea how many churches there are in this country? Tens of thousands! All creeds and ideologies find a home. How could we possibly-"

"Eschaton Sanctuary, Last Light Cathedral, Twilight Ark," Rogers said swiftly, reading from a list. "We have records on them all, Director, as you know. All have affinity with domestic terror groups, all have ideologies that are extremely troubling, all preach fire and brimstone and the end of the Republic as a good thing, because it heralds the return of Jesus and his Kingdom. It's not difficult to find people who believe this, just like jihadis believe they'll get 66 virgins in heaven. Those three churches are just from the most recent FBI terror watchlist. There are more. We do know these people, Director."

"So you want to start raiding churches, Agent Rogers?" There was a note of warning in his voice.

"Not yet. I can start pulling together intel on their funding, see if they have the capacity to buy an orbital weapon from Russia. I can see if any of them ever crossed paths with Faraday."

"Faraday," Humphreys breathed. "You think she converted?"

"I show her as always being a Christian, Director, just lapsed. We're talking now about extreme radicalization."

"So you want to go after churches on the say-so of a Satanist."

Rogers didn't like his tone. "You want to clear the fog? The Islamist raids must've started. How are your interrogations going? Have you found the kill codes to the Miest yet?"

Humphreys said nothing for a moment, then continued in a downbeat tone. "Half the raids are complete. Interrogation has begun. So far, there is nothing."

"Nothing. OK. Maybe something will come from that, maybe it is Ravi Sharma and Iran, there's every chance they're still the real enemy and this symbol is a red herring. But the lead before me is this Calvary Cross. Are you going to order me not to pursue it?"

Seconds ticked by. Rogers felt the weight shifting. It would be simple for Humphreys to take her off lead, even off the investigation completely. Then she'd be powerless.

"No. Do it. But do not release the Satanist or any of his people. I consider him a hostile. Gather what you can, be as discreet as you can, and run any physical strike past me directly. Is that understood?"

"Yes, Sir."

He hung up.

Rogers stared out of the windows at the steep San Francisco streets rising away. A tram clattered past. She had a new direction in mind.

"The nearest apocalypse church on the watchlist," she said to Marcus Chang. "Where is it?

Chang brought up his tablet and tapped in the search parameters, then opened his mouth to speak, but before he could get the word out, the window by Rogers' head blew inward.

Glass slashed her face, the crash assaulted her ears, then more bullets struck the side of the SUV. Rogers barely had a moment to comprehend what was happening, then one of the wheels burst, the truck bucked, the driver swiftly overcompensated and the vehicle flipped on the spot. It ripped over the median on its roof, narrowly scraped through a gap in oncoming traffic then rolled onto its side to batter along the bumpers of a line of parked cars, until finally it crashed through the window of an artisan burger joint, where it rocked to stillness.

Rogers jerked back to consciousness, hanging upside down, suspended by her seatbelt. Blood was dripping down her temple to patter on the padded roof of the SUV below her. Her brain felt jammed up with too many sudden events. The glass was supposed to be bulletproof, she found herself thinking, still stuck on the very first. They had to be heavy armor-piercing jackets, hollow-points probably, 50. caliber at least.

Military-level gear.

More bullets thundered in, punching holes in the truck's rear and side. One hit the driver with an explosive thud, splattering the interior of the windshield. She looked to the side. Chang was dead already, half his head torn away, his laptop shattered. Reyes hung slack from the front passenger seat, dead or unconscious.

Rogers reached up, pulled her seatbelt and dropped with a crunch onto her shoulder. The bullets kept coming, seemingly from all directions now, chewing through the truck's glass and metal.

25

ARTISANAL BURGERS

Rogers scrambled through the truck's shattered rear window, drew her Glock 19 as she exited and ran deeper into the burger joint. People lay on the floor, knocked flat by the crash of the truck or caught in the crossfire. Bullets chewed splinters out of the counter and smashed the neon menus off the walls.

She scrambled into the kitchen, where the fry cooks had already fled, leaving fat burgers sizzling on the island counter griddle, a pile of oysters ready to shuck by the sink and fries bubbling madly in oil. Bullets raked a shelf of ingredients in glass jars, erupting dry pasta and clouds of wheat flour. At the end of the kitchen she found a staircase leading up, and barged up two flights while shouting into her radio.

"Taking heavy fire on Mission Street, need immediate reinforcements."

The radio crackled back but no response came, then she emerged onto a landing, reorienting swiftly as the fusillade of bullets marked out below. She kicked through a door on the street side, entered an apartment with the drawbridge bed down and two young lovers staring back at her, wrapped up in the covers.

"Get out the back," she rasped, reached the open window onto the fire escape and leaned out.

Muzzle shots barked from cover behind a pair of armored black SUVs across the street, bludgeoning the burger joint below. She counted seven men with automatic weapons, two already crossing the street along the wreckage trail of her crashed truck. It was a thirty-yard shot with her handgun, with targets on the move from an overhead angle, but she aced harder shots every month at the range.

Adrenaline sharpened her. She made the calculations for trajectory rise and drop instantly, dropped the reticule below the lead man's nose and squeezed the trigger.

His head burst and he slapped to the blacktop like she'd hit him with a baseball bat. The second man had no time to respond before she'd plugged him in the head too.

Five men left.

Automatic fire strafed the window in a lead hailstorm, shattering the glass and pulling shrieks from the lovers, but Rogers was already on the move.

"Out the back, now!" she shouted, shepherding them half-naked ahead of her.

Across the landing lay another door, but there was no time to ram it; both lovers went down as a burst of gunfire shredded them from below. Rogers emerged through the smoke with her Glock leveled, staring down into the eyes of a man in tactical black, standing halfway up the stairs.

She fired. The bullet took him in the throat and he reeled backward, spraying arterial blood and bullets. His body thumped down the stairs, followed by shouts from the kitchen.

"Backup now!" Rogers shouted into the radio, but still nothing came in response. They had to be jamming comms, which meant no one had heard her and no one was coming to save her. The uncertainty she'd felt before was replaced by sharp conviction.

She was not just going to survive this. This was going to be her next lead.

Without further thought she vaulted the railing, dropping down onto the head of a man stalking up the stairs. Her right knee hit his shoulder, the muzzle of her Glock found the hollow of his clavicle, and she fired twice. Bullets drilled through the soft layer of skin and burrowed down through his heart, lungs and guts to burst out through his pelvis.

He fell and Rogers landed hard, rolling chaotically into the next man. He fired as he went down, rifle ripping lines of automatic fire down the plasterboard walls. Rogers' pistol bucked in her fist as his back hit the steps, shattering one of the kitchen lights. Her shoulder hit next, his fist caught her chin as they tumbled the final roll to the kitchen floor, then her Glock pressed into his side and discharged three times, blowing his innards out through his left hip.

Rogers stood. Her body throbbed and her head reeled from the fall, and she caught her balance on the steel worktop. More would be coming. Three, now? Or maybe five still; she hadn't seen these two enter. She checked her Glock, but she was out. She scanned the man at her feet, eyes fixing on his Beretta 92FS and the ammo magazines at his waist.

Then one more came in.

He was big, neck bugged out with muscle atop a pyramid of gym-baked mass. He stared and she stared. He saw the dead man on the floor and the flood of blood and homed his rifle in. Rogers was already flinging a deep fat fryer basket full of fries coated in boiling oil at his face.

The fries flew. The bullets slammed into the counter where Rogers had been, then the fries hit. Rainbows burst across the man's face as boiling oil spattered in a cloud, blinding him. Still he fired, until Rogers swung a meat cleaver like a tennis pro, burying it three inches deep into the side of his head.

He went down, skin sizzling and body convulsing.

Just then metal clinked as a grenade bounced in. She ran and dived over the island counter. The grenade blew as her hip cracked down on the far side of the metal counter, filling the space with light, sound, smoke and fire.

Rogers rolled and crawled to get the full length of the counter against her back. If she was them, she'd follow with another grenade, and sure enough one came. On the left, one bounce, and she threw herself to the right.

This time the whole island counter shredded under the blast, its supports chewed out, collapsing upon itself. Rogers rose to her feet, pulled a long knife from a wooden block and flung it just as the first man came through the door. It took him in the chest, he looked down, then Rogers charged him.

He slammed backward into two other men behind him. They all went down, but Rogers kept her feet. Five steps back, she scooped up the rifle of one of the fallen men, then turned it on the three as they struggled to get their dying colleague off them.

Bullets cut them nearly in half.

The rifle clicked empty.

Rogers panted and spun in the dark and smoke, coughed hard, then took a crumpling body blow in the belly from a huge man.

She reeled back.

He'd come out of nowhere, and was the biggest man yet, nearly 7' tall and easily three hundred pound, a hundred-twenty more than her. She couldn't breathe after the blow. All she could see in a flare of light from outside was the brightness of his eyes, and a familiar tattoo etched in black ink onto his forehead: a figure 8 with a cross crowning it.

The giant man smiled, then brought his big foot stamping down.

26

MARK

"Matthew!" Rogers shouted, forcing her lungs to comply while her hands scrabbled for any kind of weapon in the wreckage around her.

The big foot halted its descent atop her chest, breaking no ribs but pinning her like a bug. Uncertainty broke across the giant's face.

"Matthew's my brother," he said. "I'm Mark. How do you know him?"

"My team ..." Rogers gasped, "ran into him in Siberia. Now they're ... hunting him."

The big man's expression shifted. "The CIA team? They're dead."

Rogers laughed, and her left hand closed around the handle of a tiny oyster-shucking knife. "They're not ... dead."

Mark's expression hardened. "Then they will be. We're apostles of the new Kingdom. We cannot be killed."

"Let's test that, shall we?"

His foot came down and Rogers' left arm whipped around, stabbing him just above the ankle with the oyster knife. The force of his downward stamp raked the razor-sharp, three-inch blade up through the meat of his calf almost to the knee, ungloving his right shin and unleashing a torrent of blood.

His foot still thumped against her chest, driving any wind from her lungs and sending stars across her vision, but the force was diminished. Rogers could scarcely see and couldn't breathe, but continued by feel as the big man staggered, reaching over to his left ankle and slitting his Achilles tendon.

He toppled forward with a bellow and hit the kitchen floor with a boom that rattled the wreckage, too much weight to catch on his hands. Rogers jerked and tried to get up, but the silver motes were thickening and her muscles had no air. Her lungs burned and her ribs cried out, and she remembered how it had felt at New Orleans, burrowed in under the weight of her dead friends, waiting for the killer to leave.

She hadn't fought then. She'd barely survived.

The giant was moving. Reaching for her. Shouting something. He was far from dead, she knew that. Blood loss from the wound in his calf might kill him without medical attention, but not yet.

He crawled closer. His huge fists found her ankles. He had the strength to rip her in half like he was tearing a piece of paper, and she couldn't hope to break free. But then she didn't need to.

She'd trained for a decade for a moment like this. Every day five hundred pushups, fifty pullups, three mile runs in twenty minutes, two hundred sit-ups with the weight of a partner holding down her feet, then into the gym.

His hands on her ankles only made her hips the pivot point, and she shot up in the fastest sit-up of her life, stabbing the oyster shucker into his right eye. The blade penetrated to the hilt.

He gulped once like he had something more to say, then collapsed forward. Rogers kicked away from his falling chest before it could break her ankles, then lay panting in the wreckage.

Gas lines hissed and water trickled. She felt hot and cold at the same time, panting crazily. Finally, the sound of sirens rang in the distance. She lurched up too quickly, almost passed out, but steadied herself on the wall. The burger kitchen was destroyed with the island counter on the floor. Oyster shells lay strewn across the steaming griddle, with knives, chopping boards, pots, pans and hundreds of broken jars and dented canisters of ingredients scattered everywhere.

There was smoke and blood and small fires starting in the burger grease. The air smelled of gas. The kitchen didn't have long.

Rogers kneeled beside 'Mark's' body and searched his pockets. She found no ID, no phone, then his giant body abruptly jack-knifed. Like a corpse reanimating, his forehead struck hers and almost knocked her out cold.

She rocked back on her knees, feeling the blood flow from the slit of the impact, instantly blinding her. Everything became blurry and nightmarish, a ruin seen in double and painted red. With a terrible cry the giant reached up and yanked the tiny blade from his head.

Blood streamed out. He wheezed wildly, sucking great lungfuls in through his mouth and blowing them ferociously out through his nose.

"Through all your … filth," the giant roared and wheezed. "Through all your … sins and false idols. The Kingdom will … rise."

The blade shot towards Rogers' eye and she just managed to twist and lean back, so the shucker landed in her shoulder. It punched through her muscle and hit like a gunshot against her shoulder blade, knocking her flat. The giant rolled atop her and his hands closed around her throat. Blood aerosolized across her face as he sucked breath and shot it through his nose. She couldn't breathe. Her trachea was crushing. Her arms and legs kicked and grasped, her hands found plates and shattered them across his back, but that did nothing. He was half-dead already, reduced to this roaring, sucking mess, but he'd live long enough to kill her.

Rogers' left eye winked out.

"Can't be … killed," the big man rasped.

Then Rogers hand closed around something hot, slick and yielding. Not another knife, but a raw burger patty. It was useless, except… She brought it up, timed her strike then shoved it into the giant's mouth.

He sucked it in on his next almighty wheeze, dragging the meat deep into his windpipe, then sprayed fragments of it out through his nose with a honking bark. Instantly his hands went from Rogers' throat to his own, as the burger lodged in place, blocking both airways. He tried to suck in another breath, his chest palpitating with the effort, but barely made a sound as the burger only crammed deeper down his esophagus.

Rogers wriggled and kicked out from under him.

He made no further sound after that, all the air bottled tight inside his lungs by an artisanal burger, only strange croakings and tickings as his lungs pulped themselves against his ribs. He reared back, rolled over, bucked and frothed.

Rogers backpedaled as fast as she could. The shucker was in her shoulder deep, weakening her left arm. The gas was hissing and the flames were rising. Any minute the whole kitchen was going to-

The fireball blasted outward, driving her body tumbling back across the burger's seating area. Barely conscious, she looked back down the line of her body to see the kitchen becoming an inferno. The giant was lost in searing orange flames. The sirens were louder. She forced herself back to her feet and limped out onto the street, where emergency

response police had formed into a ring with their weapons drawn.

"FB … I," she called, dropping to her knees.

"Stand down!" somebody shouted.

Then they were there at her side, holding her until the paramedics arrived with a gurney.

"Get … DNI Director Humphreys!" she managed, catching the eye of the man tending to her. "Tell him-"

The darkness gathered her down before she could say any more.

27

CONTRAIL

Wren dreamed of a vast atomic bomb exploding in a sky-burst over the Burning Man festival. People became carbon shadows on the ground. Glass droplets rained down from sand sucked up into the fireball.

At one point his satellite radio squawked with Director Gerald Humphreys' voice, but the sound didn't rise above the din of the engines, and Wren didn't wake. After that the radio spoke at ten- then five-minute intervals, until the transmissions wore the battery down to nothing and it fell silent.

After several hours, Wren woke to a freezing chill and piercing shafts of light cutting through his eyelids. He opened his eyes and held up a hand, trying to look ahead, but the light of the rising sun was blinding.

"Where are we?" he shouted, but Ivan didn't seem to hear, so Wren unstrapped and clambered up to the cockpit, dropping into the co-pilot's seat. He placed one hand on the old spy's shoulder and shouted the question again.

"End of rainbow!" Ivan shouted back. "Look."

Wren peered into the glare, but could make out nothing.

"Here," Ivan offered a set of polarized flight glasses with silvered lenses. Wren pulled them on and instantly the glare cut. He could see the sun off to the side, low over a horizon of pure white mountains.

"What am I looking at?"

"Three hundred miles north of Yakutsk," Ivan answered. "Deep into Sakha Republic."

Wren racked his memory of the last deep dive he'd done on Russian geography. Yakutsk was a capital, he remembered, a mining town experiencing fast growth despite the wildly inhospitable climate, just south of the Arctic Circle.

He peered out over the panorama of white mountains. "We're in the Arctic?"

"This seems likely," Ivan answered.

Wren raised his gaze to the pale blue sky, scouring for the thread of contrail, but he couldn't see it anywhere. "Where's our bread crumbs?"

"Gone. Either jet has ascended very high, out of range, or descended for landing. We cannot go higher, though, we have no fuel." Ivan tapped the dial, verging into the red. "Very little left. So I am looking for landing site."

"When did they descend?"

"Contrail died two minutes ago. In jet, at jet speed, this allows thirty miles of descent time. We have covered twenty. So, somewhere ahead."

Wren leaned forward and peered down. It was hard to pick out anything below; just the endless crenellation of white mountains and valleys with frozen rivers. Then he saw something. "There!"

"What?"

"That straight line? It's a train track, probably built to transport rare earth metals in their mines. Land on it."

"Land on it?"

Wren scanned the mountains ahead, but saw nothing. Wherever Matthew and Faraday had gone, it could be tucked into a valley just one mountain range over, and he'd never see it from the air until he was right on top of it. "We can't land where they have. We can't let them see us. Land on the tracks and I'll find them on foot."

"And me?"

"You'll be alive."

Ivan laughed. "This is good answer. Very well. Attach harness. We will descend."

Wren did as he was told, bringing the flight harness over his shoulders and strapping in.

"Beginning descent," Ivan said, and pushed the controls forward. Their dive began. In the distance, in amongst the spiky valleys and mountains, Wren thought he picked out the silvery flash of a glassy structure reflecting the dawn light, but it was swiftly eclipsed by the crags as they dropped.

Within moments they were flanked either side by mountains, bare Jurassic rock whipping by like the walls of a cavern. The air roared against the flimsy cockpit window and sang through the bullet holes. Below the tracks straightened to run along the long, flat side of a heavily quarried mountain, dropping off in a steep ravine to the right. Several miles ahead lay a tunnel, its dark mouth barely a pinprick of black, expanding swiftly.

"It has to be here," Wren shouted, thinking about the structure he'd glimpsed ahead.

"Impossible," Ivan shouted.

"Here or they'll see us and shoot us down."

"Then here," Ivan resolved and steepened the dive.

The whole craft began to shudder. The wind beat against the Antonov's belly and the rails shot toward them. Maybe five hundred feet. Four hundred. Three. The black eye of the tunnel loomed large. The engine bucked in the nosecone, propellor whining madly against the wind shear.

Ivan pulled back on the controls, instantly hammering the craft with its own inertia and skipping the wind resistance like a ricocheting bullet. The tunnel mouth whipped closer.

Wren reached over Ivan's hands and pulled on the controls with him, gaining an extra few inches. The metal ligaments of the plane strained and squealed under the pressure, the flaps to either side extending to their fullest as the plane bucked backwards. G-forces hit hard, slamming them all into their seats.

A flap on the right wing sheared and rocketed away, then several on the left stripped like roof shingles in a tornado, followed by the tail fin as they dropped the final fifty feet.

Wren's stomach jumped up into his mouth, then the Antonov hit the narrow rails like an inert missile, wheels crashing into the wooden sleepers and ripping away instantly, dropping them with a massive jolt onto their belly. The reinforced metal undercarriage split open with an almighty crack, and a flurry of earth and gravel tore through the gouge into the fuselage.

Ivan's shout was buried in the awesome shrieking of metal on the rails as their momentum skidded out, racing toward the widening tunnel mouth. The plane veered left until the wing hit the rock wall to the left and disintegrated in a spray of shrapnel, tossing them into a violent counter-clockwise spin. The front spun to the rear, the tail led the way and the belly teetered out over the drop that now hung to their right, then the right wing slammed into the wall and erupted too.

Everything jolted left, the plane was knocked off the rails and teetered toward the valley floor below, just as the tail section of the plane concertinaed around the tunnel's right corner with a gargantuan crash, wrapping them like a DUI truck around a lamp post and halting their slide down.

Suddenly, there was silence. The roar of the engine was gone, shredded away with the wings, and the squeal of metal faded, leaving Wren still gripping the controls over Ivan's with every muscle braced. He let out a cautious breath, afraid even the slightest movement might dislodge their position.

To his left lay only empty air. He turned; the fuselage behind him looked like it had been hit with an avalanche, with the rear section filled to the roof with a gritty mix of snow and gravel. Kiefer's head lolled, while his legs were buried in the silt.

"Anais?" he croaked.

There was no answer.

Wren turned back and patted Ivan's shoulder. "Good job. I call that a perfect landing."

The old spy said nothing, though. Wren unclipped his harness and leaned further forward. Ivan had been skewered through the sternum by a sliver of metal, maybe from one of the wings. Blood pooled in his lap. For a moment Wren stared. There was a similar-sized rectangular hole in the cockpit glass.

He looked down and saw the bloody tip of it emerging through the back of the pilot's seat, barely an inch away from driving into his own chest.

Ivan was dead.

"Spasibo," Wren said, then turned and crawled back. The plane rocked dangerously. Over the earth and gravel mix, he reached Anais Kiefer.

"Chris," Kiefer said. His right eye seemed sharper, while the left had turned a gangrenous gray. "I am sorry, you know."

Wren started to dig Kiefer's legs out of the dirt. "Sorry for what?"

"Burning your friends."

"Thanks, now dig yourself out."

The plane shifted again, twisting so the floor angled sharply down over the drop.

"Those are not my legs," Kiefer said.

"They look attached to me," Wren countered, digging one leg out.

"I'm dead already," Kiefer said, then the plane tipped into its terminal slide. Wren grabbed Kiefer's wrist, took two big steps and jumped through the gouge where the wing had been. He hit the track and grabbed the rails with one hand, as behind him the ruptured body of the Antonov toppled, with Kiefer dangling over the edge.

In seconds there came a crash from far below, answered by a whuff of heat as the last of the gas in the tank ignited.

"Climb, Anais!" Wren grunted, at full stretch with every muscle in his arms and chest pulled taut.

Kiefer began to climb. In moments he was kneeling next to Wren, and Wren rested his head on Kiefer's shoulder, panting from the exertion.

"You big idiot," he muttered.

"I'm not here," Kiefer replied flatly.

"For someone who's not here you sure weigh a lot," Wren muttered, then looked up. He took Kiefer's face in both hands and looked into his eyes. "Enough with that talk, OK?"

"It's how I feel."

"What you feel doesn't matter. Listen to what I'm telling you. You're here and you're going to survive, and whatever's wrong with you, we'll fix it. Do you understand?"

"I don't understand."

"Doesn't matter. Now stand up. I am not carrying you down off this mountain."

28

THE WORD

Wren's radio was dead, the battery long-drained. His Makarov was gone, lost with the Antonov, and the temperature had to be thirty below, with the wind blasting painfully through his thermal jacket. He was hungry, thirsty, and already icicles were forming in his beard and hanging from his eyebrows.

He held one arm around the massive bulk of Anais Kiefer and ran.

Kiefer ran like a machine. When Wren pushed, he responded. He didn't seem to even tire.

The wind in the tunnel was worse, freezing Wren's fists and his feet, his face and his neck. The engine of his heart pumped blood and tried to spread the heat, but it was a losing battle. By the end of the tunnel, Wren could feel his systems failing. He knew frostbite on exposed skin at those temperatures could happen in less than ten minutes, and he'd been out for longer than that.

Beside him, Kiefer stood upright, barely breathing hard.

"How are you doing that?" Wren asked.

Kiefer didn't respond.

"Come on."

He pumped his arms and ran harder. Beyond the tunnel the tracks were loaded with several feet of fresh powder snow, which made the going harder. Lifting his legs for every step became agonizing. Soon it felt like Kiefer was dragging him more than the other way around. When the tracks inclined upward, Wren held on like a cowboy on a wild bronco, letting the big man break the snow and do the work. Still, his vision grayed, until they reached the crest of a ridge, with something bizarre below them.

In the broad basin of a karst depression lay a huge white bowl, like the bottom third of a geodesic dome. It was easily four hundred yards across and framed out of thousands of large white triangles arranged on an intricate scaffold platform.

Wren stared.

A massive satellite dish.

He rubbed his eyes and his gloves came away rimed with crushed ice. He'd read about similar structures in his research, radio telescopes built on an epic scale, designed to capture waves from astronomical objects thousands of light years distant. The bigger it was built, the further away it could reach, with the ultimate goal of reaching out to capture the distant spreading echo of the Big Bang itself.

His mind reeled, trying to calculate the costs. A structure like this, in a place as remote as the Arctic Circle, would require hundreds of millions. And to keep it quiet? That meant dark money, and dark workers, perhaps lifted from a Siberian gulag, and dark experts like…

Like Genevieve Faraday.

It was possible.

He looked wider. To the right lay the tail end of a runway cleared of snow, with an Embraer Phenom 300 light business jet parked on the verge near a fuel pump. Nearby were buildings, a cluster of silver and white structures of boxy design, like some kind of research station.

None of it made any sense, but it soon would.

He led Kiefer down.

The giant bowl grew larger, then the pair of them dropped below its lip and entered the forest of scaffolding suspending it above the icy black earth. Wren collapsed beside a concrete piling, panting hard, while Kiefer stood over him like a sentinel. The wind was gone, now they were sheltered by the giant dish above. Wren sat back and noticed the great dish's dark underside. It took his worn eyes long moments to resolve a familiar pattern carved into the nearest triangular section, then his attention sharpened.

It was close to the figure 8 with the cross on Matthew's head: two circles atop each other, but open on the left side, closer to the number 3; a squashed cross offset above and to the right; and one additional component, a third circle underneath the cross, open on the left like a mirror letter 'c'.

He looked wider, and his jaw dropped. That symbol was carved into every panel. Wren gazed up at them, trying to determine what they might mean, until the triangles began to move with a deafening metallic screeching.

Wren covered his ears but the sound was all-consuming. He pressed his hands tighter against his head and watched as the dark heavens contorted, tracing back the mechanism. It seemed the triangles were motorized, now shifting position.

The huge array was reorienting itself. After perhaps thirty seconds, the cacophony ended. Wren racked his mind, but could only think of one reason for the dish to re-orient.

An imminent strike.

He surged up, grabbed Kiefer's arm and ran.

The cold had numbed his muscles, so he lumbered and loped, stumbling over scaffolds and thudding off concrete pilings, until he left the shelter of the great satellite dish and emerged onto a bare stretch of blacktop, veneered with tracings of frost but cleared of snow.

They were in a parking lot stocked with several large coaches. They looked like tourist coaches, which seemed bizarrely pedestrian.

The research center lay ahead, spiked by an entrance foyer which rose up like an iceberg shard of clear glass. Within lay a space filled with hundreds of people. Wren stopped and stared. All wore black thermal clothing similar to his, many had their heads tilted back as their bodies swayed in rhythmic motion, all raising their voices in some kind of grand choral song which carried out into the lot and encircled Wren and Kiefer.

Wren was stunned, uncertain of what he was seeing. Was any of this was real? Was he hallucinating from the cold?

The glass doors to the foyer opened and a stocky man in a thermal black tunic approached. He carried no weapon and had a friendly expression.

"Brothers, you've sojourned under the dome too long," he said warmly, reaching out to take both Wren and Kiefer's arms. "I roamed for far too long as well, stricken by the love of the word. Join us."

"Join you?" Wren asked. "What word?"

The man chuckled. "What word. Were you out there during the repurposing? I've heard it can scramble the mind."

Wren didn't know what to say. This was too much. He looked beyond to the glass hall full of people, singing rejoicefully. Maybe he was still sitting beneath the satellite dish, hallucinating while he froze to death, but this was too bizarre a vision.

"Who are you people?"

"Only the same as you," the man answered. "One beneath the word. Come."

He pulled again, and this time Wren let himself be led.

The man chattered something about the word and the voice, then they pushed into the hall.

A wave of wet heat washed over Wren and Kiefer. The door closed behind them and the man strode to a trestle table holding several silver coffee urns and a large dish stacked with raisin Danishes.

"Please, replenish yourselves," the man said.

Wren numbly poured a coffee. It was black and steaming. He offered another to Kiefer, who took it and held it. Wren sipped. It was surprisingly good. He munched on a Danish. The sugars lit up his palate while his mind worked to make sense of all this.

"Was anything revealed to you, beneath the dome?" the stocky man asked.

Wren just gazed out over the crowd, caught up in the scale of all these men and women. They were beaming as they sang, lost in a moment of bliss. It felt as if he'd pushed his way into a faith revival in the Louisiana bayou. The music was radiating from above somewhere, but Wren saw no speakers, no band, no preacher in a pulpit.

"All religions have their pilgrimages," the man said in his ear, leaning in. "Muslims go to Mecca. Catholics go to Lourdes. Hindus go to the Ganges and pagans go to Burning Man." He winked. "But can any of them beat this?"

Wren looked at him. "What do you know about Burning Man?"

"Only what we all do. They fill the air with their heretic chatter swamping the signal."

Wren frowned. "What are you talking about, signal? Do you know where Matthew or Faraday are?"

The man beamed. "I don't know everyone, but I'm sure you can find them here somewhere. Oh look!" He pointed upward as the song climaxed and the hundreds of voices reached and sustained a note as overwhelming as the screeching of the dish's triangles.

Abruptly a golden cloud of tiny glittering flakes burst into existence high overhead.

"Glory clouds!" the big man cried, and a tears ran down his cheek. The cry was taken up by others and carried, just as a second cloud of golden flakes appeared further along the hall, then a third. There was shouting and weeping, and the note of the masses trembled then redoubled as the people gave everything they had.

Wren watched in mounting disbelief as a fourth cloud burst, catching the light and refracting it. Golden flakes twinkled down around them. One fell onto the surface of Wren's coffee, no more than a tiny piece of golden glitter, but the big man at his side instantly reacted.

"A blessing!" he boomed, holding up Wren's cup. "A blessing for his pilgrimage, a blessing of the word!"

The crowd took up the chant, bellowing about the word.

"You have to drink it!" the big man hollered. "Swallow it all. Swallow it so we might hear his word!"

Wren looked into their expectant faces. None recognized him. Finally he was beginning to grasp what was happening here: these were not soldiers, they were rubes, taken in by some kind of cult that he'd never heard of; a cult with resources unlike any he'd seen before, but featuring the same parlor tricks of the cheapest trailer-park 'religions'. It took a special breed of blasphemous arrogance to pour glitter into the vents of a building and try to pass it off as a cloud of God's glory.

Wren could work with that.

He held the cup up. The people boomed their approval. He brought it to his lips and drank it all down, ignoring the scalding heat. They roared. They clapped him on the back. Another glory cloud burst overhead, and then they were all singing and swaying and wailing. The stocky man regarded Wren with a tear of pride in his eye.

"You found him out there, didn't you? You heard his voice."

Wren nodded. "Yes. I need to speak to the leader. I need to share what I've seen."

"Of course," the man said, nodding firmly. "I know where he resides. Come."

He strode deeper into the crowd. Wren glanced at Kiefer, who stood silently by the trestle table, still holding his coffee. He seemed fine.

Wren pressed deeper into the crowd.

29

OM VEDICS

Wren passed through the crowds, coated with glitter by the time he reached a door leading out. There was a corridor lined with framed prints of wavelength signals. The stocky man led Wren along, up a flight of stairs and along another corridor to a door.

Wren's heart beat hard.

Another attack could be imminent. If Matthew stood behind this door, Wren was unprepared. He had no weapon. The last time they'd met, on the train, Wren had been beaten.

"I can take it from here," he said to the stocky man.

"Of course," he allowed, pulling his hand back just prior to knocking. "I'll leave it to you."

He left. Wren walked back down the corridor, picked up a fire extinguisher, and returned to the door. He considered different approaches, then simply knocked.

"Come," came the response.

Wren knocked again.

"Come!"

He knocked a third time, and now there was a thump and footsteps approaching. Wren raised the fire extinguisher, the door swung inward, and there stood a man Wren had never seen before. He was tall and thin, late-twenties, and uncommonly handsome, with sharp, pale gray eyes and a square jaw, wearing a long black tunic.

"What have you found there, brother?" he asked, looking calmly at the extinguisher.

"A conversation starter," Wren said, and took the man by the scruff of his tunic, lifted him onto his tiptoes and walked him back into the office. It was simple inside, a desk, two bookcases, a potted plant and no windows, with the same symbol he'd seen under the great dish framed in black and white above the desk. He kicked the door closed behind him, laid the man across the desk like he was laying out a shirt to wear, then raised the extinguisher over his face.

"I'm happy to talk," the man said, staying remarkably calm. "There's no need for-"

"So let's talk. There are two people in this facility who just landed in a private jet, and they're about to launch tungsten missiles from orbit to strike targets on the ground. Their names are Matthew and Genevieve Faraday. You are going to tell me where they are, or your head's going to meet the bottom of this metal canister at an uncomfortably high velocity, and we'll see what spills out. Do you understand?"

The man shook his head. "I'm afraid I don't understand."

Wren frowned. "What do you not understand?"

"Who you're looking for," the man said, keeping his calm. "What these people are doing. Even who you are."

Wren considered. "You don't know Matthew? Or Faraday?"

"I don't."

"And your dish out there, you're not using it for directing tungsten missiles at the Earth?"

"Tungsten what? At the Earth? No, of course not! We don't have any missiles."

Wren glared at him. With the extinguisher hanging over his head, he remained extremely calm.

"Then what are you here for?"

"It's our retreat."

"What retreat?"

"It's more of a pilgrimage, actually. We've been coming here annually for five years. We have all the paperwork. Everything is paid for, and-"

"Who are you?"

"Who? We're, uh, I take it you're not actually a member, then? It's just, you're wearing the black of the void before-"

"Of course I'm not a member!"

"Ah. Well, then we're called the Om Vedic Circle. We book the radio telescope to search for signs of God's Word. We've been coming for years, investing in the search for the origins of the universe."

"The origins of the universe?"

"Yes! We believe in science as much as we believe in Vishnu. We're all Americans, though, like yourself."

It was getting to all be too much. "That doesn't mean anything to me. I'm a CIA officer in pursuit of dangerous terrorists. Their plane landed here. The man has a tattoo on his head, right here." Wren touched his forehead. "It looks a little like your symbol there." He nodded at the framed picture. "The woman is a brilliant theorist in orbital mechanics. I believe they're using this radio telescope to upload high-bandwidth instructions to an orbital platform, which is dropping tungsten missiles onto America. The first strike took out the Burning Man festival in Nevada. Don't you know about that?"

The man gawped. "Burning Man was hit with a tungsten missile? I don't, uh. I don't really know what that means."

Wren shook him. "Where are they?"

"I don't know! I haven't seen them. It's a retreat! We're peaceful!"

"Peaceful?"

"Don't you recognize the symbol?" the man asked, his eyes glancing to the side. "That's 'Om'. It's one of the most famous symbols in the world. It's Hindu. It means the word of God, or the first word, or the voice of creation. The Big Bang, basically; that's the first word. That's why we're here. We're listening for God's voice with the radio telescope, dating back billions of years. We're here to celebrate his creation of the universe, and-"

Wren tuned him out, mind spinning like he was seeking a wavelength he couldn't quite fix on. There was something else he was missing here. Something the stocky man had said, something about pilgrimages that…

"How many people have you got here?"

"How many? Uh, three hundred? Three hundred and twelve followers, with another hundred or so support volunteers. I mean, ninety-six. Four hundred and eight all told. It's a great honor for us all. If there's something wrong with our paperwork, then I'm happy to pay whatever fine I must."

Wren put the fire extinguisher down. Maybe he'd got this all wrong. The symbols were somewhat similar, so he'd thought maybe…

But no.

"You need to go," he said, and turned to the door. "All of your people, you need to get out of-"

Then he heard it, distant and clattering up from below; the brutal hammering of automatic weapons fire, followed by screams.

Everything clarified.

These people weren't in league with Matthew. They were his next target.

30

SLAUGHTER

Wren scooped the fire extinguisher and ran back along the corridor, down the stairs, along one more corridor then burst out into the glass hall.

The glass ceiling was gone. The hot warmth was a memory, the golden flakes replaced by the crushed ice of shattered glass on the floor, with a fresh fall of snow swirling in. Rejoicers wearing the black of the void ran and ducked and convulsed as bullets streamed back and forth across their bodies like scythes harvesting grain.

They fell in waves, hit from multiple angles. Wren picked out the gunmen, black-clad operators wielding AK-47s, five of them at the points of a pentagram, spraying calmly and repeatedly, taking their time to reload. Bodies lay in swathes, men and women, young people, the aged. Bodies jerked and screams replaced the joyous song of earlier.

The nearest gunman was five yards to the right. Wren wasted no time and launched the fire extinguisher like a shoulder-mounted rocket. It zipped out and hit the man on the chin, knocking him out standing up. In seconds Wren was there, snatching up the AK-47. It was loaded with an extended magazine and the gunman had a dozen more.

It was a slaughter just like Burning Man.

Wren hoisted the fire extinguisher and hurled it up in the air, then trained the AK-47 and fired. The bullets ruptured the canister, causing an explosive escape of the sodium potassium bicarbonate powder inside, bursting outward like a 'glory cloud' of white flour.

The rain of bullets sputtered to a halt, and there were uncertain shouts across the freezing hall. Wren was already running to the next point of the pentagram. White dust drifted, obscuring sight lines and starting the surviving Om Vedics coughing. Wren vaulted bodies and picked out his next target.

The man wasn't looking. He didn't know what hit him, as Wren surged from the fine white mist with his right elbow already locked and loaded, which he unleashed into the man's temple. The blow was solid, a mighty thunk, and the figure went down.

Wren ran on.

The rain of gunfire began again. The impact thuds and the screams restarted, then Wren reached the third man, standing near the spot where Wren had first entered. Now the glass wall had been obliterated. The man was spraying wildly with his rifle, looking in all directions except for behind him, so Wren looped around, came at him from the parking lot and rammed him in the lower back.

Together they flew forward, the man struck the glass-strewn floor on his belly and slid, screaming as the shards dug in. Wren slid, rolled him over and silenced him with a punch that crushed his trachea.

Up again, Wren just had time to see the next figure in the pentagram swing his rifle around, cutting a swathe through the survivors toward him. There was no time to dive, no time to do anything but absorb the stream, until out of nowhere Anais Kiefer appeared and caught the barrel in one hand.

The gunman looked like a child next to Kiefer, who simply stood there, holding the rifle. He tried to yank it back, but on his third try Kiefer lashed out without looking, sending a punch that whipped the man sideways. He might have flown three clear feet if he hadn't had the rifle strap around his neck. It caught and snapped tight, as Kiefer's grip didn't allow for an inch of budge.

The man's neck broke. He fell. Wren stared in disbelief. Kiefer was looking in roughly his direction. The fifth stream of bullets had halted.

"You owe me, now," Kiefer said.

Wren ran. "They're about to launch another strike," he shouted over the glacial wind and the fresh influx of screams. "Come with me."

Kiefer didn't move but Wren kept going, past the fifth point of the pentagram where hundreds of spent brass shells lay in piles amongst the bodies and glass. He scanned the route ahead, but it seemed the only way into the research facility was through the door he'd already taken.

He bolted inside. Now there were specks of white powder on the floor, leaving a new trail of crumbs for him to follow. It bypassed the office of the Om Vedic's leader for another route, off to the side and up another flight of stairs, which was where he met the fifth man.

He fired down at Wren from the landing above. Bullets crashed into the concrete steps, just a millisecond before Wren reached them. He stopped on a dime, flattened himself against the wall, held the AK-47 out at arms' length and angled back over his head, and pulled the trigger.

The weapon barked through its extended magazine in seconds, drilling ten-plus rounds per second up toward the hiding place of the fifth man. There was a shriek, his stream of bullets ceased, then Wren ran on, slapping another extended magazine into place.

The landing was extensive, more of a gantry encircling multiple open squares, below which lay various laboratory and control spaces. The gantry allowed more people to gather and watch. Wren ran past the control room for the telescope, equipped with wall-mounted computers and control systems; a backend office with spectrometers and correlators to analyze the frequency of signals; and a storage space filled with maintenance and safety equipment. Beyond all that, there were more steps leading up.

He took them three at a time, climbing up to the top of the structure and into a bulbous glass dome reminiscent of the flight deck at Vostochny, tiered with ranks of work stations around a central screen. Most striking was the 360-degree view out over the complex and the dish. Directly below lay the broken bodies and glass of the Om Vedic group in the foyer, already half-buried in fresh powder snow. The parking lot was a slushy moat, beyond which lay the great white valley of the telescope's dish.

The Om Vedics had thought to use it to reach back into the distant past. Matthew and Faraday wanted to wreak destruction in the present. The skies above swirled gray with an angry storm.

Wren focused on the central screen. It showed a blue ring enveloping the sphere of the Earth, what he assumed to be a Middle Earth Orbit, with a blip that had to be the Miest passing through eastern Siberia. Arcane data rippled down either side; calculations, equations and coordinates passing too quickly for him to read.

"There, it's done!" called Genevieve Faraday from her desk near the front, tapping final keystrokes. "You can't stop-"

Bullets ripped into her chest and flung her backward across her screen, where she gasped a breath, looked at Wren then slid down to the ground.

Gunpowder smoke rose from the front row of seats. Wren stared as a figure emerged, his massive frame unfurling like a flag in the wind, rifle already trained in. He was truly enormous, seven feet tall and built like a buffalo. The black tattoo on his forehead seemed to glow in the strange, seething gray light.

An 8 and a cross.

"Christopher Wren," he said, his voice as deep as the grinding of the radio telescope's frosted gears. "America's saint."

"Matthew," Wren answered, "the lost apostle". Snow whipped around the dome as the storm surged in, making it feel like they were trapped in some strange snow globe. "Why kill Faraday?"

"I was always going to kill her," Matthew answered calmly, "or at least render her inert." He pointed a finger at his left eye. "The Egyptian pharaohs did it. Kill the architect and all the builders, so no one could ever find their tombs."

Wren glanced at the screen. Whatever process Faraday had begun, it seemed she'd completed it, and now the Miest was preparing to strike.

"What's the target?"

The giant man looked over his shoulder then back. From outside, there came the grinding sound of the dish shifting position again.

"You'll find out soon enough. I don't want to spoil the surprise."

"I hate surprises." Wren bunched the AK-47 harder into his shoulder, sights pointing at Matthew. "I'm the kind of guy that jumps to the end of the book."

"Impatience is a sin," Matthew said, then started stalking up the steps. "I learned patience over many years. I can teach you, like I taught your friend on the train."

Wren gritted his teeth. "I'll pass."

"It won't matter. We've waited for so long, Christopher. Dreamed for so long. The Miest is our weapon, and only one man on this Earth can control it; a man you will never find and cannot stop."

Wren considered his options. It would be easy to shoot Matthew now, but a wounding shot to a shoulder or limb was risky. The big man was fast, and only had to shift an inch or two the wrong way for the bullet to hit his chest or head, or worse yet, ricochet into the delicate equipment behind him. Then there'd be no way of finding out what Faraday had done.

"Stop there," he barked, as Matthew crested the top of the stairs.

"I only obey one master," Matthew answered, then lowered his rifle onto a nearby seat. "And his commands are clear. He says you can be taught. He wants me to relieve your burden, like I did for your friend." This time he pointed his finger at Wren's left eye. "I live to serve."

"Stop or say goodbye to your knees."

Matthew took another step. "So fire, Saint Christopher."

Wren backed up, mind racing. A shot was a risk, but he wasn't at all sure he could beat the giant in a fair fight.

"Last chance," he warned.

"Last rites," Matthew said, then lowered his head and charged.

31

MATTHEW

The giant man lowered his head like a bull charging a matador, his massive thighs propelling him across the polished marble floor in barely a second. Wren was ready, feet set and stance firm, and brought the grip of the rifle up in a sweeping upper cut, aiming to catch Matthew full in the face.

He missed.

In a bizarre maneuver, Matthew hit the ground hard on his chest a foot in front of Wren, then slid. His right shoulder hammered into Wren's leading left leg and swept it backward under his immense weight, following through to hit Wren's right leg a millisecond later, dead-stopping with almost enough force to wrench his knee out of joint.

Wren was twisted on the spot, off-balance and teetering with both legs wrapped in Matthew's embrace. He managed to bring the rifle down on the big man's swollen back with a bass-drum thud, then there was nothing to hold onto and he toppled.

He slammed hard onto the polished marble, blasting the air from his lungs, but managed to crane his neck up and avoid cracking his skull. At once he began to twist, trying to kick his legs free, but the giant had already wrapped his left leg in an ankle-breaking lock.

"This is your first lesson," Matthew rumbled, and hyper-extended Wren's ankle.

The ligament snapped with a sharp pop. Wren gasped at the sudden intensity of the pain. On an intellectual level he knew exactly what had just happened; at the least the anterior talofibular ligament connecting his shin to his foot had come unmoored from the talus bone, with a high likelihood of spreading damage to the posterior ligament, the calcaneofibular ligament, all surrounding connective soft tissue as well as the two bone anchor points.

The sudden pain brought a rush of adrenaline, and he managed to reel up to a sitting position and drop a haymaker elbow toward Matthew's head.

The blow hit only air. Matthew had already pushed off Wren and scooted away, already rising to his feet.

"I understand," he said in his foghorn voice. "The first lesson comes the hardest, especially to a man like you."

Wren pushed himself to his feet too, facing the giant. His right leg was fine and held his weight, but his left was useless; he could barely rest any weight on it. The fight had just changed, and they both knew it.

Wren still had the rifle, though, and dragged it around.

Matthew was ready for that, catching the barrel and easily swiping it off to the side. With one leg out of commission, Wren had no hope of standing his ground, leaving him with only two choices: cling to the rifle and get spun, or let go.

He let go.

Matthew hadn't anticipated that and overstretched a little, opening an avenue for Wren. He plunged into it, leveraging the firm base of his right foot to shoot a whole-body uppercut punch into the base of the giant's jaw.

It hit with a sound like an axe felling a tree, rocking the

big man backward and to the side. Wren leaped forward, throwing all his body mass at Matthew and grappling around his neck.

The big man took two steps but it wasn't enough, and fell. He came down on his side, ignoring any attempt to cushion his fall and sending both arms back to grasp at Wren's throat.

Wren had other plans, though, dropping straight for the big man's ankle. His calf was as thick as a normal man's thigh, his booted ankle more like the knotty branch of an ancient oak, but he managed to get the lock on.

"I learn best by example," he rasped, then pulled with all his strength.

The gunfire pop of Matthew's ankle filled him with a fresh surge of aggression. Matthew gasped but immediately swung around just as Wren had, trying for a big elbow into Wren's back, but he didn't wait for it to land.

He attacked.

The elbow hit him in the left shoulder, only half of its turning circle completed so punching with only half of its force. It was almost enough to crack Wren's clavicle and throw him off, but not quite. It did spin him lopsided onto his right side as he came down across the big man's chest, but he'd anticipated that, and drove another blow with everything he could muster.

His left hand shot out in a blade shape, whipping over Matthew's deployed elbow and driving hard at his exposed throat. At the last moment the giant realized the threat and yanked his head down, taking the blow in his cheek. Wren's fingers punched in and through, ripping the big man's face open on his own teeth, burying his momentum as the blade collapsed into a fist to finish by hammering his knuckles into the base of Matthew's right eye socket, hard enough to rap his head off the floor below.

Wren closed his fist, snatching at the big man's jaw, but it was a mistake.

Matthew swept both hands to his face, wrapped Wren's left hand even as he readied to rip off the big man's jaw, and locked it.

Then twisted backward.

More pops burst like firecrackers as Wren's left distended; tendons and ligaments cracked and sheared. The shock was all-consuming, the sudden dump of cortisol into his system filling him with nausea. Still, he flung his right hand at Matthew's left eye, but the big man batted it away easily, yanked Wren close with his ruptured hand, and encircled his head with his huge right arm.

Wren's legs windmilled on the marble as the arm tightened, instantly locking off the flow of blood to his brain. His right hand flailed helplessly.

"Second lesson," the giant rumbled into his ear. "Obey."

The world grayed as consciousness dwindled, but it didn't fade out completely. Rather he lay cocooned in the huge man's grip long enough to watch his body fall limp, staring through gray curtains as just enough blood crept through for him to stay awake.

Matthew dragged him. Across the marble they slid together, to the very edge of the glass bowl, until Wren was splayed facing out with the giant behind him. Ahead through the gray mist lay more churning gray, as the storm barraged harder. Below was the shattered foyer with the bodies of all the Om Vedics, now coated in snow, and beyond that was the white bowl of the space telescope, even now pumping directions up to the Miest.

"Witness the wages of defiance," Matthew whispered, his lips by Wren's ear. "these people were warned, as we warned the miscreants of Burning Man. In a thousand ways, the Lord gave them warning, and still they sinned. Still you sinned, Christopher Wren. Which brings us to the third lesson." Matthew rustled at his right sleeve. "The most important one."

Across Wren's reduced vision he brought some kind of long, twisted metal needle. It had a dull point but a sharp edge, with an angular bend in the middle.

"It's a surgical tool of my own devising," Matthew rumbled, "based on an endoscopic probe. It fits in a sleeve down my forearm, so it's always ready. It was ready for the Vostochny director. It was ready for your friend on the train."

Wren felt a dull sense of fear gnawing through the numbness. He tried to kick free and watched his right leg flop pitifully.

Matthew held the tool in front of Wren's eyes. It blurred and twinkled. "Get a good look. The procedure I've mastered in the field is called a 'corpus callosotomy'. I insert this tool into your brain through the corner of your left eye. You see, the bend?" He demonstrated. "That allows me to get behind your nasal bone and into your brain."

Wren jerked again. This time his right leg barely twitched. The world became grayscale as snow rushed in closer, obscuring the dish.

"Better," Matthew said. "You see, there are twin hemispheres in the brain. One side leans toward reason, science, logic, the other toward faith, and there is a thin, delicate fiber bridge between them, called the corpus callosum." He paused, taking the moment to wrap his legs around Wren's midriff like a python immobilizing its prey. "This device permanently severs that bridge. The hemispheres no long communicate, and the man that remains is reborn. He can be taught to reject the lies of our modern world. He can be taught to obey. Even you will become this man too, Saint of America."

The silver device twinkled closer. Wren thought it looked like a star.

"Prepare to be born again," Matthew whispered, and pushed the needle into Wren's left eye.

32

ANAIS KIEFER

Anais Kiefer lived in a world of uncertainty.

Ever since the giant had cracked his chest on the train, speaking strange things into his ear and pushing a silver device into his eye, nothing was clear. Words failed him. The world failed to resolve. His own body felt alien, so when he looked down at what he knew were his arms and his legs, they looked like the arms and legs of somebody else.

He couldn't feel them.

It was hard to focus. It was hard to gather the motivation to act.

After the attack, he'd woken in a tent and felt wrong. Unsafe. Crawling out, finding his weapon and taking up cover in the snow had all been automatic responses to that feeling of danger. He hadn't had to think about them so they'd just happened, but once he was in the snow, trying to figure out exactly what the danger was, he was stuck.

He couldn't grasp it. He couldn't think.

He'd become aware he was swiftly freezing, but still couldn't budge. He'd stared at his bare hands, clamped to the barrel of the AK-47, as they turned blue. These were hands he thought his knew, but now looked like a stranger's, somehow bolted to his body. He'd tried to tell those hands to let go of the rifle and push him up. He'd tried to tell his legs to stand.

Somehow the signal hadn't gotten through, and the effort was exhausting. Inside he'd felt only panic and fear, though not a word of that escaped his lips. He knew he was dying. Then a voice had come from the distance.

"Kiefer?" It occupied a space beyond his body which he could scarcely comprehend, let alone see. "It's Wren."

That meant something. On some level, he understood who Wren was. Wren was a pivot point about which his life revolved. Kiefer had gone to prison for Wren, and fought alongside Wren, and attacked Wren, and…

It was all a jumble of times and moments. Still, under Wren's call, he'd made a supreme effort to stand, then to speak.

"Chris," he finally managed. "Is it you?"

Wren had looked after him. Kiefer didn't understand why, or what had happened, but he knew that Wren had always been good. They'd fought the Taliban together. They'd served undercover in ISIS together, and though the world around him now was foggy and unclear, he remembered those days vividly. He remembered the stink of hiding in goatskins in sweaty, smoke-filled caves as American Predator drones scrolled on overwatch above. He remembered the moment their cover had blown in the Hindu Kush, when the terror cell they'd embedded with got word of who they really were. He remembered how Wren had tried to come back for him in the midst of their escape, but failed.

Then he'd been alone.

They'd kept him in a tent, only breaking the darkness for beatings and torture. They were inventive. Months had passed. At times he'd forgotten who he was. By the time he finally escaped, crushing the throats of his jailers in the midst of an intertribal war, he was a new man.

By then, he hated the CIA, and most of all he hated Wren. They hadn't come for him. Nobody had come, and he'd suffered alone. He'd wanted nothing more than revenge against Christopher Wren.

But here was Wren, helping him.

"Are you hungry?" Wren asked. Time spooled and unspooled between mouthfuls, as he fed Kiefer like a baby. Now they were on a plane. Now they were in a truck. Now they were in the snow. In each moment, he couldn't remember how he'd got there or why.

Wren laughed.

It was a single moment, and he didn't know why, but it felt strangely all right. Then there'd been the warm space, and people singing all around, and he'd finally started to feel better. More like himself. He'd looked at his arms and seen something about them he recognized. He began to remember some of what the giant man had said to him, and what he'd done, and then there was gunfire.

People screamed. Images jolted and combined.

Again, he reacted without thinking, in line with decades of training and experience. People were dying and it was his job to stop that. He was a protector. Every fiber of his body knew how to do that job, and though he could barely see, and his body still felt foreign, he moved. He found a man with a rifle and took it. The man lay on the floor motionless, and Kiefer looked for the others. He wanted the noise to stop.

Then it was cold.

Snow fell and there were bodies on the floor, and people shuddering and crying. He looked around himself, trying to understand what had happened. Snow landed on his face, and he looked up, and there kneeling at the edge of a bubble of glass that looked like a gumball dispenser, he saw Wren.

He was kneeling. His face was pale, his arms were limp, and the giant man was holding one arm locked around his neck.

It all came rushing back then. The feel of the metal as it slid into his eye, and the awful scratching as it worked up and down, and the sense that his own mind was being erased.

He couldn't allow that to happen to Wren.

His body lurched into action, moving on muscle memory with absolute fluidity, every fiber firing at and beyond his earlier capacity. He was a protector and had been all his life. He sped through the crowd of lost souls, through the door and up. His brain saw the powder trails and his eyes remembered 'up' and he ran.

Then he was in the giant gumball. Snow was everywhere, and screens, and blood, and there was Wren, wrapped like a child in the grip of the giant,

"Third lesson," the giant said, and Kiefer's mind jammed up again. He didn't know what came next. Had this already happened, or was it the future? Was he the one in the giant's arms, or was he the giant, or was he another man, just watching?

He looked down at his own arms. Big hands, strong arms. They'd done so many things over the years, some good, some bad. He could be both proud and ashamed. But right now?

The giant raised the silver needle to Wren's eye. He was still talking. He pressed it in. And then Anais Kiefer knew with absolute certainty what came next, as if it had already happened.

He strode in. He plucked the needle from Wren's eye with one hand even as he wrapped the other around the giant's thick neck and squeezed with everything he had.

"Fourth lesson," he grunted, the words coming unbidden, "talk less."

He pushed the needle deep into the giant's eye, and raked it up and down, until he stopped struggling and shouting and fell limp to the floor.

33

QUESTIONING

Wren blinked as blood flow returned to his brain. His left foot and hand sang with pain but he could ignore that, and turned to see Anais Kiefer kneeling over the still body of the giant, Matthew. In his hands hung a long, bloody needle. Matthew's left eye was red.

Wren shuddered. This was the fate he'd just barely escaped.

"Thank you, Anais," he said.

Kiefer said nothing, just stared past him at the snow.

"I'm sorry that happened to you. I'm sure there's something we can do."

Kiefer didn't budge.

Wren pointed at the needle. "Can I take that?"

Kiefer's hand jerked forward awkwardly, and Wren tentatively took the needle with his right hand.

"OK. Good. Thank you. Now, Kiefer." He thought for a moment. The pain from his ruptured wrist and ankle filled his head but he clenched his teeth and pushed it down. "I need your help. I need to get down to those computers, but I've broken my ankle and my wrist. Can you help me-"

Before Wren could react, Kiefer lunged at him. His left arm scooped under Wren's neck, his right looped under his legs and he hoisted him like a damsel in distress.

"I didn't mean-" Wren began awkwardly, but already Kiefer had straightened up like he weighed nothing and started striding down toward the big screen. "OK, well, this'll do I guess."

Kiefer reached the bottom of the steps, beside the workstation where Faraday's body lay sprawled on the floor, then stood.

"If you could put me down on the-"

Kiefer dropped him. Wren's good arm shot out and managed to arrest the fall, his right leg caught most of his weight, and he ended up sitting flat on the floor. It would've been comical if the big screen weren't showing four Hammers on an orbital path, already deployed from the Miest and heading for America.

His mouth ran dry.

"That's bad," said Kiefer beside him.

Wren looked from Kiefer to the screen. "You can read that?"

Kiefer said nothing.

Wren hoisted himself into Faraday's seat and tapped the keypad, but the screen did not respond. He tried various key combinations but nothing worked. He leaned over, momentarily leaning his weight on his left ankle, which was agonizing, to check the cables. All were attached to ports and docks and seemed correct.

He was locked out.

"I need a satellite radio," he said to Kiefer, but Kiefer only stared at the screen. "Anais, listen to me. I need a satellite radio, now. One of the men we killed downstairs must have one. Can you fetch one for me?"

Kiefer twisted his head down toward Wren. This time his

eyes seemed to be focusing a little better, almost meeting Wren's. "Fetch" he repeated slowly. "Like a dog?"

"No, like a lieutenant," Wren countered swiftly, reading the threat in those cloudy eyes. "My foot is busted. I can't run. I need you to do it or things are going to get very bad."

Kiefer stared a moment longer, then nodded. "You're the captain." He turned and ran up the steps, stopped briefly at the body of the giant to plant a hefty kick into his side, and ran on.

Wren was left gazing at the big screen. Four Hammers. The pain was a storm to match the snow beyond the glass, but this was worse. As he watched, the Hammers trickled east. He imagined them in the upper exosphere, released in MEO somewhere between 2,000 to 36,000 km and plummeting faster with every second. Four great rods of tungsten ripping down from the heavens to the Earth, their tips blazing red-hot, their trajectories set by a genius and a madman and a secret puppet-master Matthew thought he never would find.

At Burning Man they'd lost 70,000 souls. How many innocents would four Hammers kill?

The facility around him was silent but for the rushing of the snow. He brought up his left hand and inspected the damage. There were no breaks in the skin; his hand simply sagged uselessly. He tried moving his fingers. They worked, but it was agonizing and there was no power or traction behind them.

He leaned over and looked at Genevieve Faraday. Her chest was bloody, but her face was surprisingly lifelike. If anything she looked surprised. She was the knot that had bound them all together.

"Why?" Wren whispered.

She did not answer. As per Matthew's intention, she'd carried all her secrets to the grave.

Wren tugged her jacket off her shoulders, knotted it with

one hand then slung it over his right shoulder, resting his left arm in the cradle it provided. At once the pain reduced. He looked at his left foot. What he needed was an orthopedic boot, but failing that, he could bind it.

After hopping awkwardly up the stairs, he found the giant lying still. Wren stripped his jacket then wound it firmly around his left foot. Pulling the knot taut was agonizing, but in moments the pain receded somewhat. He tried to take a tentative step and immediately regretted it, but at least he didn't pass out.

Anais Kiefer bounded up, holding out a satellite radio. He looked at Wren accusingly. "I thought you couldn't walk."

"I can hop. Can I see that?"

Kiefer thought for a moment, like a sulking child, then held the radio out. "Is this right?"

"It's perfect," Wren said, and tuned the radio into Humphreys' frequency, dialed the code and waited. In moments only the DNI answered with a shout.

"Wren?"

"It's me, Humphreys. I found the facility, it's a giant radio telescope three hundred miles north of Yakutsk. Faraday's dead and the giant's incapacitated, but they managed to launch four more Hammers from the Miest."

Seconds passed, then Humphreys' voice blasted back through the line, warped by static. "Four! How did they launch four?"

"That doesn't matter now. What matters now is the targets. You have SAMs batteries in place over sensitive locations, right?"

"Not enough to protect the whole US, and they won't do much if we can't detect the Hammers coming in! How long have we got?"

Wren scanned the big screen. In the last few minutes, the red Hammers had covered perhaps an inch toward America, but what did that mean, really? He had no idea what their orbital paths were. One might hit on the first pass, the others might circle the world several times before finally striking, building more destructive kinetic energy with every loop.

"I have no idea. The soonest strike could be within an hour. I don't know beyond that."

"That's useless, Wren! What about targets?"

"I can't say. That might become clearer as they get closer."

Humphreys laughed. It sounded frantic to Wren. "We need you to be precise, Wren! Four attacks like Burning Man? I don't know if we'll survive it. We only dropped two atom bombs on the Japanese and it broke them for eighty years."

Wren racked his mind. He looked at the screen and the calculations spinning down the side. If Faraday was alive, maybe he could've compelled her. If he had a video link, maybe someone on Humphreys' end could make sense of the numbers. He had neither, though. He looked at Matthew. Maybe if Kiefer hadn't cut his brain-bridge, they might've got something out of him, but probably not. Torture wouldn't have worked.

Then something occurred to him, something Matthew had said.

"One second," he said to Humphreys, and looked up at Anais Kiefer. "Anais, would you obey an order I gave you?"

Kiefer stared.

"Anais," Wren barked sharply, which grabbed the big man's attention. "Would you obey any order I gave you?"

Kiefer seemed to think about it. "Yes," he finally said. "You're my captain. I'm your lieutenant."

"Good. Pat your head and rub your stomach at the same time."

Kiefer stared.

"Do it," Wren ordered again. "Pat your head and rub your stomach."

Kiefer's arms began to move. Even he seemed surprised. One rose up to his head and began to pat his disheveled hair, the other went to his stomach and began to rub.

It sparked a light of hope in Wren's chest. He looked again at Matthew. He was out for the count, sleeping off major amateur brain surgery. There was no telling what damage Kiefer had done with that needle, but there was a possibility he remembered the targets, and a chance he might tell them to Wren.

A chance he would obey.

"Get a bucket of water," Wren said to Kiefer. "We're going to wake him up."

Kiefer stopped patting his head and rubbing his stomach, then turned and ran off again.

"What have you got planned, Wren?" Humphreys squawked down the satellite line. The signal was growing scratchier, most likely thanks to the storm.

"I'm going to interrogate Matthew. Maybe if I pose as an authority figure he recognizes, it'll help; he mentioned one man pulling the strings. Did Rogers find out anything?"

"I don't know. She was attacked in San Francisco, looks to be by the twin of this 'Matthew'. He's dead along with almost a dozen other men. Rogers is in intensive care."

Wren didn't have time to parse that, other than that Rogers must've discovered something if they were coming after her. He stared at the screen, watching the Hammers crawling further east with every passing second.

"There's a quarter million lives at risk, Gerald. Get her on the line now."

34

CALVARY

Minutes ticked by. Kiefer came back with a bucket, and Wren directed him to set up a chair looking out of the glass bowl into the storm. Together they hefted the giant into it, then lashed his arms and legs firmly down. His head lolled and his left eye had crusted over.

Wren stood with the radio in his hand, waiting for the static to break.

"Agent Wren, this is Dr. Lila Vale," came a voice down the line eventually. The connection was worse already, barely audible. "I understand you need to speak to Agent Rogers, but I must warn you, her condition is critical. She's sustained substantial lung contusion and concussive effects from multiple grenade blasts, as well as several knife wounds. She's lost blood and she's-"

"She's my friend," Wren kicked in, cutting him off. "Wake her up."

A lag of a second followed. "Very well. I'm administering an intravenous anticholinesterase to bypass the anesthesia. She should be conscious for several minutes. Any longer than that and the exertion could cause her to crash. I will not let her die."

"Good. How long until-"

A gasp came down the line.

"Agent Rogers," said Dr. Vale calmly. "You're in Saint Francis Memorial Hospital. You've had treatment, but your condition is weak. I've temporarily woken you from anesthesia, but you won't be awake long. You've sustained serious lung damage, but you should be able to speak. Now, on the line I have Agent Christopher Wren. He has questions for you of urgent national security to discuss. Do you understand what I've explained to you?"

Seconds passed, and Wren hoped Rogers was signaling assent.

"Let the record show the Special Agent nodded," said Vale. "Agent Wren, she can hear you."

For a moment Wren's throat thickened. The thought of Sally Rogers, so young and full of ambition, laid up in a hospital bed barely able to speak struck him cold. But there was no time for emotion.

"Sally," he said. "Humphreys told me you fought someone. He said you were onto something."

"Chris," came her reply. She sounded breathy and hoarse. "Yeah. He," she stopped to cough, "he had the tattoo. Eight and a cross. He called himself …" she coughed harder, sounding like she was about to bring up a lung. "Mark."

Wren blinked, pairing that with Matthew. "Mark. Like Jesus' apostles?"

"Right. He called himself … an apostle. Talked … about sin. Filth. About wiping away … false idols."

Wren reeled. That was new. Extreme religious cults were common. Puritanical groups willing to resort to extreme terror in striking down unbelievers, who named their leaders after the apostles from the Bible, though? That was rarer. Maybe unique.

"I've got Matthew here," he said swiftly. "He tried to cut my brain in half, Rogers, but Kiefer beat him to it, and-"

"Kiefer cut your ... brain in half?"

Wren almost laughed. "No. He cut Matthew's. But before that, he talked about one man controlling the Miest. I'm thinking he's in America. He's got to be rich, a zealot, with a support organization around him and a connection to Faraday. Faraday's dead now, along with any way to use her to stop this attack, so you need to find that man."

"I'll ... try."

"Good. Now I'm going to interrogate Matthew, and I need to pass myself off as his superior. Maybe he'll spill targets, cut-off codes, even the location of the Miest. Do you know anything else about this group I can use to convince him? "

Seconds ticked by. Wren thought he might've lost her.

"The symbol," she said, then coughed again. "It's the ... Calvary Cross."

"Calvary Cross? I don't know it."

"You ... wouldn't. Very ... rare. It's made up of the ... Russian Orthodox cross and two triangles. The bottom triangle ... symbolizes Calvary hill, where Jesus ... was crucified. The top symbolizes ... two halves of the spear in Jesus' side."

Wren blinked. Two triangles and a cross. A figure 8. Calvary hill. That took this group and their symbol right back to first principles. Jesus. Dying for all our sins.

"Do any known groups use that symbol?"

"Ask ... Humphreys. He has a ... working group at Langley. I do know ... it was used by fanatics monks in the ... Middle Ages. They wanted ... to enshrine religious law. Religious ... rule."

Wren cursed.

"And Chris?"

"What is it, Sally?"

"Mark said he ... couldn't be killed. He almost ... couldn't. I think he was ..."

"Built in a lab?" Wren finished.

"Right."

"I thought that, too. Matthew is huge. Bigger but faster than me. It's not natural."

"There's drugs ..." Rogers wheezed. "Illegal treatments. Gene therapies. Growth hormones. You could build ... men like that."

"I'll tell Humphreys. OK, Sally. You need to rest."

"There was something ... else. I can't quite ..."

"Anything that could help."

"The Kingdom," she blurted, coughing. "That's it. The new Kingdom ... he called it. The Kingdom ... will rise."

The words rang in Wren's head, forging unexpected connections. Kingdom. In his study of cults, he'd researched the Bible extensively. Matthew and Mark were two of the three 'Synoptic' Gospels that mentioned the Kingdom of Heaven on Earth, along with Luke. Usually that phrase was interpreted as the spreading of peace under the spiritual halo of Jesus, but not always.

For some it meant the end of the world, brought about by the Second Coming, the arrival of the Antichrist or the Rapture. Essentially, doomsday, and Wren knew all about doomsday cults. He'd grown up in one, the Pyramid, which ended with one thousand followers burned alive in the Arizona desert. For doomsday cults, like the Unification Church or the Solar Temple, the Kingdom of Heaven on Earth was a cast-iron prophecy where the world would end and begin again better. Billions would die in the wars of purification, but that was acceptable. Preferable, even. Many such groups had tried in the past to bring on the End Times.

None of them had had Russian exotic weapons in orbit, though.

"That's good. I can use that, Sally."

"And tell that bastard ... I killed his brother."

"I'll slip it into conversation. Now get better and find the guy, OK?"

"I'll be-"

She coughed and kept coughing for long seconds, each one deeper and louder than the last, until the voice of Dr. Vale cut back in. "I'm ending the interview to render life-saving aid."

The line died.

Sally Rogers was eight thousand miles away again.

"Wren," came Humphreys' voice. "I've relayed all that to the working group. The symbologists and cult experts should be back to you with something in minutes. Kepler's working on possible orbital calculations right now. Most of all, we need the target of those Hammers."

Wren set his teeth. These zealots had attacked Rogers. They'd attacked his country. He refocused on Matthew, sitting unconscious on his chair, the 'apostle' for this new movement.

"Stay on the line, Gerald. I'm going to get those targets for you."

He straightened up. The pain in his hand and foot only sharpened him, now. He'd worked mind games on cult leaders before. He'd brought them down from within. Matthew should stand no chance.

He nodded at Kiefer, and Kiefer tossed the bucket of water on Matthew's head.

For seconds nothing happened, then the giant man gasped awake.

35

APOSTLE

Matthew's left eye was ruined, but his right darted from side to side, taking in the snow, the flight deck, Wren and Kiefer, then his own bound body. He struggled, jerking to get free, but couldn't.

Then he began to laugh.

He threw back his head and roared.

Wren reached out and took hold of his chin beneath his ruined cheek. The big man tried to bite Wren's fingers, still strong despite the amateur surgery, but Wren was stronger.

"Calm down," he soothed, holding his jaw gently but firmly, speaking as he would to a skittish horse. "Matthew. You're amongst friends."

"Friends?" Matthew shouted. "Friends? You dug into my brain, didn't you? But you missed. I don't know what you hit. I don't know. This isn't right. You hit something."

He began laughing again. Thick dark blood oozed from his left eye, then began to trickle from his nostrils.

Maybe there wasn't long left.

Wren squeezed his jaw. "Apostle Matthew," he said firmly. "This is your final test. The Lord comes in many guises. He tested Job nearly to destruction. Did you think you would be any more privileged?"

That partly stilled Matthew. He blinked and tried to focus on Wren. "Job? How can you-"

"The Kingdom has come," Wren interrupted. "The Hammers have fallen. Now you answer to me."

Matthew blinked and weaved. "You? I answer to you? But you're not-"

"Be not wise in thine own eyes," Wren intoned, "fear the LORD, and depart from evil."

Matthew gasped. "Parables, 3:7. Are you-"

"The light of the body is the eye," Wren raced on, "if therefore thine eye be single, thy whole body shall be full of light. But if thine eye be evil, thy whole body shall be full of darkness."

Matthew's jaw dropped and all his struggling ceased. "Matthew, 6:22, 6:23."

"Your own Gospel," Wren said. "See not with your eyes, my apostle. See with faith."

"But, but," Matthew whispered, his one good eye darting over Wren's face. "Who are you?"

"I am Luke," Wren said.

"Luke," Matthew murmured. "Not an ... apostle. I do not answer to-"

"Luke," Wren repeated steadily, gaze boring into Matthew's one good eye. He'd made his choice for good reason. "Luke the evangelist, one of the 70 apostolic men, and author of Acts."

Matthew breathed out and his jaw slackened. "Acts of the Apostles."

"Acts of the Apostles. The Fifth book of the New Testament. Our whole vital history, from Calvary through the Pentecost to the first church in Antioch."

Matthew gasped and his good eye fluttered. "Calvary. Did you say Calvary?"

"It is our history," Wren said gently, playing into his delusion. "It is also our present and our future. Luke wrote it then. I will write it now."

A tear beaded and ran down Matthew's cheek. "You're lying. The Kingdom is not … really here. Not yet, it can't-"

Wren smiled, and ran one finger up Matthew's cheek, rubbing away the tear and quoting from the Gospels again. "'Take no thought for the morrow, Matthew. Sufficient unto the day is the evil thereof. Seek ye first the kingdom of God."

More tears flooded from Matthew's one good eye. "My own Gospel."

"I carry them all within me," Wren said.

"So it's true? Is it done?"

"Through the tender mercy of our God. Don't you feel his love all around you, Matthew?"

Matthew began to sob, then laugh, then blood gushed from his right nostril as if someone had switched on a faucet. "Luke 1, 78. Your Gospel! I do feel it. But Luke?"

"Yes, Matthew."

"Where is Mark? He said he would be with me, when the Kingdom comes."

A shudder ran up Wren's back. "Mark is here with us." He gestured to Kiefer.

"Mark," Matthew whispered. "I longed for this. I-" He abruptly retched. Bile splashed out over Wren's right hand, but Matthew continued trying to talk as if he hadn't noticed, his right eye roving wildly, trying to fix on Kiefer. "I wrote our letters many times, seeking the right words. Are you truly here?"

Wren looked up at Kiefer. Kiefer said nothing.

"Say yes," Wren whispered. "Now."

"Yes!" Kiefer blurted.

"My brother," Matthew said.

"There isn't long," Wren pressed. "Matthew. I have everything already recorded in the New Acts of Luke, all except the remaining four targets and the name of our master."

Matthew smiled and weaved side to side, now drenched in his own blood. "Luke. The New Acts. I cannot tell you that which I do not know."

"You don't know the targets?"

His head flopped forward and his body slumped. Wren barely caught his head, and jerked forward onto one knee to catch the big man's body as he tipped to the side, leaning the chair with him.

"I know the targets," Matthew whispered. "But his name? How could I know the true name of our Lord come again?"

Wren gritted his teeth. "Then the targets?"

"The targets," he muttered, his hot blood soaking through Wren's thermal jacket. "The first five, or the final?"

Wren stiffened. That was new to him. "Ten targets?"

"Ten targets," Matthew mumbled, his weight pressing his face into Wren's chest now. "Ten commandments. Ten summits."

"Then the first five. Tell me now, Matthew, before our Lord claims you as his own."

"Yes! Luke. Our Acts. First are the godless creatives of Burning Man. Second are…"

He rasped on, then he whispered, then eventually he slumped against Wren, and the chair toppled, and Wren pulled back. Matthew hit the marble and lay still.

Wren gazed out at the snowstorm, struggling to think. Four Hammers, then five more. Unstoppable. Unavoidable. It was too much.

"Wren?" crackled the satellite radio. Humphreys' voice was barely distinguishable for the thickness of static. Wren turned back to the big screen, where the four Hammers had spread out and were even now approaching the West Coast. If anything, they'd picked up speed.

Wren understood the attack, now. It was like a full-body version of Matthew's field 'corpus callosotomy' surgery, rendering America a paraplegic, inert and unable to defend itself. Burning Man symbolized creativity and culture. The others symbolized knowledge, history, the police and the military. To destroy all five would crush America's ability to resist, and the Hammers could take them all in one fell swoop.

With all five gone, the people would be broken. They would listen. Under the threat of five attacks to follow, they would obey.

He took up the radio.

"I have the targets, Humphreys. Maybe you can stop some of them."

"Repeat that, Wren. You said you have the targets?"

"They're all in or near Washington. The Library of Congress. The National Archives. The FBI Headquarters on Pennsylvania Avenue and the CIA headquarters at Langley."

For a long moment Humphreys said nothing. "You're certain?"

"Yes."

"I'm at Langley, Wren. The working team's here. Everybody's here."

Wren slumped down beside Matthew. The pain was suddenly too much. "Try to get out."

"How long have we got?"

Already the Hammers had crossed the line of the West Coast and were picking up speed. Across the Pacific they'd spread out, each taking distinct tracks through the five layers of atmosphere, but now they were tightening together again.

Four bullets fired on looping tracks from the same gun, heading for the same batch of targets.

The devastation would be incredible.

"Minutes," he said numbly. Now the Hammers sped across California and into Nevada, across Nevada and into Utah. "Maybe one minute."

"One minute?"

"I'm sorry, Gerald. I really am."

Humphreys said nothing for a long moment. Wren thought he heard him breathing, or maybe he'd already fled. On foot, he'd barely make it out of the building in time. Each Hammer was equal to a nuclear bomb. The blast crater at Burning Man had been vast, almost a mile across. Langley would be decimated. Washington would be shredded.

Wren pictured him running. They'd never been close. They'd never liked each other. But he'd never wished for this.

Then Humphreys' voice came back, stronger and clearer than before. "I've notified the President. If you're right about those targets, she should be safe. Washington is well protected by SAM batteries, so we may save the FBI headquarters, God willing. The other two, I can only hope." He took a breath. "I've given directions that Sally Rogers be maintained as lead on the investigation, but this is all-out war, now. There'll be a new DNI and new directives. There'll be a push to strike Russia or Iran immediately, and another push to appease and negotiate. I need you and Rogers to find the real perpetrator; you're our only hope to stop this. Get to Sapporo, Japan if you can, there'll be a fast jet waiting for you. No matter what's to come, no matter what they say, this country needs her heroes more than ever. I'm dumping everything the working group found into the cloud. You'll know how to access it. And Wren?"

Wren felt like he'd been punched in the gut. Breathing was hard. "Yes."

"I found the man backing your wife. He's a real son of a bitch. That's all in the file too."

Wren didn't know what to say. The Hammers were over Kansas now. "Thank you for your service, Director."

"My pleasure. Now, I'll call my family. Good luck. End this, Christopher."

Humphreys was gone. Still Wren held the radio pressed to his ear, eyes fixated on the screen as the Hammers soared east over Missouri, then Illinois, then Kentucky. He pictured Gerald Humphreys' alabaster face hanging over his cadaver-like frame, looking out of his office window over Langley's leafy lawns, waiting for his wife to answer his call.

West Virginia.

Virginia.

Wren hoped she'd answer. He hoped Humphreys had a chance to say everything he needed to. I love you. I'll cherish you. I'll wait for you.

Through the window of his office at Langley, it was possible Humphreys would see the other Hammers strike. Perhaps he'd watch the mushroom cloud rise up from the wreckage of the Library of Congress, depository of all America's science, logic, knowledge and understanding. Maybe he'd see the fire and dust erupt over the National Archives, home of the Constitution, the Bill of Rights and the Declaration of Independence; all the stories American told itself that enshrined democracy and equality in the country's DNA, that had made the United States the shining city on the hill for over two centuries.

Then, at last, perhaps for a split second he would glimpse the Hammer fall upon Langley from the sky, a red streak followed by a blast that obliterated everything.

The satellite radio line died.

On the big map all four blips of the Hammers fizzled out.

It was done. Wren felt hollowed out. He couldn't believe

it. Perhaps the President remained, perhaps Congress still existed, but that was surely a matter of intent. To truly take a country, you needed its leaders to kneel. They needed to teach the others to obey.

Wren looked up through the glass to the snowstorm above, where the Miest still circled.

Five Hammers remained.

36

EMBRAER

Screams filled the air, but that was nothing next to the devastation in Wren's head.

He saw Washington burning. Four vast craters blown into the national psyche, at the heart of American power. The DNI lost, along with every agent at Langley, the spiritual home of the CIA.

Wren's colleagues. He knew hundreds of them. He'd given them orders and taken them. America's foreign intelligence infrastructure had just been catastrophically beheaded. Hundreds of CIA stations based around the world were suddenly adrift. The attack was stunning, 9/11 to the tenth power, and still they had no clear enemy.

They could attack Russia. They could attack Iran. But none of that would lift the threat of five more Hammers off America's neck.

All it took now was one man with an app. Faraday's genius was baked into the Miest, and with her dead there was no unpicking it. Algorithms and decision trees and expertise and the 'artistry' of dropping telephone poles out of orbit to wreak havoc had been automated and reduced to a button on the screen of a man who wanted to reorder the world completely.

All they had to-

"What do we do?" somebody was shouting repeatedly.

Wren blinked and looked out through a large glass window into the space that had once been the foyer. Now it was a lumpy wasteland of snow. Flakes filled the air in a blizzard. All the bodies had been obscured. All the blood and shells and weaponry were hidden by the thickening blanket of white.

He looked at the man before him. He was familiar. The leader of the Om Vedics. He was short. His cheeks were stained with tears. Wren had trouble connecting to his pain.

"Half of our people are dead, dozens are wounded! I don't know what to do. The facility is falling apart. What are we supposed to do?"

Wren looked over at his people. They were innocent. They filled the corridor around him, some stretched out on makeshift blankets clutching wounds, some shrieking, some sobbing, some just staring into space. None of it felt real, like a movie with the sound dialed down.

He looked into the leader's face. He felt so tired. Every muscle and joint hurt. His head throbbed. His hand and foot burned.

Shock. He recognized it in himself. He was numb. But he knew how to deal with shock; you pushed through it one step at a time.

"Do you have a pilot and a doctor?" he asked.

The leader frowned. "What? A pilot?"

"There's a plane," Wren said, as the noise began coming back at full volume. "A jet. If you have a pilot we can board the worst injured. I can work with a doctor to keep them alive until we reach a friendly airport."

"A friendly airport?"

"It depends on fuel supplies, but I'm thinking Sapporo, Japan. Ulaan Baatar is also possible, or Seoul, but both might be out of range."

The man stared, seemingly beginning to understand. "I believe we have a pilot. We have at least one nurse. If they both survived. But what about a Russian city? Or a Chinese city?"

Wren shook his head. "Not our allies. They won't help us. Find the pilot. Find any nurses you've got, along with any medical kits they can find. Wrap up the fifteen worst injured people as best you can and carry them out to the jet. Meet me there in twenty minutes."

"Twenty minutes? And what about the rest of us?"

"The jet's small," Wren said. "You'll have to get back in your coaches and get out the way you got in."

"But-"

"No buts. Pilot, nurse, wounded, in that order. Go!"

The man stared a second longer, then nodded firmly and strode off.

"Take me to the jet," Wren said to Kiefer.

They exited through the side of the facility, into the storm. Snow whipped into Wren's face, reducing visibility to several yards. He guided Kiefer by memory, until the fuel pump appeared in the blizzard, and alongside it, the Embraer Phenom 300.

Room for 11 occupants. Range of close to four thousand kilometers. They'd be pushing both of those numbers beyond the limit.

Wren reached the fuel pump under its snow-capped awning, touched the side and sent up a silent prayer. It was warm, which meant the hoses and the fuel itself were heated. Jet fuel froze at temperatures below minus 40 Fahrenheit, and it was easily that out here.

Attached to the pump was a small booth. It was locked, but Wren hit the glass with his elbow, reached through and unlocked the door. Inside, the keys for the Embraer hung on a hook. There were also controls labeled in Russian and Wren scanned them. He recognized one to release the fuel, one for heating the fuel, and several marked runway.

Wren flipped them all.

Outside, bright red lights flashed up in progressive banks with audible thuds as electricity expanded the cold filaments. They flashed up through the snow cover, illuminating the runway for several hundred yards.

Wren snatched the keys, stepped back into the storm and directed Kiefer out onto the runway. In the shadow of the Embraer he sank to one knee, pushed his right hand deep into the clear foot of snow and touched the blacktop beneath.

Warm already.

As he'd suspected from the controls, the runway was heated. A ludicrous expense, but a necessity given the telescope's location. The longer he kept his hand on the surface, the warmer it got. The snow melted and ran to slush.

"What are you doing?" Kiefer bellowed.

"Talking to the runway," Wren shouted back, then hopped over to the fuel cap. One of the keys on the ring opened it up. It was cold, which presented a problem.

"What did the runway say?" Kiefer asked.

"It wants you to get that fuel hose over there," Wren shouted, pointing. "And attach it here."

Kiefer nodded, then his eyes screwed up in thought. "Should we listen to it?"

Wren grinned. He felt ludicrous, outmanned and outgunned, no more than a mote in God's eye, but here they were. "I think so. I think it knows what it's talking about."

Kiefer studied Wren, then nodded. "Yeah. OK. I like this runway too."

"Then let's go."

Kiefer ran. Wren limped and hopped to the stair control under the Embraer's door. He unlocked the cover, inserted the activation key and turned it.

The door opened and the stairs deployed. Inside lights flickered to life. Wren climbed up into the cabin and was struck for a moment by the passenger bay. Laptops lay on seats amongst half-empty chip packets and bottles of water. Here Matthew, Faraday and their six faithful had sat, heading toward a future that was now crashing down around Wren. He hadn't stopped them, but at least they were all dead.

In the cockpit he dropped into the single pilot's seat. He could fly a jet, but had no intention of flying this. There were too many other things he needed to do. Thankfully, the controls were in English, and he hesitantly flicked switches, activating the fuel transfer heater and checking the current supply. The tank was three quarters full.

He looked out into the storm and figured he'd need to overfill as far as he dared. Given the conditions they needed an Instrument Flight Rules, or IFR, top-up.

Back at the stairs, he watched Kiefer dragging the hose over. He attached it to the fuel nozzle, then laughed and looked up at Wren.

"It's hot!" he shouted.

His simple joy was strangely infectious. Everything was going to hell, but here they were in a bubble of unreality. Wren had intel he could use and they were on their way. It offered a glimmer of hope.

The level of snow on the runway was already lowering as it melted.

He hobbled down the steps and back to the booth, gave Kiefer a thumbs up, then hit the switch to release the fuel. Pumps circled up and hummed, and the line bounced in the snow as the fuel filled it.

The leader of the Om Vedics appeared through the storm, followed by a line of believers carrying makeshift stretchers. Beside him walked a woman in her thirties and bedraggled, with loose strands of wavy red hair clinging to tear trails down her cheeks. Her eyes were wide and she looked terrified.

"This is our pilot," the Om Vedic leader said.

"Welcome aboard, captain," Wren said, offering his hand. She shook it uncertainly. "The cockpit's yours. Begin pre-flight checks, we're leaving in ten minutes."

She stared at him numbly. "What's our destination?"

"Sapporo, Japan, if we can reach it. We have no flight plan. You'll have to wing it."

She whimpered, and Wren figured that passed for a laugh. He hadn't even meant to make the joke. "Yes, Sir."

"I hope you can get out in this storm," the leader said, and looked upward into the maelstrom.

"We'll make it," Wren said, and moved on to the line of wounded people. He instantly knew that he'd be sending half of them back.

They weren't going to survive the flight. Travel time to Sapporo would be at least four hours, if they were lucky. The last thing he wanted was literal dead weight slowing them down. Better to give more attention to those who had a chance.

He began battlefield triage. He'd done it before and it was horrible, but ultimately logical. He'd save any he could, and then they'd fly.

Within ten minutes it was done. He'd turned away five then shepherded the injured into the fuselage. The runway was almost clear of snow. The pilot gave him the thumbs up from the cockpit. The leader of the Om Vedics watched. Kiefer stood at his side. wren looked one last time at the great satellite dish, from which the order had gone out to devastate America, then he lurched up the steps.

They closed behind him. The jet engines fired up. Within five minutes they were in the air and rising hard.

37

EIGHT HOURS

Sally Rogers woke in the hospital room in Saint Francis Memorial, head pulsing and lungs itching to cough. There was an oxygen mask over her face, so she pulled it off then coughed long and loud.

Her lungs burned. Breath came in short, sharp gulps. The room was dark, lit by faint red LED bulbs on the monitoring equipment around her, chiming with the sound of her pulse. It sounded fast. Off to the right lay a large window with a crescent of daylight cutting in around the edge of a heavy blind.

Dawn, maybe.

She remembered waking here earlier, and speaking to Wren with full dark outside. She remembered the crash cart and the paddles on her chest. They hadn't used them in the end, but they'd come close.

"Agent Rogers," came a voice from her side.

She turned. A black man in his fifties sat there, dressed in olive army uniform, tall and thick with broad shoulders and five golden stars on his epaulets. His tight-knapped gray hair was buzzed close to his scalp, and his eyes were a piercing hazel. "Who are you?" she asked, her voice croaky.

"General Andre Vicker," the man said. "You've been unconscious for four hours. There's been a further attack on the homeland while you slept, and DNI Gerald Humphreys is dead. His last act was to safeguard your position as lead on this investigation and send me to help, but events have overtaken us. We're at DEFCON 1 now in the run-up to first nuclear strikes on Iran."

Rogers stared. She couldn't quite believe what she'd heard.

"What?" was all she managed.

"Two Hammers landed approximately three and a half hours ago," Vicker pressed on. "One hit Langley and killed the DNI and many of the key staff working on this threat. One hit the National Archives in Washington, but we managed to shoot down the third and fourth with SAMs batteries on their way to FBI headquarters and the Library of Congress."

Rogers jaw dropped. She became aware of a tugging in her left wrist, and looked down to see a drip needle tugging at the skin. A line of her own blood was feeding back up the tube toward an empty bag. She pinched the tube to stop the flow, then pulled the needle out and clamped her thumb over the pinprick hole.

"Two more Hammers hit?" she repeated.

"I have footage in my debrief," Vicker said. "Would you like to see it?"

Rogers shook her head. Would she like to? The answer was an easy no. She never wanted to see that.

"Yes," she said, then kicked her legs out of the bed, took her own weight and managed a step. She was weak and her legs uncertain, but she could feel the strength coming back already.

Vicker opened his laptop, swiveled it so she could see and hit play on a video.

A timestamp began to run on the image of a familiar building, designed in the monumental, neoclassical style. It had colossal Corinthian columns in white marble, standing at the top of an elevated bank of steps and crowned with a massive triangular pediment carved with intricate scenes.

"That's the National Archives," Rogers said.

"It is."

The timestamp advanced, then there was a near-invisible blip down the center line of the building, after which the huge structure simply disappeared in a vast ball of dust and fire. In less than a second the camera was whited out as the spreading ball engulfed it.

Rogers felt the terror of Burning Man coming back. Sweat broke out down her back and a shock reaction kicked in, flushing her hot and bringing on nausea, but she could not look away.

"Why destroy the National Archives?"

"Wren thinks it's for the symbolism. The Archives housed the Constitution, the Declaration of Independence and the Bill of Rights. He thinks they were targeting in particular the First Amendment, written in the Bill of Rights."

Rogers racked her mind, then understood and gasped. "Separation of church and state."

"That's right," Vicker said.

She couldn't fault it. It was methodical. Separation of church and state was a core tenet of US democracy, and a clear obstacle to anyone seeking to establish a religious theocracy. By destroying the founding document itself, these fanatics were paving the way to change America forever.

"Show me Langley," she said, her voice tight but firm.

He clicked play.

The George Bush Center for Intelligence was nothing special to look at. It had no sense of historic style like the National Archives, and no such aspirations to inspire. Still, seeing it at the tail-end of this triptych of destruction hit Rogers the hardest.

The CIA was where she'd found purpose. At Langley, she'd harnessed the shapeless rage she'd felt ever since New Orleans. Under the tutelage of first Gerald Humphreys then Christopher Wren, she'd become somebody new. She'd made a new life.

The complex was vast. The largest intelligence headquarters in America. She knew every inch of its accessible grounds, from the four giant copper plates of the encrypted Kryptos sculpture to the underground exchange where thirty miles' worth of outmoded steel pneumatic tubes still dead-ended.

It mattered to her.

The Hammer fell, and in a second all that was gone.

The feed died but Rogers kept staring at the screen, feeling the depth of this new wound digging into her soul.

She felt sick and furious at the same time. Tears poured down her cheeks. This was everything she'd believed in, destroyed as if by the hand of God. Countless more Americans had just died. Langley alone had more than ten thousand staff, and the Hammer on Washington could have killed anywhere up to a hundred thousand.

The country would be different after this, no matter the outcome.

She edged toward the shuttered window, head spinning and shoulder throbbing, trying to work all that through. Humphreys was dead. The CIA was headless and hamstrung. At the window she turned.

"And we're attacking Iran?"

"The President determined, on best evidence, that an immediate retaliatory strike was essential."

"But it's not Iran." Her mind raced back over the encounter with Mark in the burger joint, rasping about the

'Kingdom'. "This is not Islamic terror, General. If anything, it's the American equivalent of ISIS or the Taliban, in line with the destruction of the First Amendment. Didn't they see my investigation?"

"Where you cleared Ravi Sharma as a target? Where you interviewed Satanists? We're past all that, now. We need an enemy, and Iran fits that bill."

"What about Wren? Did he turn up anything?"

"It's thanks to him we saved the FBI and the Library of Congress; he got us just enough warning. He's also provided a lot of intel since then, but it's all conspiracy theories about fundamentalist Christian doomsday cults, trying to bring about the 'Kingdom of Heaven' by force, just like you're talking about now. None of it's solid."

Rogers turned and swept open the blinds. Harsh summer light flooded in, forcing her to squint. There was San Francisco, and the bay, and the sea stretching away like a twinkling desert of sapphires. Everything looked normal. It didn't feel real.

She turned back to Vicker. "So we're ignoring Wren?"

"Not ignoring," he countered. "But he's given us nothing specific. Not yet. He killed everyone who might be a witness, which leaves us with only hearsay and rumor from a man with a complicated past with doomsday cults."

Rogers felt her anger surging. "So they're disregarding him because of his past. How many times does he have to save the country to get a pass on that?"

"Not my department," Vicker said flatly. "Not our decision to make."

That left her reeling. "We have to do something."

"We are, Agent Rogers. The investigation continues. But in the meantime, with our enemies salivating at the gates, would you suggest we just start dropping bombs on American churches who share some Ascendancy theology? If you include the

Second Coming, the Rapture and the Antichrist, that's probably half the churches in the country. Christianity's a big tent, and the President would be signing her own death warrant if she went off half-cocked. We need the one specific group that's perverted the faith to this extent, but we don't have them. Without that target, we're in the wind, and Iran is far better than nothing."

"But you're talking about nuclear weapons," Rogers countered. "That's a doomsday scenario right there. If Iran has bombs, which they may well do by now, they'll drop them on us. It spreads, it escalates, then there's nothing left."

Vicker just gazed at her. "It's war, Agent Rogers. We can't do nothing. They'll all come for us, then."

Rogers bit her lip. He was right. "OK. How long have we got?"

"Until first strikes? I'm only partly in the loop, but best evidence suggests less than twenty-four hours."

Rogers grunted. "Twenty-four hours to save the world."

"And eight to save America," Vicker countered.

She looked up. "Eight? What, why?"

Vicker took a heavy breath. "That's the other piece of intelligence. We assumed the Miest only had five Hammers, because there was one Persona launch." He paused a moment. "But Wren is certain there were at least five more aboard an earlier launch to the Miest, and right now these extremists are using them to target major US cities."

Rogers felt herself slipping deeper into the nightmare. "For what? They already blew up the Bill of Rights. What more do they want?"

Vicker took a heavy breath. "You aren't classified to hear this, but I think you need to know. Three hours back, right after the Hammers struck, we received a message claiming credit and listing demands."

"What demands?"

"The list is long. It begins with the resignation of President Ablas, followed by the immediate foundation of the new role of Prophet, as ordained directly by God. This Prophet would have absolute executive command of the military, the courts, the media, and all branches of government. The Constitution would be replaced by a new document titled the Apostolic Covenant, enshrining a new fourth branch of government called the Apostolic Council, formed of Apostles appointed by the Prophet. Countless laws will change on day one."

Rogers' mouth ran dry. "That's a theocracy. That's exactly what Iran has."

Vicker's expression darkened. "You were right to call these people the American Taliban. The laws they're proposing will throw us back at least a hundred years. Further, maybe. They open the door to the possible return of slavery. Women would lose the vote, lose their positions, passports and driving licenses, and be bound to male relatives, needing permission to even leave the house. Homosexuality, transgenderism, and any other behaviors considered 'deviant' by the Prophet would be made illegal, with draconian punishments immediately set in place."

Rogers didn't know what to say. "I don't … that's not possible."

"Perhaps not today," Vicker allowed. "But if they drop a Hammer on New York and kill eight million in one blow, with four more Hammers in the chamber? That mood of defiance might change."

Rogers felt like she was drowning. This was worse than anything she could've imagined. She didn't know what to do. She didn't know where to start.

"But ...," she began, then faltered, like a drowning woman looking for anything to cling onto. Her mind spun back over all the briefing books she'd read, about orbital mechanics and the mass of the Hammers and-

"Faraday!" she blurted. "You said she's dead?"

"Wren said that. Yes, we believe she is."

"So how are they targeting us? Everything I read about dropping a Hammer said it was an art as much as it was a science. They needed Faraday in person to guide them. It couldn't be automated!"

Vicker's expression paled. "We've had theorists working that problem for hours. Apparently, with five Hammers already dropped, they've gathered enough intel on specific orbital descent paths to bypass the need for Faraday, especially if they don't need extreme precision."

Rogers tried to comprehend that. "So they're using the same descent paths? The same sets of calculations?"

"Exactly."

"Doesn't that help us intercept the Hammers?"

"Only if they hit the exact same targets. But they're threatening cities. That means minor alterations to the calculations, but the targets are big. The theorists are saying that Faraday started with Burning Man for a reason. On a flat desert plain, they could hit anywhere within several miles and still kill most of those people. Then they fine-tuned and became precise, with the strikes on Washington and Langley. Now they just need to be roughly on-target. Big cities are big."

Rogers felt the chill spreading through her. "So it's really automated."

"It is. They don't need Faraday to kill millions. One person with a trigger can activate the Miest."

She felt sick. This had to end.

"Where's Wren?"

Vicker nodded. "He stole a jet at Yakutsk and made it to Sapporo, Japan. He transferred an hour ago and is coming

here now on a Blackbird SR-71, travelling in excess of Mach 3, with a mid-air refuel about to happen any moment. He should be here in two hours."

Rogers stared. She didn't know much about hard military materiel of the last millennia, but everyone had heard the name Blackbird. "That's a spy plane. Weren't they retired twenty years ago?"

"They were." Vickers said, and offered no more.

Rogers brushed it aside. It didn't matter. They had eight hours. "And what are we doing? What's the plan to stop this?"

He shook his head. "Honestly, other than seeking scapegoats to fend off further attacks, we have none. We have no leads, Agent Rogers. Only you and Wren."

She swallowed hard. Her mouth felt like a desert. "Then I need to talk to him."

"I agree. He's online in the Blackbird, ready to debrief. Here."

He tapped several keys, the laptop briefly rang, then a video feed opened up.

It was Wren, wearing a thick headset in a heavily cushioned co-pilot's seat, looking considerably worse for wear. His face was bruised and scratched, his left arm hung in a sling, but the furious light of purpose still shone in his eyes.

"Sally," he said, and his voice came through clearly via the laptop's speakers. "It's good to see you. I know what we have to do."

38

ASCENDANCY

"Chris," Rogers said. Just seeing him almost broke her. They hadn't been face-to-face in months, not since the Russia operation. Despite the sling, though, and the injuries, he looked even larger than life. He'd put on muscle, she figured, maybe twenty pounds. "What happened to you?"

"That freak Apostle Matthew broke my left wrist and my left foot. He's dead now. But there's things he said, Sally, building on what Mark said to you. Things that have sent me down the rabbit hole. Humphreys had all the working group's findings uploaded, and I've been sifting through them, looking for anything that links up."

Rogers felt her heart lift. "You found something?"

"The core of it, I think," Wren said. "What this all means, and where it's going. If we can narrow that down, we can find the man we're looking for."

Rogers nodded. This felt like hope in the darkness. This was what she always expected from Wren, and he always delivered. "Tell me."

"I'm sending you the full annotated findings, but in brief, has Vicker told you about the Apostolic Covenant?"

"He did. Apostolic as in apostles."

"Apostles under a single Prophet. It's a budding religious dictatorship. But it didn't come about in a vacuum. There's been a loose religious movement called 'Ascendancy' building for years now, this idea that society should not be governed via democracy and votes, but by divinely appointed men, with God's own right hand sitting on the throne."

"Right. The Prophet. "

"Yeah. I got close to this with Matthew; he told me there are ten Hammers aboard the Miest, ten for the commandments and ten for the summits."

Rogers frowned. "Ten for the summits? What does that mean?"

"I didn't think anything of it at the time, but there's a theory in Ascendancy called the 'Ten Summits Sanction'. It's metaphorical, where each 'Summit' represents an area of society the Ascendants need to capture in order to prepare the Kingdom of Heaven."

"And sanction, like in authority?"

"Right, as in permission granted."

"OK. So what are the ten?"

"Family, religion, education, culture, business, health, government, courts, military and police," Wren spooled off. "Matthew laid out the first five strikes in terms of these 'Summits'. So destroying the free-thinkers and creatives at Burning Man was striking a blow for control of culture. When they hit the National Archives, that was education."

Rogers' mind raced. "What about the other three?"

"The failed strike on the FBI was police. The Library of Congress was education. The CIA must symbolize military, or at least the ability to project power overseas."

"But now they're threatening major cities, not social 'Summits'."

"I know, because they think they've already won. They're

ready to claim their throne. The point is, this Ten Summits Sanction pre-exists these Apostolic Covenant freaks. At some point, the guy running this show crossed paths with it. If we can narrow that moment down, maybe we can find him and shut down the Miest."

Rogers thought that through. "OK. So how do we do that?"

"Follow the only lead we've got," Wren said. "Faraday."

Rogers said nothing for a long moment. She looked at Wren. Maybe he'd taken one too many hits to the head. "Faraday's dead, Chris. I went to see her family. They don't know anything."

"I read your report on the ranch," Wren said. "The paddock and the stable door forming the figure 8 with a cross? That's genius. Well spotted. But I think there's more."

Rogers considered. "Her husband's an overworked, emotionally stunted wreck. Her kids are little study automatons who rebel by playing video games. She was a control freak, Chris, and she engineered them all to be that way, so they'd never ask questions and never figure out what she was up to."

"Exactly like a cult," Wren said. "Keep the faithful so busy with bullshit tasks they never have time to think critically."

"Right. She gave nothing away. There's nothing there to find."

"Except you found something. Her arrogance let it through and you saw it. I know there's more; we just have to ask the right questions."

Rogers sucked air through her teeth. "I don't know. Is it really the best use of our time?"

"It's the only one," Wren said. "Remember Alexey Platnov?"

"Who?"

"Platnov. I got his name from a Spetsnaz officer at Vostochny. He's a Russian spymaster out of Moscow, and he ran middleman for the fire sale of the Miest to this group. He brought in Director Voronin and helped make all this happen."

"OK. What about him?"

"Hours back Humphreys located him and sent a team of Delta Force Marines to run him down. They tracked him to a luxury yacht off Archangelsk, north-east of St. Petersburg. He didn't know anything, though; said he received a substantial payment from an anonymous cryptocurrency wallet, and that was it. No names, no schedule, no idea of the Covenant's plan for the Miest."

"He sold out."

"He was one of the officials asset-stripping the Russian state. It was a dead end."

Rogers gritted her teeth and glanced up at Vicker. She was beginning to see what he'd meant about Wren having nothing concrete.

"Is that it, then? Just a feeling about Faraday?"

"We also looked into the human-augmentation direction. Remember the size of Apostle Mark? Remember you said it was like he was built in a lab?"

"Of course."

"Matthew was the same. I've been looking into it. It may go some way to explaining how the Calvary Cross conjoins with the Transhumanist movement to make the 8-cross symbol. There are recent investments in human growth hormone, genetic engineering and muscle augmentation that have exploded the field. Making giants is possible. It's happening right now, and I think these Apostles were some of the first out of the vat."

Rogers began to feel some of Wren's zeal rubbing off on

her. "OK. So you're hunting down those investments? Finding the labs?"

"There aren't that many. We have them all listed on a map. Of course, there could be dark labs, secret labs, whatever, the kind of place where the apostles learn to perform field corpus callosotomies."

"Field what?"

"Cutting the brain in half. I told you, Matthew did it to Kiefer, so he did it right back. It causes massive confusion, muddling all the sensory signals and interrupting the regular flow of command and control decisions within the brain, making the victim extremely amenable to coercion. It allows forceful faith conversions."

Rogers shuddered. "You think he was planning to perform these 'callosotomies' on the American people. En masse?"

"I don't know. I hadn't thought of that. Maybe."

"That's terrible. It's just … the Hammers are one thing. The Kingdom, too. But cutting into peoples' brains to make them believe you? It's …" She trailed off, finding no words for the disgust she felt. "OK. So, you found some locations. Can we tie any to the Apostolic Covenant?"

"Not yet. Vicker's got multiple teams out there renditioning known Ascendants. There's easily two dozen strident Ascendant churches in the US right now. Every one of them has either already had, or is about to have, a knock on their pastor's door. Questioning's already begun. If any of them knew about this plot, then we'll get a name that way."

"But you're not hopeful?"

"I think this group hid too well. I still think Faraday's our best angle of attack. We just need one thing to shake loose, and along with all the rest, we'll have him."

Rogers began to feel the passion. Wren was winning her over. None of it was concrete, that was true, but it felt like they were swimming closer to shore, about to feel the sand beneath their toes.

"It's a lot," she said.

"It's all happening. We've got every resource at our fingertips. Ask Vicker."

Rogers looked up. Five-star General Vicker nodded. "I'm your liaison to the President, to the Pentagon, to the NSA. Whatever you need."

"We can do this, Sally. Unless you have a better idea, we go back to Faraday. This whole thing started with her. I'm pretty sure that's where it ends."

She nodded. "OK. You got me. I'll get on a plane and head back to Houston."

Wren grinned. "There's the spirit. I'll see you on the ranch in two hours."

39

HOUSTON, TEXAS

Wren's Blackbird approached Ellington Field Joint Reserve Base, seventeen miles southeast of downtown Houston, at Mach 3 and 40,000 feet high.

"The runway isn't long enough," the pilot said when they were fifty miles out. "We're going too fast. Mach 3 requires a triple-length runway."

"So air brake," Wren shouted.

"Not enough."

"Drop altitude sooner."

"Still not enough."

"Then shut off the engines. I need to land right here, right now."

The pilot turned around to look at him. "Turn off the engines? These are twin axial-flow turbojets. The second the afterburners are off, we'll drop like a rock. The Blackbird has no glide capacity."

"So take us low, air brake, then kill the engines. You won't need to glide far."

"And hit the runway?"

"Yes, hit the runway! Give me control and I'll do it."

The pilot laughed then turned back around. "Don't be ridiculous. You'll pancake us."

"There's the spirit. Can you do it?"

"I'll have to switch off first, glide into a vertical then kick the engines back on to straighten us for the landing. That should slow us down."

"Or crash us into the ground. Go for it."

Now the pilot laughed. "You know a Blackbird's never been shot down?" Abruptly he pushed the stick down, plunging the jet into a dive. "It can outrun every missile in existence. No other jet can intercept it. The only times we ever lost them were pilot error."

Wren felt the G forces hitting as the plane shot down faster than gravity. "So you can do it?"

"We're already committed now." He reached out and flicked three switches, hit an override, turned a key then hit another button, and instantly the ramjets powered down. Sirens filled the cockpit until the pilot powered them down too. "Into our glide. Tell me when you feel like we're slowing down."

Wren laughed as the blood flooded to his head.

The plane shot down silently, skimming through the sky at a steepening angle.

"This feels like a nosedive," Wren tried to say, but it came out garbled. He felt lightheaded and heavy at once. Dead ahead he saw the leafy gridwork of downtown Houston rocketing closer.

"Engines restarting in ten seconds," the pilot said, his voice coming as if in slow motion. "That'll be your air brake."

Wren tried to count, came close to blacking out, then there was a kick in his back that ratcheted the jet upright. He saw blue sky, then clouds, then Houston again, then skies, then slammed into something, bounced, slammed again and the engines entered reverse burn. The pilot shouted something, and only after the engines' roar faded and the jet fell still on the runway did Wren realize he was laughing.

"Need to puke?" the pilot asked.

"Yes."

"Me too. I'm never flying one of these again."

Wren kept laughing as he unlatched the cockpit cover and the warm air of Houston flowed in. He barely got himself up on one foot with his upper body over the edge before his last meal escaped.

His eyes blurred and he rubbed them, wiping his mouth. A stair car was racing down the runway toward them. He blinked again. They were off the end of the blacktop and onto the grass overflow area. The air stank of spent jet fuel and burned rubber, the skies were clear and blue.

The stair car pulled up and a figure stepped out, stocky with a tight blond ponytail.

"Hell of an entrance, Boss," called Sally Rogers.

Wren managed a laugh. "I didn't puke on myself. That was the pilot."

She laughed. "Looks like he puked on both of you."

"It was projectile."

The pilot laughed nearby then vomited again.

"Bring the stairs up," Wren said, barely controlling his stomach. "I can't climb right now."

Rogers dropped back into the stair car and drove it up to the Blackbird's side with a clank. Wren pulled himself carefully out of the seat, crawled over the edge, then let Rogers guide him down onto the stairs. The orthopedic boot on his left foot hit the metal with a thunk.

"I killed my giant without any problems," Rogers said.

Wren snorted and tossed an arm around her shoulders. "You had a burger. I didn't have anything."

"Never underestimate raw meat," Rogers said, and led him down the stairs.

"Six hours," Wren said.

"Six hours," Rogers repeated.

At the bottom she guided him into the cab, got behind the wheel and whipped off.

"How do you feel?" she asked.

"Thirsty. Broken." Wren caught her eye. "Angry."

She nodded. "Humphreys."

"That bastard had to go and die like a hero, after a half-ass career of bumbling and making excuses. They'll give him the Medal of Honor."

"He sent you a Blackbird; last I heard, they were retired twenty years ago. I think we both owe him one."

"Yeah," Wren said, and looked out as the runway sped by and the low assortment of buildings drew near. "RIP Gerald Humphreys. I'm not sorry I shot you."

Rogers laughed. "Yeah. You shot me too."

"I shoot a lot of people," Wren said, then sighed and looked into her green eyes. "Thank you for coming, Sally."

"Where else would I be?"

"Oo-rah." He held out a fist and she bumped it.

"There's water in the door," Rogers said. "You stink."

Wren laughed. "No shower in about three weeks now."

"It's the blood, I think."

"Not mine. Not most of it, anyway."

"Faraday's going to love that."

"Fred Faraday," Wren murmured, then popped the cap on the water bottle and knocked it back. "He's in custody?"

"We never let him out of our sight. You're sure he knows something?"

Wren came up for air. "If he doesn't, we're screwed. I don't know, we head to NASA and start bracing all her old colleagues? Maybe something would spill loose."

"But you've got a good feeling about him?"

"Don't you?"

"The man was a wreck. If he knows something, he doesn't realize it. We'll have to dig it out."

Wren finished the bottle and dropped it. "Our specialty."

Rogers grunted then pointed ahead. "Our onward ride."

They'd passed into the Coast Guard Air Station part of Ellington Reserve Base, where a massive olive-green CH-47F twin rotor Chinook helicopter stood.

"Good," Wren said, "more speed."

Rogers laughed and pulled the car up twenty yards from the Chinook. "Come on, old man. Let's get you out of here."

She pulled. Wren pushed. Together they got him out and hobbling toward the Chinook. In moments they were strapped in, the great rotors fired up and they were away, winging west toward the Faraday ranch at 200 mph.

40

RIP

The Chinook put down on the paddock in the center of Genevieve Faraday's ranch. FBI vehicles filled the driveway, and several agents were standing out by a large conservatory.

Rogers strung Wren's arm over her shoulder and helped him in.

"I know him," she said. "I'll take lead. You sit there and look terrifying."

Wren just grunted.

Within moments they were inside the conservatory, sitting across from Fred Faraday. His eyes darted wildly from Rogers to Wren, taking in his sling, his boot, his blood-spattered strike suit.

"What?" he began, but didn't know where to go after that. Wren was just too unexpected, some kind of giant monster birthed from a war zone. "Who is this?" he settled on.

"My colleague," Rogers said. "I'm afraid he has some sad news, Mr. Faraday."

Fred Faraday looked at Wren, but had trouble meeting his eyes. Wren didn't blame him. "So, uh? Sad? What do you mean, sad?"

"Your wife is dead," Wren said, his voice grinding out like the rumble of an approaching storm. "In a secret research facility in Siberia, killed by an apostle named Matthew. She was their engineer. She designed the Hammers that have struck our country. She prepared the algorithm to fire them." He paused for a long moment, letting the man take that in. "She was a traitor to us all. Now we're here to determine if you are, too."

Faraday's eyes widened. It was a lot to take in. "What? That's … I don't know. What are you saying?"

Wren said nothing more. Instead, Sally Rogers leaned in. "It's all true, Mr. Faraday. Now we're going to have a conversation. It will be short. If this conversation does not give us what we need, you will leave this property in FBI custody, likely never to return. As the husband of the worst traitor in American history, you will be presumed guilty. You will never see the light of day again. You will stand trial, but it will be no trial. The people are ready to kill, and you will not be the first nor the last to die for what was done to us in Washington and Nevada. If you are innocent, then it will not be fair. It will feel like justice to the masses, though. Your family name will enter history alongside Benedict Arnold and Aaron Burr." She paused for a moment. "Unless…"

Fred Faraday looked like a drowning man. His eyes were wide and watery, his mouth a round 'O', his skin paling.

"I don't...," he mumbled, "I don't understand. Unless what?"

"Take a moment," Wren rumbled. "Figure it out."

They sat in silence. Nobody spoke. Faraday looked from side to side. He began to sob, then stopped, casting fearful glances at Wren.

"How could she … I mean. I don't know anything. I would tell you if I knew anything!"

"We think you do know something," Rogers said. She

leaned forward and took his hand. "Last time I was here, you told me she had no strange associations. She had no enemies but landscapers. We need to revisit that."

"Revisit it?" His voice spiked toward falsetto. "There's nothing to revisit. I don't know anything. I don't know her colleagues. I don't know her friends. I don't even remember the names of the landscapers!"

"I don't care about the landscapers," Rogers said, then shook her head, almost sadly. "And also not true. You told me herself, you used to be closer. You've been together for over twenty years, correct? You bought this ranch together. You did know her then. At some point, though, she drifted away. She turned inward, possibly around seven years ago, the same time she reworked the ranch to match the symbol of her new group." She took a breath. "We need to know about anything unusual during that time, any interactions that seemed strange."

Faraday jawed at the air. "Seven years ago. I don't know. I can't remember."

"Then I'll remind you," Rogers said, bringing up a research docket on her tablet. "Seven years ago, you were named Head Dealer at the Honda Dealership in Bellaire. Your wife had been working on Stardust for two years. Your boys were close to finishing elementary school. Tobias was getting As in Math but dropping in science. Your wife scheduled a parent-teacher meeting to remedy that." Rogers looked up at Faraday, who licked his lips. She scrolled onward. "A year earlier, you both inherited a substantial sum when Genevieve's father died unexpectedly. That allowed you to buy this ranch and take the holiday on Hilton Head. A year later, you made a substantial bequest to Harvard. Some call it a placeholder bequest, all but guaranteeing your boys a place. You also-"

"It wasn't a placeholder," Faraday said.

Rogers studied him. "That hardly matters right now, does it?"

He glared at her, finding some defiance, then looked down at his hands in his lap. "No, I guess not."

"But you do remember seven years ago." She didn't say it as a question. It was a fact.

"Yes. But I can't think of anything like what you're looking for. You're looking for a traitor? For something unusual? How do I know what that looks like?"

Rogers looked at Wren. He nodded.

"In particular, did she have any religious associations at the time?"

Faraday frowned. "Religious?"

"Did you attend church?"

"No. Not for years."

Rogers perked up. "But you had?"

"We did, for a time. When the boys were born we looked at baptism for them both, but decided against it."

"You lost your faith?"

"Not exactly. Just, it didn't seem important?"

"Was that your decision or hers?"

Faraday opened his mouth, then closed it. He thought for a moment. "I don't know. Maybe mine."

Rogers nodded. She looked at Wren again, and he took that as his signal to come in.

"It's likely your wife continued attending religious services," he rumbled, causing Faraday to startle. "We show no record of that, but we're confident she did. There are thousands of churches in Houston. Tens of thousands in Texas within a reasonable commute. We need you to help us narrow that down."

"Narrow it down?"

"We need to know which church she went to."

Faraday looked lost at sea again. He puffed and looked around the conservatory. "I, uh. Let me think."

"Did she ever mention anything?" Rogers prompted. "The name of a pastor. A denomination. Did she ever mention a sermon?"

Faraday just stared, then shook his head. "No. Nothing."

"Think harder. It wouldn't have to be a sermon or a service, even. Maybe a wedding, a funeral, a fundraising cake bake, a-"

"Wait!" Faraday barked, jolting in his seat.

"Wait what?"

"Nebula."

"Nebula?"

His hands worked the air like they were searching for words. "Her horse. Nebula! She was Genny's favorite."

Rogers squinted. She remembered the framed photograph of a horse on Faraday's desk, with the letters RIP. She'd thought it a cute memento of her childhood horse.

"What does a childhood horse have to do with this?"

"Childhood?" Fred Faraday countered, seeming perplexed. "Nebula died only eight years ago."

Rogers looked at Wren. "Eight years ago?"

"Yes. It was her horse, so she handled all of it herself. I wasn't involved." He sped up, perhaps feeling he was onto something. "I went to work one day and there was a dead horse in the paddock. I came home and the horse was gone, but there was a framed photograph on her desk. And…" he stopped, waving his hand as if he could wind the memory into focus, then snapped his fingers. "An order of service."

Wren's heart skipped a beat. "A funeral service? You saw it?"

"Only for a second. I don't remember. There were flowers too. I remember I wondered about it, but I didn't ask her. I didn't want to get into it. It seemed like another fight in the making."

Rogers stood abruptly. "Where's that order of service now?"

"I don't know. I have no idea."

Rogers exchanged another glance with Wren, and he nodded.

"I'll be back in a moment," she said.

Wren and Faraday sat in the conservatory. Faraday looked up then down, then finally up again. "What happened to you?"

"I had a fight with an apostle."

Faraday's eyes bugged. "An apostle? Like, from the Bible?"

"Pretty much," Wren allowed. "It took a long time. He kept turning the other cheek."

"Is that… wait. Is that a joke?"

Wren shrugged. Then Rogers was back, clutching a framed photograph of a horse. It was a handsome chestnut stallion. "Nebula, RIP," she read off the frame, then opened the back. The only thing inside was the photograph.

"Nothing," Wren said.

"I checked it last time, too," Rogers said.

Wren considered. "What about the body? Horses are often rendered or cremated. The order of service could be with the remains."

Fred Faraday snapped his fingers again. "That's it! Cremated!"

"She had Nebula cremated?" Rogers asked.

"Yes! At least I always assumed that. I remember now." He thought for a second, then stood. "Yup. It's here."

"On the ranch?"

"On the ranch. In the stables. She didn't exactly tell me, but I saw her standing there a few times, like she was praying. I don't usually go in her spaces, but I couldn't miss it. I'll show you."

"Lead on," said Rogers.

Faraday raced out of the conservatory and across the paddock. Wren and Rogers hobbled swiftly after him, through the strange cross-shaped entrance into the stables, and into cozy brown shadows.

The floor was russet clay coated with fresh golden hay. A handful of horses nickered and huffed in the set of eight stalls, while riding crops, saddles, tools and bags hung from the redwood pillars. Fred Faraday was dipping his head in and out of stalls. Wren and Rogers watched until he found the one he was looking for, in the far right corner.

"Here," he said excitedly, pointing. Rogers and Wren advanced. "It's right there, carved low in the wood."

Rogers brought up her cell phone and switched on the flashlight. In the corner of the stall words were carved into the post.

NEBULA – MY HEART

Rogers looked at Wren, noted his sling and his boot. "I'll get the shovel, shall I?"

"Put that gym muscle to good use."

She found a shovel outside and stabbed it into the clay. It didn't take long. About a foot down, the shovel thumped on a hollow wooden casket. Rogers dug it out, an oak box a foot square.

"It's heavy," she said.

She set it down out in the center of the stables, popped the brass clasp then swung open the lid. It was filled to the brim with gray ashes, but inserted neatly into a slot in the underside of the lid was the order of service.

She snatched it up, holding the flash light close.

"That's it," Fred Faraday said. "I'm not a traitor. I helped you."

At the top of the order of service was the name of the church, and the attending pastor.

HEAVENLY RENEWAL TABERNACLE

PASTOR ELIJAH CROSS

"Heavenly Renewal," Rogers said. "That sounds like a Kingdom of Heaven kind of place to me."

41

HEAVENLY RENEWAL

The Heavenly Renewal Tabernacle was a small evangelist church with a modest congregation of two hundred, according to its website. It was situated on the west side of Houston, on Richmond Avenue near Levy Park. From above in the Chinook it looked like a quiet, leafy neighborhood where the church fit right in.

The helicopter put down on the street in front, drawing several people out from the Tabernacle's white clapboard façade. The wrought-iron steeple mounted on a faux bell tower wavered in the downdraft from the Chinook's rotors, and the vibrant flowers and shrubs lining the entrance path through the small gardens shimmered in the wind.

Wren stepped out onto the blacktop.

A wealthy area. Well-dressed clientele. Stained glass panels in arched windows brought elegance to the simplicity of the clapboards, displaying scenes of Jesus on Calvary hill, surrounded by beams of orange and yellow light.

The resurrection. The renewal.

He could just pick out the sound of voices raised in joyful song. A white marquee tent had been erected by the entrance and stacked with numerous white cakes studded with strawberries.

"I don't like it," Wren rumbled.

"I'm with you," Rogers agreed.

They'd come direct from the Faraday ranch, barely two minutes of flight in the Chinook, just long enough to check the website and for Rogers to request a full FBI workup on everyone associated with it.

"He's still the pastor," Rogers said, taking Wren's left arm over her shoulder. "Elijah Cross. This mass is not on the schedule."

Wren wasn't surprised to hear that. They started toward the double doors, and an older woman with perfectly coiffed hair stepped in front of them.

"May I ask, what are your intentions here?" she asked.

"Pastor Cross," Wren said, but did not slow down. At the last moment the woman stepped aside. "Is he here?"

"This is God's house," she called after him. "You can't just-"

Rogers pushed through the heavy double doors into a spacious lobby, with shiny herringbone floors, pale cream walls and tall, bright works of art depicting more scenes of Jesus' life after the resurrection. The rolling back of the stone. Jesus on a throne holding a rod and scepter. The apostles dressed like holy knights but kneeling in prayer, as if engaged in spiritual warfare.

"This is the place," Wren said, and they swept past the information desk, banked up with colorful church pamphlets, into the sanctuary.

The singing stopped.

The sanctuary was an intimate, circular space bathed in the warm glow of sunlight through stained glass. Curved mahogany pews were arrayed in a half circle around the pulpit, lined with plush cushions and filled with congregants, all of whom were now staring at Wren and Rogers as they stalked up the central aisle toward the stage, where Pastor Elijah Cross stood.

He was no more than six foot tall, with short, silvery hair and a neatly groomed beard, but his demeanor commanded the room. He was calm and still, quite in contrast to the surprise of his flock, with expressive eyes. He wore a buoyant gold tie over a snug white shirt with the sleeves rolled up.

"Pastor Cross," Wren called, interrupting the sermon. "We need to speak with you."

"Can it not wait until the brethren are departed?"

Wren and Rogers breached the stage. "I'm afraid not. Let's go to your office."

Rogers took the pastor by the arm and guided him to the side. Wren took the pulpit and looked out over the flock as sirens pealed up from outside. "I need to ask all of you to stay here."

He limped after Rogers and Cross, as the doors opened behind them and the local PD flooded in.

The pastor's office was in back, small and business-like with a tidy desk and a bookshelf lined with leatherbound books. Rogers gently deposited Cross into his chair then took one of the seats opposite. Wren remained standing, feeling his anger surge.

"What's this about?" Cross asked, maintaining his poise.

"The Hammers," Wren said. "Are you celebrating?"

A flicker of annoyance spread across Cross' face but was swiftly smoothed away. "Of course not. Why would we-"

"A marquee outside. Cream cakes for all. And Psalm 16, 'Fullness of Joy'?" Wren paused. "That's what you were singing, correct? Hardly a classical arrangement. Not a minor key. It sounded upbeat to me."

Cross eyed him. "I don't like your implication. Not that

the psalms my congregation sing is any of your business. I would like-"

Wren surged up, reached across the desk and took Cross by the tie, yanking him back to his feet and summoning the words to a Psalm he'd memorized a long time ago. "'I say of the holy people who are in the land, they are the noble ones in whom is all my delight. Those who run after other gods will suffer more and more?' Sounds to me like you're reveling in the punishment the Hammers delivered."

Cross stared at Wren and Wren's fist knuckled around his tie. "They're ancient words. They can be interpreted in many-"

"'You will fill me with joy in your presence,'" Wren went on, "'with eternal pleasures at your right hand.'"

Cross opened his mouth then shut it. "I don't have to explain myself or my choice of psalms to-"

Wren dragged down, bouncing the pastor's head off his own desk. The wood made a loud thud. Rogers let out a small gasp.

"Do you know how they celebrated 9/11 in Egypt, Syria and Lebanon while the towers still smoldered? They sang. They handed out candy. They had parties in the street. How is that any different from you're doing?"

Cross blinked, rubbed his head then tried to snatch away Wren's fist, but there was no removing that grip. "There's no law against seeking joy in the worst of news! There's no law against-"

Wren dragged him back down to the desk, so hard this time that Pastor Cross' forehead split open and a trickle of blood ran down his nose. He cried out and shot his hand to his forehead.

"What are you doing? You can't do this!"

"Three Hammers have hit American soil now," Wren seethed, "with well over a hundred thousand dead. I can do what I need to. And you should be rallying donations. You should be in the midst of a prayer drive. Not singing of joy. Not celebrating the conquering of three of the ten Summits."

Cross' jaw dropped and his eyes widened, but he tried to cover it up. "I don't know what you're talking about."

"So you're not an Ascendant?"

"I'm not a what?"

"An Ascendant. Conquer the Ten Summits. Bring the Kingdom of Heaven to Earth. You don't even need to answer that, it's written all over your 'Tabernacle'. It's in your church's name. You want a new Apostolic Covenant with your people at the top and American democracy left in the trash. You groomed Genevieve Faraday, and now we're all paying the price."

A flash of terror came into Cross' eyes. "What did you just say?" he whispered.

"Genevieve Faraday. We know she came here at least seven years ago, maybe many times since."

"I know who you're talking about. I know that name!"

"Think fast," said Rogers.

"I, uh-"

Wren looked down at the desk, then back up again. The message was clear.

"I understand your concern," Cross said slowly and steadily, trying to get back control of the situation. "Yes, I get it. We are celebrating. But it's not what you think. This is not a terror cell. We have nothing to do with the Hammers. Yes, we pray for the Apostolic Covenant, and the return of our Lord and Savior to rule over his Kingdom, and-"

Wren tightened his grip on the pastor's shirt.

"But we would never do anything violent!" Cross blurted. "Never, I swear it. I cast those out who would throw the first stone. I've banned dozens of congregants who sought a faster track to the Kingdom. I've always counseled patience and faith and-"

Wren dragged him down to the desk again, pulling a high shriek from Cross' lips, but paused before his head struck the wood.

"Faraday. Was she one of those seekers? Did you ban her?"

"Yes! That's exactly it. I did!"

Wren gritted his teeth and glanced at Rogers, who nodded.

"Tell me everything."

"What is there to tell?" Cross babbled. "She came for months. She mixed with other congregants. She joined prayer meetings. Then she raised the possibility of taking action."

"Action to bring on the Kingdom?"

"Yes! From then on, I sought God's counsel and I asked her to leave. That wasn't an easy decision for me. She was a high-profile member of the church. Respected. It hurt me and the Tabernacle to do it."

"And that's it? She just gave up on taking action?"

A moment passed before Cross answered, and Wren saw him spooling up the lie. "I have no idea. She was gone. I wasn't responsible for her, and I'm not responsible for-"

Wren leaned in, braced his weight on his right leg and lifted Cross bodily by the scruff of his shirt. The man yelped, then cried out as Wren swung him and slammed him down flat on his desk.

His legs kicked and his arms scrabbled, but Wren had him pinned like a bug, shifting his grip to wrap around the man's throat.

"You're lying to me," Wren said. "So here's what we'll do. I'm going to squeeze your throat until you can't breathe anymore and you die. What do you think will happen then, now that the Kingdom of Heaven is on Earth? Do you think you'll reincarnate right here, like you just lost a life in a video game?"

Cross struggled to get any words out through his constricted throat. "I, n-no, it..."

"Maybe you'll be more inclined to answer my questions in your next life. Hopefully it'll just take a few minutes."

"Wait, no! It doesn't work like that. It-"

Wren smiled. "Let's find out, shall we?"

He squeezed. Cross kicked and thrashed. His face went red. Wren looked at Rogers. She looked back at him, deadpan.

"My money's on him not coming back," she offered.

"Yeah," Wren said, and let go.

Cross blustered and panted. Wren gave him thirty seconds, then leaned in. "The next words out of your mouth better be the truth, the whole truth, and nothing but the truth, so help you God. Is that clear?"

Cross wheezed and sprayed spit, then managed to croak out words. "There was ... another man. I banned him ... the same time. He and ... Faraday talked ... a lot. They ... I banned them together."

"Who was the man?" Wren pressed.

"I don't ... know his name. But I heard ... after. He'd set up ... his own church. Temple. Something. Not Apostolic ... C-Covenant. Not even ... close. Congregants saw ... her there ... too."

"What church?"

Cross whispered it.

"Louder!" Wren boomed.

"Something ... Hindu," Cross rasped. "I think ... Om Vedic ... Circle."

42

OM VEDIC CIRCLE

Wren was stunned. He let go of Cross' shirt and took a step back, forgetting his left foot was in an orthopedic boot. His weight came down and his leg gave way, dropping him into the chair behind him with a thump.

"What is it, Chris?" Rogers asked.

"I know that group," Wren muttered, feeling the world spin around him. Abruptly he was nauseous. The Om Vedics had been slaughtered. He'd had the leader of the Om Vedics Circle literally standing right there, with a fire extinguisher raised to crack him in the head.

It made no sense, but it was so unlikely it couldn't be a coincidence.

"Who are they?" Rogers asked.

Wren turned to her, mouth running on autopilot while his mind churned in the background. "They were in Yakutsk. Hundreds of them. They said they were seeking the Word of God with the radio telescope, hunting for the sound of the Big Bang. The sound of creation. They said they'd been coming there for years. Then Matthew's men started killing them."

"Killing them?"

Elijah Cross slid off the desk and slinked into his chair, looking more scared by the moment.

"Kiefer and I stopped it halfway," Wren said. "After Matthew and Faraday were dead, I talked to the Om Vedics' leader again. I evacuated some of his worst injured members to Sapporo. But he ordered that strike?"

"He killed his own people," Rogers said.

"It was a cover," said Cross.

Both Wren and Rogers looked at him, and instantly he looked like he regretted speaking up.

"What do you mean?"

"Uh, I mean, I always thought that. When he made that church, or temple, the Om Vedics? You don't just go from extremist Apostolic Covenant to that. You're in too deep. So I read his Om Vedic materials. They were big hippies, most of them; no talk of Jesus, no talk of the ten Summits, just 'Om' and the Word. I thought it was too big a shift."

"But a cover to achieve what, throw off the FBI?"

"Exactly," Cross said, leaning forward now. "Even my tabernacle is on the FBI watchlist. Undercover officers attend services about twice a year, auditing my sermons. But a group of stoned hippies trying to link pseudoscience to faith? Nobody cares about that. So what if they take trips out to Russia? They're just going to chant around a radio telescope and pretend to hear signals from the deep! They're not hurting anyone."

Wren nodded along. The trips out to Russia could have allowed them to set all this in motion years ago. "Cover, OK. He preaches the 'Word' for the masses, while meeting freely with an inner circle to plot the rise of the Kingdom."

"His apostles," Rogers said. "And uses dark money to invest in making them man mountains."

"And he recruits Faraday," Wren added.

"That's all he needed, once he knew about the Miest. Plus the money to fund it all."

Wren cursed. "Money. Where did it come from?"

"That's the other thing," Cross offered. "I dug around a little when he started coming here. I found no records, no businesses, no name, but I saw his cars. He always had nice cars. Like, deluxe brands, top of the range, Ferrari, Tesla, Lamborghini. He parked them several blocks away, like he didn't want us to know, but I followed him." He paused a moment, looking at them. "He's rich."

"But you don't know his name?"

"I don't."

"What about the Om Vedic temple?"

"Gone. A few years back. I don't know if he moved it or shut it down, but it's a dry cleaning place now."

Wren cursed. "I had him."

"You couldn't have known."

"I should've known. There was something about him. Too confident. I almost battered his skull in with a fire extinguisher, and he didn't even raise his voice. I just thought he was stoned."

"People were getting killed, Chris. Don't beat yourself up."

He put that to one side. They needed solutions, not blame, with less than five hours remaining. "OK." He put one hand to his head. "I took his plane, but I doubt he stayed in Russia. If he's building the Kingdom of Heaven in America, then he needs to be here to rule it."

"He's the Prophet," Rogers said.

"I'm sure that's what he plans. Why else do all this?

"OK. So he had a second plane."

Wren shook his head, thinking back to the icy telescope and surrounding area. "Not at Yakutsk. So he must've had a backup plane. There were plenty of vehicles there. Maybe there's another airfield nearby, another jet. He could just go get it. It wouldn't be as fast as the Blackbird." He looked up at Rogers, running the calculation. "If he is coming here, he'll still be in the air now."

"It's gotta be twelve hours from Sapporo to the US, in any normal jet."

"Right. Probably he didn't transfer through Sapporo, though. Too many records. Maybe a Russian coastal town, or China, even North Korea."

Rogers nodded. "So we get satellites up. Or better yet, send the Blackbird. It's a spy plane, faster than anything else. It can find him."

Wren shook his head. She made a good point, but it was flawed. "Needle in a haystack. He won't be on any standard flight path, and I'm sure he's not going to rock up at a big airport like LAX."

"So how do we find him? Set up surveillance over the whole West Coast?"

"Same thing. That's thousands of miles. Not feasible, besides which, he could come up from Mexico or down from Canada."

"Of course."

"We need to know where he transferred, and we need to know his onward flight path." His mouth went dry as a thought struck him. "Maybe there's a way."

"What way?"

Wren stood up and jabbed a finger at Elijah Cross. "Put away your marquee. No more cakes, no more Psalm 16. Expect FBI undercover agents every week from now on, and steer well clear of any activist role in the Covenant."

"Yes, sir," Cross barked.

Wren was already lurching out, Rogers trailing behind. "How do we find this guy, Chris?"

Wren waited until he was outside the tabernacle and well out of earshot, then stopped and looked in Rogers' eyes.

"I asked Humphreys to put a satellite over Vostochny. I asked several times, then I demanded a spy plane."

"OK. But that's Vostochny. Not Yakutsk."

"I know. But Humphreys was an efficient, by-the-book man. Cross every 't', dot every 'i'. I'm thinking, if he ever got around to shifting a satellite or a spy plane out to Vostochny, that he would've had it stick around. Maybe put it on automatic overwatch above Yakutsk."

Rogers' eyes widened. "That would be neat. He liked things to be neat and he hated waste."

"Call Vicker, Sally, and any FBI contacts you think might help. I'll hit up everybody I can at the Pentagon, the NSA, wherever. There's got to be someone who tracks our satellites and spy planes and can tell us what assets we've got out there."

She brought up her phone. "If it's out there, we'll find it."

43

WRAITH

They had their answer within fifteen minutes. By then they'd set up in a chain coffee shop near the tabernacle, laptops and phones spread out around them, glugging hot black Americanos and working their contacts.

Vicker came through with the goods via the US Air Force remote piloting system.

"You're right," the five-star General said. "DNI Humphreys did send a spy plane up to Yakutsk, a Lockheed Martin RQ-170 Sentinel, nicknamed 'Wraith', out of Tokyo. We have the feed it captured."

"Send it," Rogers said.

In seconds they were streaming top-down footage from over the Yakutsk radio telescope. There was a block of shifting data in the corner, scrolling by rapidly, detailing precise coordinates, height, fuel use, and other information.

"Oh man," Rogers whispered, surveying the great dish. "That thing really is huge."

"Fast forward," Wren said.

The footage wound ahead. Wren watched as two tiny dots

emerged from the surrounding mountains and ran under the satellite dish.

"That's you," Rogers said.

"Me and Kiefer."

They sped inside, then within seconds the great glass foyer collapsed and muzzle flashes sparked within.

"They really executed them," Rogers said coldly. "Maybe they knew too much?"

"He didn't need them as cover anymore."

The storm kicked in, obscuring the view.

"Can we compensate for this?" Wren asked, as flurrying flakes erased all sign of the telescope."

"Uh, I think," Rogers checked a block of shifting data in the corner. "Yes. It looks like the Wraith's dropping altitude."

The facility came back into view, far closer now; so close Wren could see himself within the glass orb fighting with Matthew.

"Ugh," Rogers gasped as the giant wrenched Wren's ankle to the side.

"I'm right here, Sally. I'm fine. Fast forward."

She did. Soon Wren and Kiefer were hobbling to the plane, and the runway began to melt, and a stream of Om Vedics carrying stretchers came out to the plane, and-

"Wait," Wren snapped, almost tossing his coffee. "Right there. Go back three seconds and freeze."

Rogers worked the controls. The figure of Wren had just met the Om Vedic leader, the 'Prophet', and shaken hands with the pilot.

"Advance frame-by-frame," he said, and Rogers did, until something happened that Wren had forgotten about in the crush, but that changed everything.

The Prophet looked up.

It was a full-face image of him, only slightly blurry thanks to the snow, but easily recognizable.

"That's him," Wren breathed.

He was younger than he remembered in the crush and violence, certainly no more than 30, but with piercing gray eyes framed by sleek designer glasses, exuding a smug confidence. Wren hadn't noticed it at the time. His face was chiseled, with a well-defined jawline and high cheekbones. His hair was long and tied back. He did not look stoned; if anything he looked like a playboy billionaire, supremely confident in his power.

"It's like he's looking right at us," Rogers said.

"Maybe he is. Maybe he knew the Wraith was up there."

"Impossible," Vicker interrupted down the open line. "The Wraith is undetectable. And in a storm like this?"

"Then maybe his God told him."

"Don't even joke about that," Wren said, staring into those steely gray eyes. "Get a screen grab."

"Screen-capping," Rogers said, then dropped the image into a chat box. "General Vicker, can you run this through facial recognition?"

"Inputting it now," Vicker replied.

"Roll forward," Wren said.

In moments Wren, Kiefer and all the wounded were on board the plane. It took off and left the telescope facility.

The Wraith followed.

"No!" Rogers shouted.

"It already happened, Sally," Wren said, as the facility peeled out of view and the Wraith tracked the Embraer. "We got his face, and that's better than…"

He trailed off as the Wraith circled back.

"What just happened?" Rogers asked.

"Standing protocol on automation," Vicker answered. "A plane like the Wraith wants to maximize intel. It followed your jet long enough to mark a flight plan, then went back to the target."

"Smart automation," Rogers said, and scrolled the feed further forward. Within less than an hour on the timestamp, one coach filled rapidly with Om Vedics and departed.

"I didn't see him get on board," Wren said.

"Me either," Rogers agreed.

The Wraith tracked the coach for fifteen minutes, to the only main road near the facility where it headed west. Once that route was logged, the Wraith returned to the telescope again, just in time to see a final vehicle leaving, a dark truck.

"That's got to be him," Wren said.

The Wraith followed it on a winding track through the mountains for thirty minutes, to a private airfield in the mountains ten miles away, where a Bombardier Challenger 605 was waiting.

"That's it," Wren blurted.

Range 4,000 miles. Sixteen seats. The lap of luxury.

The Prophet transitioned on board alone, and the Wraith tracked it as it taxied, took off and established a flight path.

"Uglegorsk," Rogers said, reading the assumed destination off the data block in the corner of the Wraith's screen, given fuel supply and direction. "Where's that?"

Wren was already bringing it up on Google maps. "Sakhalin Island. A thin strip of land just north of Japan and east of Russia. Uglegorsk's tiny, a backwater, but it does have an airfield."

The Wraith returned to hover over the radio telescope, seeking further intel, but they both knew the facility had revealed all its secrets.

"Uglegorsk," Rogers repeated, looking up. "So we're thinking he refueled there, then broke for the West Coast?"

"That's the theory. We just need to know where. We can still beat him to it, if we can figure that out."

"That could be anywhere in the country, Chris."

"Not with the fuel supply of a Bombardier. He'll barely

reach the West Coast. We'll intercept him when he puts down."

"OK. That's solid."

"Vicker, any luck with that face recognition?" Wren pressed.

"I have him," Vicker replied. "Collating everything from different agencies in a cloud file. Sending that link to you now."

44

PROPHET

Both Wren and Rogers clicked the link, which opened to a cloud document rapidly populating with birth record, social media photographs, financial records, employment history, Deed Poll, tax data and two sets of social security papers.

"Nolan X," Rogers said as they both swiped and scrolled rapidly, scanning data and moving on. "Not his birth name, of course. He's 27 now. Seems he changed it at age 18."

"Birth name Howard Gibney," Wren read. "Looks like a heavily religious upbringing in small-town Nebraska; Dad was a struggling evangelist preacher, Mom a 7th day Adventist. Lots of friction in the ideology there."

"So a troubled youth, mixed up heavily in religion." She found something in his tax record. "Then, and you won't believe this, our old friend Mecklaren came to town."

Wren looked up. "What? You don't mean Lars Mecklaren?"

"Not personally," Rogers said swooping deeper into the documents. "Look at this article about big investments he was making in Nebraska, then it's matched by Gibney's social security filing number. It seems Mecklaren's social media site, NameCheck, set up a moderation depot on the outskirts of North Platte."

Wren frowned. "Moderation? You mean the people who go through posts on social media, the content that's been reported?"

"Exactly that," Rogers said, scrolling further. "Sometimes it's for violence, dangerous ideology, hate speech, incitation, things like that. And Gibney went to work there at 16."

"Too young," Wren said. "I've sat in on those moderation sessions, I've seen the material these moderators have to look at all day, every day. It's soul-crushing. It can give you PTSD, the amount of bile, rage and violence that people post. Torture, abuse, violence, hatred, and it's all so banal. So commonplace. It's a backdoor into the worst side of the darknet."

"Agreed. It seems NameCheck were cutting corners, though, and technically you only need to be 16 to moderate, at least that's the case in Nebraska."

Wren looked up. "Vicker, can we get a record of what he moderated at NameCheck?"

"I don't think that will be possible," Vicker responded. "Mecklaren is infamously strict about privacy. We've had run-ins with him before. There's no way-"

"Then you didn't read the whole brief," Rogers interrupted. "I already threatened to bury him in an iron coffin. If we ask, he'll deliver."

"Then I'll ask. What are we looking for?"

"Apostolic Covenant content in his moderation queue. Maybe a lot of it. Or Ascendancy. Ten Summits Sanction. It could be where he got radicalized."

"That and lots of other things, I'd wager," Rogers said. "Down the rabbit hole, and he was paid to fall through the cracks."

"Looks that way." They kept scrolling as more documents

flew up into the cloud. "Anything on where he lives?"

"Nothing yet," Wren said. "I'm seeing Nebraska, the Nolan X name change, then it's just a blank."

"Where did he make his money? We're still thinking the Miest cost him millions, right?"

"Absolutely. Platnov on his yacht paid for with anonymous cryptocoins confirms that. But OK. The next we know, a few years later he shows up in Houston at Heavenly Renewal Tabernacle."

Wren nodded. "Near NASA. That's no accident. He targeted Faraday."

"Or someone very much like her. He had his plan for an orbital strike already in place."

"And that was just 7 years ago. He would've been just 20 years old."

"20 years old," Wren said, and whistled low. "With the confidence to try and hook a celebrated astrophysicist and the money already in his pocket."

"So somewhere between 16 and 20 he made millions."

"At least. And maybe kept on building. And he already had his vision, an Apostolic Covenant convert by 20, with the dream to become Prophet of all America."

Rogers cursed. "I'm still amazed he managed to get Faraday."

"He's clearly impressive. He fooled me once. His Apostles nearly killed us both, and he successfully dropped three Hammers onto the homeland. But, you're right. Faraday's a genius too, but I'm thinking she was a seeker already," Wren said.

"Seeker?"

"Someone looking for something, trying to fill a hole. It's what made her easy to recruit as a CIA operative on the side. She needed more."

"A lost soul," Rogers whispered.

"Right. He just gave her something to bite into, then he recruited her to the Om Vedics, his cover group for the Covenant, and strung them along with BS about the Word while plotting the Kingdom with his inner circle, and building up his Apostles to take control. There's probably more of these giants. After that, it's just a question of waiting until the means of conquering the ten Summits became available."

"Russia's dissolution and sell-off," Rogers said, picking up the thread. "Do you think he learned about the stockpiles of Russian exotic weapons, about Miest and the Hammers, from his NameCheck moderation queue?"

Wren looked up. "Possible. It's the kind of thing that would get moderated. State secrets."

"And that would've appealed to a lost soul strung out on the wrath of God."

"How do we know he was a lost soul, too?"

"He was a teen in rural Nebraska," Rogers countered. "I'm from small-town Middle America. That describes just about everybody I grew up with."

Wren laughed. "I think we've been to different parts of Middle America, Sally."

"Like you said, his parents' faiths are in conflict; that makes for an uncertain youth. He's clearly intelligent, and there's not a lot of outlets for that kind of intelligence when you're flanked for hundreds of miles by cornfields. Then Silicon Valley rolls into town and he jumps at the chance to break out, thinks he's going to make his fortune, when all that happens is he gets corrupted, jaded and radicalized."

"He did make his fortune."

"Yeah, how did he do that?"

"Who cares? He paid for the Miest in cryptocoins, maybe he gambled and won. Maybe he read something in the moderation accounts that gave him insider trading knowledge. Maybe-"

"I can confirm that," Vicker interrupted. "We just got Gibney's moderation log from NameCheck and I read the topline. It's going in the cloud, but it's broken by percentage of content; the areas he leaned into moderating the most. It looks like he spent most of his time on the Apostolic Covenant, cryptocurrencies, human augmentation content and anti-feminist beliefs."

Rogers cursed out Mecklaren. "So he got radicalized on four fronts at once, at a time when his brain was still highly plastic. He bought into it all."

Wren took a long slug of coffee, nodded at Rogers then brought up the log. It confirmed everything Vicker said, but offered no further onward path.

"OK." He took a breath and looked up from the documents. "We know his story. We believe he's heading to the West Coast. Now we need something concrete on where. Home ownership. Deeds. A location for his temple." Wren thought a second, then snapped his fingers. "The Om Vedics! His plan was to kill them all, probably because they knew something about him. Just like Matthew killed Faraday, he wanted to clean up his trail."

"But they're alive," Rogers breathed, then her tone dropped. "On a coach in Siberia, headed east on a mountain road. We'll never find them, let alone reach them, before the next Hammer falls."

"Not all of them were on the coach. I took a dozen with me on the Embraer. I dropped them in Sapporo with Kiefer." Wren stood up, again forgetting about his left foot, which sent a jolt of pain up his spine. "Vicker, get us on a line with them. Ten of them were too sick to talk, half may be dead already, but the pilot and the nurse. They'll know where the temple was."

Rogers' mouth opened in a wide O.

"Putting the call through now," Vicker said.

45

PACIFIC CITY

"There is no temple," the pilot said, moments after the call had gone through and Wren explained what they were looking for. She was nervous but Wren spoke calmly and slowly. "That's not how it worked for the Om Vedics."

"I understand. So where did you meet?"

"At a range of places," she went on, eyes flickering between Wren and Rogers on the video call. "Retreats. I've been to dozens. I'd been to Yakutsk three times already. I-"

"Locations in the United States, please."

She'd thought. Then she'd spilled five different sites. One in Gibney's old home town in Nebraska, one in Maine and three on the West: Fresno, California; Olympia, Washington; and Pacific City, Oregon.

"Could you tell if your leader, Nolan X, had a preference for any of those sites?"

She'd shaken her head.

"Thank you. We'll be in touch if we need more."

As soon as the call ended, Wren had brought up the map of human augmentation labs, looking for crossover. Within seconds, he had it.

"Pacific City," he said. "There's a human augmentation lab there called the 'NeoGenesis Hub'."

"That's exactly the kind of Biblical-tech fusion name he was into."

"Vicker, can you launch spy planes now to check out a potential flight path from Uglegorsk to Pacific City?"

"I can do that. How many planes?"

Wren looked at Rogers, and she nodded. "All of them."

"Sending the order. You have four hours until the next Hammer falls."

"It's one of those," Rogers had said. "Let's get on a plane to the West Coast."

Within a minute they were on the Chinook. Within three they were back at Ellington Field Joint Reserve Base, and within ten they were tucked into the co-pilot seats of F-15 fighter jets, racing up into the skies at 1,500 mph.

Wren looked out of the cockpit cover to the land receding below. He thought about Mecklaren, and Russia, and the Apostolic Covenant and Miest. It felt like a long line of chickens coming home to roost.

"I don't think Gibney will be amenable to coercion," he said.

"Extremists often aren't."

"So how do we get the kill code for Miest out of him? If torture won't work.

Wren had been through a lot in the last day. He'd learned a lot. "I've got an idea for that."

2 hours and 45 minutes later, Wren and Rogers stood on the blacktop at Pacific City airstrip, a tiny burg in northern Oregon, watching the sky. Dusk was drawing in as the molten yolk of the sun sank into the Pacific.

They'd just stepped off a pair of F-15s, which had dropped them off then swiftly cleared the runway, leaving the air strip largely empty. Nothing to cause Gibney any suspicion, though they were actually surrounded by FBI officers concealed in the clothing of groundskeepers, fuelers and avionics technicians.

All stood ready to storm the Bombardier.

Gibney was due in minutes. The flight path of his Bombardier had been confirmed by spy planes.

"One man," Wren said, the rage simmering hot in his chest. He'd had time to watch the footage of the Hammers falling, now.

"One zealot," Rogers countered. "We can't let this happen again."

"Bombardier is on descent," came a crackly voice in Wren's ear.

Soon enough they saw it, a sleek jet falling from the heavens like a silver cross.

"Stand by," Wren said, looking out over the runway. His pulse pounded in his chest as the Bombardier touched down. It reached the end of the runway and stopped.

"All units go," Wren commanded.

The runway came alive with movement. Vehicles surged up to encircle the Bombardier. Wren and Rogers stepped onto the running boards of their 'breach' vehicle, a stair car which raced out in the lead and clanked loudly up against the fuselage of the Bombardier.

Despite his injured foot, Wren was first up the stairs and in front of the door to the jet as it opened outward with a hiss of decompression. On the other side stood a man who could only be an Apostle, a massive chunk of meat who filled the entryway.

For a moment, he looked surprised.

Wren shot him in the head with his Sig Sauer, and he dropped.

Beyond him stood the Om Vedic leader. The 'Prophet'.

Howard Gibney. Nolan X.

He looked even more surprised than his dead Apostle. He opened his mouth to speak, but Wren surged closer and punched him in the face. He went sailing backward to slap against the floor. Wren followed up with Rogers right behind him. Between them they patted him down, retrieving a phone from one pocket and a satellite radio from the other, which they handed off to waiting techs.

"More Hammers will … fall," Gibney muttered, clearly dazed. "Every three hours, if I don't check in and-"

"Shut up," Wren spat, and scooped him up over his shoulder.

"New York," Gibney muttered. "LA. Chicago. Could be-"

"I said shut up," Wren repeated and turned to lurch down the stairs. He tucked the man into the stair car, atop a large flat gurney-like board, where Rogers was already waiting to strap him in at the temple, shoulders, waist and knees.

The stair car took off.

"What's … this," he muttered. "Torture?"

"Would torture work?" Rogers asked.

"Never. And five Hammers will fall, if anything happens to me, and-"

She slapped his face. "Then shut up."

He was clearly stunned. "I'll never talk."

"What you think doesn't matter," Wren answered.

After barely twenty seconds of driving the stair car stopped next to a long white trailer with a red cross on the side. Cables ran into it from a raised outlet in the taxiway, beside the small hangar.

Wren took the rear of the gurney-like board in one hand and Rogers took the other end, and they carried him out of the car. Wren's left foot cried out with every step, but the orthopedic boot and the cocktail of painkillers he was on canceled out the pain.

Within five steps he was at the rear door to the trailer,

which opened smoothly. Two figures appeared from within, dressed in green scrubs with surgical masks across their faces.

"What's this?" Gibney asked.

Wren backed into the trailer. Inside it was a clinical white, with dazzling silver surfaces beneath a high-powered surgical lamp. Cabinets lined the walls, several open and revealing vials of pharmaceuticals and anesthetic drip bags, rolls of syringes in blister packs, tubs of plastic operating gloves; everything a mobile surgical suite needed.

"What are you doing?" Gibney shouted, starting to show some alarm.

Ahead stood a frame with four legs reaching up; Wren ran the gurney board into slots on the legs, pushing it forward until it locked in position. One of the two surgeons moved in beside Wren, affixing an anesthetic breathing mask over Gibney's face.

"Every three hours!" he shouted. "Starting with New York!"

The team ignored him, buckling his restraints in more tightly. One of the surgeons lifted over a large round loop of metal with multiple buckles and fasteners.

"What's that?" Gibney shouted into his mask.

"Skull restraint assembly," Wren answered. The surgeon scooped it under Gibney's head, bolted it to the gurney board, then tightened the fasteners onto his skull. He began to scream as the contact points of the assembly pushed through his skin and clamped down on bone, completely immobilizing his head.

Next up the surgeon lifted a rotary bone saw up from the side panel, trailing a power line to hanging socket above, and hit the power. The stainless steel blade inside began to whirr.

Now Gibney's eyes were wide and frantic. He tried to

kick with his legs and thrash with his arms, but barely succeeded in moving an inch.

"What are you doing? What kind of torture is this?"

"It's not torture," Wren said, dropping to one knee so their eyes were at the same level. "It's called a corpus callosotomy, but done under proper, surgical conditions. I think you're familiar with this procedure. You advocated its use on your apostles, didn't you?"

"I did not!" he shouted into the mask. "That was Matthew's idea. His fascination. I never condoned it."

"But you let him, didn't you? You considered widening it out to re-educate the entirety of America!"

"I couldn't stop him! He was the psychopath. He started all this, he wanted to-"

"Did Matthew also recruit Faraday? Was it his idea to slaughter the Om Vedics? Did he pull the trigger on five Hammers that killed over a hundred thousand innocent Americans already?

Gibney stared, then his face hardened. "They weren't innocent. Only God can make us innocent, and all those people had given up their-"

The bone saw buzzed back to life.

"Let me explain what's going to happen now," Wren shouted over the grinding sound. "We're going to open up your skull, at least the front quarter. We'll take the bone cap off completely, then the surgeon will reach in with a scalpel and cut the fiber bridge connecting the two hemispheres of your brain. That's the corpus callosum, as you know. Everything's sterile. Everything's clean. But you will be reborn. You'll be disoriented at first, seeking something to trust, an authority to obey, as your new brain struggles to understand the world in a new way. And I think you're going to see a different kind of light."

"Never!" Gibney shouted.

"We'll see. Matthew mistook me for the Apostle Luke. Maybe that guy I shot on your plane. I'm thinking you'll mistake me for God himself, or maybe the Second Coming, especially with all this white, and the light behind me? I'll look like an angel. So when I command you to give me the kill code for the Miest, what do you think is going to happen?"

Gibney's eyes flashed back and forth, from Wren to the bone saw to Rogers on the other side. "You wouldn't. It's cruel and unusual! It's against the Constitution."

Wren laughed. "You destroyed the Constitution, Howard. And this isn't a negotiation. It's one last chance to save your brain and ensure you go to your lethal injection as the guilty man you are. Give me the cut-off codes for the Miest and we end this right now."

Gibney stared. Then he clenched his jaw and began to recite Scripture in a sonorous, powerful voice. "Psalm 105, 12, 'When they were but few in number, few indeed, and strangers in it, they wandered from nation to nation, from one Kingdom to another.'"

Wren nodded at the surgeon with the bone saw, who brought it down against Gibney's skull.

"'He allowed no one to oppress them; for their sake he rebuked kings,'" Gibney went on, as the saw cut through the thin skin of his forehead and dragged against the bone beneath.

"'Do not touch my anointed ones; do my prophets no harm! He called down famine on the land and destroyed all their supplies of food, and-'"

The bone saw passed through his skull and he passed out.

"I thought he'd never shut up," Rogers said.

"Doomsday preachers," Wren grunted. "Always gotta have the last word."

46

NO GOING BACK

The operation was nauseating. Rogers looked away first, followed moments later by Wren. The blood wasn't the worst of it. It was the sounds of fibrous membranes tearing, like the husk ripping away from a ripe ear of corn.

"I'll be outside," Rogers said.

Wren followed.

They stood and watched the last glow of the sun fade from the ocean. Neither needed to say how much rode on this decision. If the operation went badly, if Gibney was unresponsive, if they somehow destroyed his memory of the Miest cut-off codes, then five more Hammers would fall.

"We made this decision together," Rogers said, as if reading the thoughts on Wren's mind.

Wren looked at her. "It's a lot."

"It is. If we left it to the President, to the bureaucrats or the Generals, they probably would have appeased."

"It's quite likely. Five cities could mean a death count in the tens of millions."

"Then we'd be a different country."

"Conquered from within."

"Losers in a civil war to the American Taliban. I'm not ready to hand my passport over to a male member of my family, though, never work again, never think for myself again, on pain of having my brain sliced into." She nodded toward the trailer. "This man needs to pay."

"No punishment will ever be enough," Wren said. "No justice. All we can do is stop him then try to heal the damage he did, become strong at the broken places."

Rogers frowned. "That's not the Bible. That's Hemingway."

Wren managed a small smile. "My interests stretch beyond religion and cults."

Rogers smiled back.

Seconds ticked by. The sound of the bone saw kicked up again from within the trailer. Wren checked his phone. They had twenty-seven minutes until the next Hammer launched. The operation should be finished in ten. His heart beat harder.

"I don't believe in healing," Rogers said at last. "Something like this, it changes you. There's no going back."

"I know."

Rogers looked at him, then took his hand and squeezed it. Wren squeezed back. She'd been there in Arizona when he'd burned his own father alive, when he'd arrested the sister he'd though he'd lost as a child and dumped her in a black site for life.

"You do. But you don't know me, Chris."

Wren turned and smiled. "I do, Sally. I checked your record thoroughly, long before I ever hired you as my lieutenant. Any time I see a hard charger like you, I need to understand why."

"And what did you understand?"

"The mass shooting," he said, and breathed out. "The man they never caught? He killed your friends. He buried you in a pile of their bodies. He almost killed you."

Rogers let go of his hand. "You've always known that? You never mentioned it."

"Why would I mention it? It's your business. But it is why I've always trusted you. People like Humphreys? God rest his soul, but he was a social climber. The CIA was a game to him, a way to keep score, maybe right until the last moment when the stakes finally became real." He let out a breath. "His whole life, he was safe. Insulated. A rich kid, a privileged upbringing, a world of comfort. He never had that moment like we did, where everything was taken and we chose to make a career of getting it back, not just for ourselves but for others too."

Rogers said nothing for a long moment. Wren could see the strong emotions working beneath her cheeks.

"I'm never getting back what I lost," she said eventually. "No more than you did."

"No," Wren allowed. "We're not cut out for peace, are we?" He gazed out at the darkening skies. "You know what else Humphreys told me, in his final moments?"

Rogers snorted. "That he'd never liked you?"

"He hardly needed to say that. No. That he'd found the person who was backing my wife. You know she's spending tens of thousands on top-flight lawyers, trying to unseal my CIA record? Maybe hundreds of thousands. I don't know what happens with that now, with Langley gone, but I know she's not going to stop. She wants to keep me from ever seeing my kids again."

Rogers breathed out heavily. "I'm sorry, Chris."

"Yeah. People like us, life just punches us in the balls."

She laughed, then sobered. "So who is it? Who's backing her?"

"A senator," Wren said wistfully. "Someone whose son I killed. Someone who's been waiting for revenge, for some way to take my kids away from me, for years."

Rogers cursed again. "Has she got a shot?"

"Probably. I'm hoping that this Hammer situation turns out well, and I'm considered such a hero that the American people will demand I get access to my kids."

Rogers laughed again. "Maybe. They've got short memories, though."

"Don't we all."

Then her expression shifted. "And if it goes badly…"

"We're not there yet."

The bone saw stopped. There was silence except for the distant lapping of the ocean on the beach and traffic passing on Highway 1. Inside the trailer, they'd be removing the front section of Gibney's cranium and reaching inside with a blade.

"I got a lead," Rogers said abruptly. "Right when Humphreys called me. On the active shooter."

"Who?"

"All I've got are fake IDs. But I think he's in England. He's some kind of aristocrat, maybe, or just a conman with a host of fake IDs. But I think he's there."

"In the UK?"

She nodded.

"And you're going to kill him?"

Rogers shook her head. "No. This is one I have to do by the book."

Wren surveyed her. "I believe you. You'll find him. You'll nail him. By the book. I always admired that about you."

"And tried to corrupt it." She smiled. "But a vigilante death's too easy for him. He's going to jail right here in the USA for what he did. No doubt." She paused a moment, maybe weighing how much to say. "There's an exchange scheme to the National Crime Agency. The British version of the FBI. I'm going to take it."

"The NCA," Wren repeated. "The FBI will miss you.

They'll be waiting, I know. Call anytime, Sally. If I can help, I will."

She patted his shoulder. "Thanks, Boss. Fix your leg first, though."

"And my wrist," he said softly.

"You'll need both to get a leg up on the bad guys, singlehandedly."

Wren winced and looked at her. "How long have you been saving that?"

"It's been in the back of my head for a while."

"It should have stayed there."

The door to the trailer opened.

"We're ready for you," said the surgeon.

"Showtime," Rogers said. "Break a leg."

Wren shook his head and headed up the steps.

47

GIBNEY

Howard Gibney, or Nolan X, was already much reduced. Beneath the stark white light of the surgical lamp, with his lank chest bared and affixed with heart-rate monitors, he looked pathetic. With his skull cracked open, he was pitiable.

This was the fate he'd envisioned for America. Brutal rule for all, cruelty for many, and catastrophic brain 're-education' for all those who resisted.

Wren felt sick.

Fory-five minutes until the Hammer launched, and not a moment to waste.

He loomed over Gibney, whose eyes spun and tried to fix on him. Wren knew the impact the light would have, haloed behind him. He remembered what Anais Kiefer had said, far back in the snow of Siberia. How he couldn't see. How he hadn't felt like himself. How he'd let Wren take his cold hands and lead him away.

Obedience came easy after a callosotomy, once authority was established.

"Hello Howard," he said in a deep, commanding voice.

Gibney's eyes whirled and locked on a spot just over Wren's left shoulder, staring directly into the blazing light.

"Who … are you?" he whispered.

"You don't recognize me?" Wren asked.

"I … I can't see. Things are … fuzzy."

"So see with your faith," Wren advised. "Use your belief."

Gibney blinked. Wren could see him straining. Trying to understand. "I don't … I can't… "

"Then let me help. Let me speak words of praise."

"Please," Gibney said. "I feel lost."

Wren had spent much of the flight in the F-15 selecting his references. Ordering them perfectly. He began with the Gospel of Matthew, 6:9, spoke with low, simmering intensity. "'Our Father which art in heaven, Hallowed be thy name. Thy kingdom come. Thy will be done in earth, as it is in heaven."

Nolan X gasped and his eyes widened, darting right to fin closer on Wren's face, seeking out the source of the Lord's Prayer. "You mean it's done? Is the Kingdom truly come?"

"My son," Wren said warmly. "I knew you would see me."

A tear broke down Gibney's cheek. "I am here, O Lord. I am here."

"As is the Kingdom," Wren said, then shifted to Ephesians, 2:20. "And the Kingdom is 'built upon the foundation of the apostles and prophets, Jesus Christ himself being the chief corner stone.'"

Nolan began to sob. "Hallelujah for the corner stone," he whimpered. "Oh hallelujah!"

Wren laid a tender hand on Gibney's cheek. "The Covenant is here, my son. Your work will be rewarded."

"Praise be!"

"Now the time for war is over. It's time to build."

"Build?" Gibney countered. "What of the world? Am I not to crusade outward to-"

"'And I will make for them a covenant on that day with the beasts of the field, the birds of the heavens, and the creeping things of the ground,'" Wren interrupted, citing Hosea, 2:18. "'And I will abolish the bow, the sword, and war from the land, and I will make you lie down in safety.'"

Tears streamed down Gibney's cheeks. "Ah, thank you. So I can rest? The work is done?"

"The work is done. It is time to put away arms and build the Kingdom." Wren flowed through to Micah, 4:3. "'And they shall beat their swords into plowshares, and their spears into pruning hooks; nation shall not lift up sword against nation, neither shall they learn war anymore.'"

"Yes!" shouted Nolan X. "Yes, I'm ready to build. Show me the way."

"The way begins with you, my son. Hand back the weapon that was granted to you, my Hammer of the heavens, for vengeance is mine, dearly beloved, and I shall repay."

"Romans, 12: 19," Gibney breathed.

"'Therefore if thine enemy hunger, feed him," Wren pressed on, "if he thirst, give him drink: for in so doing thou shalt heap coals of fire on his head. Be not overcome of evil, but overcome evil with good." Wren shifted quote again, to Leviticus 19:18. "'You shall not take vengeance or bear a grudge against the sons of your own people, but you shall love your neighbor as yourself: I am the Lord.'"

"You are the Lord!" Gibney crowed.

"Relinquish unto me the Hammers of heaven, my child."

"I will!"

"Give me the kill codes for my holy vengeance."

"I will! I will!"

48

FOUR MONTHS LATER

Chris Wren ran.

The woods of his Delaware farm, crisscrossed with hiking and bike trails he'd blazed himself, were sodden with a misty autumnal rain. The branches spidering across his path hung with fat droplets like tiny flower buds, and the trails were boggy with mud churned by his repeated passage. The air itself felt dense, every breath aspirating the cool mist into his lungs.

At the five kilometer mark he burst out of the trees and into the clearing beside his log cabin. Ahead lay the track he'd built, a twenty-yard runway of sand and gravel, atop which sat a sled weighted down by three hundred pounds of rain-sodden oak logs.

He ran to the sled, gripped the handles firmly, bent over with his toes digging into the mud and pushed. After five repetitions on the track, he switched to pulling. It was his least favorite, because it was hard not to look at the tight support bands around his left wrist and ankle.

"The threat to our great nation is ended!" President Ablas had thundered four months earlier, standing on a stage in front of the smoking ruins of the National Archives. "No longer will we live in fear of the skies, because God has chosen this land. He has chosen to make us strong!"

The crowd roared. Wren had been blurry and sleep-deprived at the time, standing in the audience, not on the stage. His ankle and wrist had yet to be treated, so even standing had hurt. He'd wanted to come to Washington, though. He'd wanted to be here for this moment of defiance and healing.

"Our enemies will never again strike us unseen," Ablas went on. "Never again will they rain terror from the heavens. Let them live in fear of us! Let them look to the skies now and fear *our* vengeance!"

It was then that Wren realized what was happening. No one had warned him, but he felt the crowd shifting in time with the President's words. He felt the world bending as the truth was corrupted and rewritten.

"As I speak these words to you, the mujahideen of Iran, the mullahs and imams, the Ayatollah and his muftis all have cause to fear us. Five Hammers of God are falling right now. They are unstoppable. In moments they will strike, and only devastation will remain. The Ayatollah will die in fire. His council of extremist theocrats will die. The system that props up his religious dictatorship dies, today. Today, the Iranian people will be free. Today they throw off their shackles and choose a fresh, democratic destiny for their once-great nation. Let the world learn that America will never meet an atrocity with further atrocity. We will meet it with freedom!"

The crowd roared.

Wren had half-expected something like this. He didn't know how he felt about it. the crowd loved it. Across America, maybe even across much of the world, it would go down well.

But it was a lie.

He turned his back and hobbled away.

Now he hit the fifth repetition and released the sled. Adrenaline coursed through his body, driven by frustration. When he'd handed the control codes for the Miest over to Ablas, he'd known this was possible. He hadn't fought to prevent it. He hadn't dumped the Hammers into the Pacific.

He'd let it happen, and now that decision haunted him.

A heavy sandbag hung from the cabin wall and he let rip. Punches and kicks flew, pummeling the bag with everything he had. His knuckles swiftly grew bloody and his shins became raw, then he shifted to elbows and knees until he was too drained to continue.

Wren entered the cabin exhausted. He didn't bother with a shower, already soaked through from the rain. He simply stripped in the doorway, pulled on some sweats and laid back on the couch with the lights off and a fifth of Maker's Mark bourbon in his hand; the only thing that could shut out the gnawing sense of impending loss.

A call woke him.

He jerked up and looked around, momentarily still trapped in the same nightmare he'd had since the Hammers fell, looking down from a Blackbird as millions died below in Tehran and Tabriz, in Mashhad and Qom and Kerman.

Women. Children. Collateral damage.

The phone kept ringing.

"Wren," he answered.

"Chris," came a deep, rumbling voice.

Wren recognized it immediately. He sat up, heart instantly pumping harder. This was the call he'd been waiting for.

"Anais," he said, head still spinning from the liquor. He checked the time. 4 a.m. "How are you?"

"Sick, Chris. Sick at heart."

Wren said nothing for a moment. He'd left Kiefer at a hospital in Sapporo and he hadn't been seen since. "You ran."

"I was sick in my mind, then. Now I've healed."

"You sound better."

Kiefer laughed. "I'll never be better. What that man did changed me, and there's no going back."

"I know that."

"I can only go forward. I can only see things the way I see them."

"What does that mean, Anais?"

"I think you know. It's like before. All I see are the lies, now. The corruption that keeps the whole beast staggering on."

"You're talking about the strikes on Iran?"

"They were wrong. We both know it. I don't care how much we hated Iran, or how much good cause we had to fight them. They did not fire those Hammers at us. I know that. I heard what Matthew said on that mountaintop. Don't you try to lie to me about that as well."

Wren said nothing.

"Ablas is a war criminal. If any other nation did what she'd done, we'd call for her to be tried at International Criminal Court."

Still Wren said nothing.

"Do you know how many innocent Iranians died in her attacks, Chris?"

Wren did. He'd run the number through his head countless times. He'd tried to find his peace with it. "Over a hundred thousand."

"More like half a million, considering the aftershocks. The refugees. The spread of famine and disease. Many were women and children, Chris. Innocents. And we celebrated that. We celebrated on the streets."

Wren said nothing. All of that was true.

"No one else can do what needs to be done now, Chris. You want justice? Help me."

Seconds passed. Wren didn't know what to say. He'd

thought he'd understood what Rogers had meant, before, about there being no going back. He'd already lost so much. His father. His children. His role at the CIA. But he'd always had his country.

Now, maybe, he wasn't so sure. It didn't feel good to be a party to this. He couldn't sleep without whiskey. He couldn't think for seeing all the small bodies of Iranian children who'd committed no crime. They'd simply been born into a vicious theocratic state. It was undoubtedly good the Ayatollah was gone, just like it was good they'd got Saddam Hussein after 9/11. It was good the people were free.

But it was all built on a lie.

"Ablas executed those people," Kiefer said.

Finally Wren found the words. "And you want to execute her. To assassinate the President of the United States. Don't you?"

"Yes," said Kiefer bluntly. "And you want to as well. I can hear it in your voice."

Wren said nothing. He didn't trust himself to speak. He didn't know what he felt.

"I'll come to you," Kiefer said. "Fight me, if you want. Or join me. Either way, we'll find out what justice really means."

THE NEXT CHRIS WREN THRILLER IS COMING

HAVE YOU READ EVERY CHRIS WREN THRILLER?

Saint Justice

They stole his truck. Big mistake.

No Mercy

Hackers came for his kids. There can be no mercy.

Make Them Pay

The latest reality TV show: execute the rich.

False Flag

They framed him for murder. He'll kill to clear his name.

Firestorm

Is the new President a traitor?

Enemy of the People

There's a target on Wren's back. Everyone's a hunter.

Backlash

He just wanted to go home. They stood in his path.

Never Forgive

5 dead in Tokyo. His name's all over it.

War of Choice

A red tide is rising in the east...

Hammer of God

Terror comes from above.

HAVE YOU READ EVERY GIRL 0 THRILLER?

Girl Zero

They stole her little sister. Now they'll pay.

Zero Day

One little girl dead in Haiti. More will follow.

Kill Zero

The past isn't dead, but it can kill...

HAVE YOU READ THE LAST MAYOR THRILLERS?

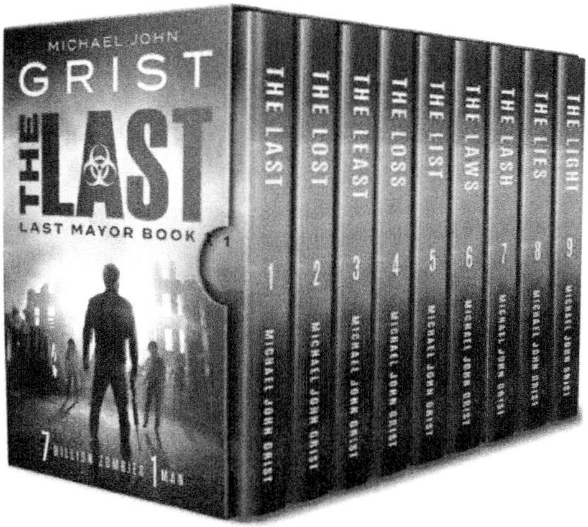

The Last Mayor series - Books 1-9

When the zombie apocalypse devastates the world overnight,
Amo is the last man left alive.
He barely stands a chance.

CHAT WITH MIKE!

Join the Mike Grist newsletter and be first to hear when the next Girl 0 or Chris Wren thriller is coming.

www.subscribepage.com/christopher-wren

Printed in Great Britain
by Amazon

44082976R00169